NO ENEMY BUT WINTER

Recent Titles by Anne Goring from Severn House

KATE WEATHERBY

NO ENEMY BUT WINTER

Anne Goring

This first world edition published in Great Britain 1997 by
SEVERN HOUSE PUBLISHERS LTD of
9–15 High Street, Sutton, Surrey SM1 1DF.
This title first published in the U.S.A.1998 by
SEVERN HOUSE PUBLISHERS INC of
595 Madison Avenue, New York, N.Y. 10022.

British Library Cataloguing in Publication Data

Goring, Anne
　　　　No enemy but winter
　　　　1.　Domestic fiction
　　　　1.　Title
　　　　823.9'14 [F]

　　　ISBN 0-7278-5269-8

Typeset by Palimpsest Book Production Limited,
Polmont, Stirlingshire, Scotland.
Printed and bound in Great Britain by
MPG Books Ltd, Bodmin, Cornwall

Chapter One

By six o'clock that June morning Carrie Linton was outside scouring the four deep steps to the front door. She had already brought up the shine on the convoluted brass door knocker and wiped yesterday's dust from the window ledges with a damp rag, taking her time, pausing often to raise her face as though to test the mild garden scents. It was no penance to be out of doors on a morning that promised a day as clear and hot as the three previous ones. Not like those raw, icebound winter days when the touch of water on her chilblained fingers brought tears of pain and caused her to skimp the front steps, despite the threat of a scolding from the eagle-eyed Miss Tucker.

She mopped the last of the suds from the bottom step and, after a glance at the upper windows to assure herself that the blinds were still drawn and Miss Tucker and Miss Amy were not astir, she wiped her hands on the sacking apron that enveloped her and crept softly along the flagged path. A blackbird in the tall hawthorn by the gate cocked his gold-rimmed eye at her without interrupting the bubbling spate of his song, his small movements dislodging a fall of white blossom that drifted down to cling like fine snow to the unruly tendrils of brown hair that escaped from her cap. She leaned on the gate and stared up the lane. A cat stepped delicately across the road from the terrace of cottages higher up, leaving a trail of dusty pawprints. There was no other sign of life. No tall gangling figure loping towards her. She frowned and scraped at

1

the white paint on the gatepost. She had half suspected that this odd feeling of tension and restlessness might have something to do with Aunt Linnie and Adele. Which meant that Jem would have brought a message. But it was too late for Jem now.

She stifled a yawn. She had slept badly last night and wakened early. Usually, after a day spent up and down the stairs of the tall house, running to do the bidding of the two spinster ladies and their bedridden mother who saw to it that their maid-of-all-work should not have a moment of idleness in which to develop mischievous habits, she fell into her bed in the attic to drop instantly into exhausted oblivion. But not last night. She had been unsettled and wakeful. Uneasy. Yet her day had been normal enough. Pleasanter than most, because Miss Tucker had decided that the gooseberries were ready for making into her special preserve, and because gooseberries were such tiresome fruit to pick, Carrie had been despatched to pick them. She had spent the whole morning in the garden and despite pricked fingers it had been a pleasure to feel the sun on her back after the gloom of the basement kitchen.

Yet perhaps the sun was the cause of her restlessness. The unusual heat had been a reminder of another time – another place. It had brought to the surface childhood memories long suppressed. A remembrance of a low red roof against a sun-bleached sky; a rioting of scarlet and mauve and purple blossom over a verandah rail; a voice chattering in a language that had once been familiar on her own tongue; the smell of charcoal cooking fires at dusk and the heavy perfume from the thick white flowers that overhung the coarse grass of the compound. Above all she recalled the woman in the pale dress, moving lightly about the rooms of the house, laughter always trembling about her. Her presence, her smile, her loving arms and gentle hands signifying happiness and security.

Yes, she remembered the heat. And so much else. That terrible bewilderment and aching sense of loss when the

2

happiness was swept away so suddenly and the house became dark and hollow and full of weeping voices. Everything had changed then. And perhaps this hot spell had triggered some suspicion that change was in the air. Change, in Carrie Linton's experience, meant only for the worse.

She stared again up the lane. The cat had disappeared into the hedge, a window was flung open in the nearest cottage and somewhere a boy whistled, but she neither saw nor heard. She was remembering how the voices had stopped weeping and started to whisper. "Such a tragedy. Orphaned and so far from home . . . What is to be done with them? Are there relatives?"

"Where is Mamma?" Adele had whimpered, clinging; clinging with her hot little fingers, afraid to lose Carrie's hand. "Why has she left us? When will she come back?"

"Mamma is dead," Carrie told her, the weight in her chest like a stone.

"Your sister is too young to understand," the voices said. "You must be brave, Caroline. Arrangements will be made. You have an aunt in Manchester, in England. She has been notified of the unfortunate circumstances."

"I want Mamma," Adele wailed day and night. "Why are we to leave Rokiah and Ah Lan?" The monkey that had been Papa's gift to them stalked the verandah rail, backward and forward, its chain clinking. "Why do we have to go and where is Manchester?"

"A long way off. A long sea voyage. It will be all right, Adele. Don't cry so. I can't bear you to cry. Aunt Linnie will look after us when we get to England. She is — was — Mamma's sister. I am named for her. She and Mamma loved each other. She will love us just as much."

The morning they left she took the monkey to the edge of the compound and removed its collar and chain. She watched it scamper off into the scrub and lalang that pressed against the fence.

"Why did you do that?" Adele demanded, her lip trembling. "We could have taken it to show Aunt Linnie."

Carrie shook her head. "It is cold in England. Papa said so. The monkey would not have been happy there." She could not explain the complexity of her emotions. She was leaving the monkey as a token. She had given it back to Papa and to Mamma. The flowers she and Adele had put on the grave yesterday would already be withered under the searing sun. There would be no more. Papa had given them the monkey. Now she gave it back to the forest. For Papa and Mamma who would lie together for all eternity under the crumbling red soil of the cemetery.

Aunt Linnie would care for them. She hugged that thought to her in the long slow months of the journey across the sea. Through the torpor of endless becalmed days and the fearsome excitement of the storms, when Adele's screams could not be heard above the screeching of the gale in the rigging. The ship creaked and groaned and dipped her bows into the green swells and Carrie dreamed of Aunt Linnie. A younger version of Mamma. Gay and pretty. 'Always sunny,' Mamma had said. 'She had many admirers when we were young. I always thought she would marry someone dashing. Yet it was I, the quiet one, who married the handsome adventurer who brought me all the way to Malaya. And dear Linnie married a doctor who left her a widow within two years and without a child to bring her comfort.'

The reality almost lived up to the dream. Different but not unpleasant. Aunt Linnie was no longer the flighty girl of Mamma's tales, but a plump woman who peered at them shortsightedly and wept over them and called them 'my darlings' and installed them with great kindness in her comfortable cottage in Cheetham.

They were not unhappy together, the three of them. When the accounting was done there was enough money to see the girls educated. "We shall enrol you in Miss Browning's school," Aunt Linnie said. "I have heard the most reassuring accounts of her methods. I intend nothing but the best for my dear sister's girls. Oh, we shall be very cosy together. I do believe Adele already forgets about that horridly hot country and you will forget, too, Caroline, in time. You see, I shall be a mother to you both."

Carrie had looked at the smiling, dimpled face of her aunt. She was so like Mamma in the turn of her head, in the colour of her hair and tone of voice, but without Mamma's tranquillity and grace. She kissed her aunt's cheek. She was grateful. The picture Aunt Linnie painted pleased and reassured her. The stone weight she had carried in her chest through the months since her parents' death lightened a little. She and Adele had truly found a haven after the long dismal months since the tragedy. She had no reason, at nine years old, to believe that adults could no more command their destinies than little children.

"You feeling all right, Carrie?"

She jumped. "Jem Walker! Creeping up on me like that! I almost started out of my skin."

"You were watching me all the way down the lane," he protested. "Looking at me right funny." Then, awkwardly, "You feeling all right? Not sickening? Ma says it's the sort of weather for breeding sickness."

Carrie's momentary irritation vanished. "It's just that you're late, Jem," she said. "I wasn't expecting you at this time." She saw that he had been running and was breathless. Under the tangle of black hair that fell over his forehead and about his ears she could see a dew of perspiration.

"Aye, I'm late," he said. "Overslept. But Mrs O'Hara give me these last night. Both of them. Said you must have them this morning."

5

She took the two letters from him slowly, almost reluctantly. Both were addressed in Aunt Linnie's hand. One to 'Miss C. Linton', the other to 'Miss R.L. Tucker'.

Bewildered she looked up at Jem. "What's she writing to Miss Tucker for? Is something the matter? What is it, Jem?"

"Don't fret yourself," he said easily. "Nobody's in trouble. It's just visitors."

"Visitors?"

"Someone as knew your ma when you were in foreign parts. Mrs O'Hara thinks it most particular that you be there when this lady comes. That's all I know."

Change. She held the letters gingerly as though they might develop snake's fangs and bite her.

"Who can it be? Did she say, Jem? Nobody's been to see us since that lady who looked after us on the ship called. But that was before . . . before Aunt Linnie remarried." She never spoke her uncle's name more than she could help. "There were letters from people once. But not for a long time."

"I must go, Carrie. I don't know more, except that you have to be there. It's all in the letter, I dare say." His bony face flushed. "I shall see you Sunday evening perhaps?"

"I expect so," she said absently. Then, aware of his hesitation, she looked up at him and smiled.

Carrie Linton was anything but vain. She did not think herself the remotest bit pretty. Her face was too sharp, her forehead too high, her complexion marred by the freckles that after the merest touch of the sun blossomed across her nose and cheeks. But she did not understand about her smile. It lit up her face, awoke a glow in her grey eyes. It was a warming thing. It made people who had dismissed her as a plain and solemn little creature notice, suddenly, the way those unruly tendrils of hair that Miss Tucker was forever ordering her to push under her cap, lay in gentle curls against her pale skin and what good white teeth she

6

had and how her long brown eyelashes were gold-tipped and curving.

The first time she had turned her smile on Jem Walker she had been a little lass of thirteen and he already a gangling youth of sixteen. For the three years since that day Jem had dismissed all the other girls he met as uninteresting creatures. Coquettish housemaids who eyed him as he lugged heavy trunks and parcels from his cart into the back doors of grand houses might pat their curls and delay him in the kitchen; mill girls, homeward bound, might giggle and cast glances at the well-set-up lad on the carrier's cart, but he kept his eyes on his horses and scarcely noticed their banter. Carrie's smile had made him immune.

Carrie now hardly noticed the flush of colour in Jem's sun-browned face, but she knew how much Jem appreciated her efforts in teaching him to read and write on her evenings off. "Yes, Sunday," she said warmly. "Of course. I shall be home then. Did Aunt Linnie give you that old copybook of mine? Good. Then I expect to see that your lettering has improved."

"Master'll be in a temper if I don't hurry," Jem said. "I have to go to Bury today." For all his words he seemed reluctant to go. His blue eyes lingered on her face.

Carrie looked down at the letters in her hand. Her face was solemn again, her mouth tight. She looked devitalised once more. Ordinary. Jem remembered her smile and saw her beautiful still. "Goodbye then, Jem," she said, turning from the gate.

"I'll be round Sunday."

But she scarcely heard the thump of his clogs as he ran back up to Cheetham Hill Road and turned down towards the smoky haze of the town and his long day's work.

There would be no time off on Sunday. Miss Tucker read Aunt Linnie's letter with compressed lips.

"It is highly inconvenient," she snapped. "When you took this place, Carrie, you seemed a sensible girl. There was no mention of how often you would be wanting to shirk your duties to run to the assistance of your feckless family."

"But it is not so often," Carrie protested, knowing as she spoke it was useless to argue. "It was just once last month when Adele had one of her asthma spells and my aunt was poorly. And before that I can scarce remember . . ."

"You have a poor memory. During the cold weather there was that business of your uncle becoming inebriated and causing a disgraceful disturbance in the street. And during the whole of last year you were finding excuses to run home."

"Adele was so much worse then," Carrie said. "She doesn't get the attacks so often now. Aunt Linnie being ill herself, couldn't cope."

Miss Tucker's long nose twitched. "The misfortunes of your family are no concern of mine. Your aunt, had she been less impulsive might have been in a very different situation today. She made a sad mistake in her second marriage. At her age she should have known better, but then some women lose all sense and reason when a man so much as looks at them." All the smugness and contempt of untempted virginity coloured her voice. Carrie hung her head, outwardly humble because argument would make matters worse, inwardly struggling with rage because she hated Aunt Linnie to be spoken of so, for all the truth of it.

Miss Tucker had made her point. Now she prepared to be benevolent. "Very well, you may go this afternoon after dinner, but you must make up the time. It is unfortunate that you have already had your day off this month, so you shall lose your next two Sunday evenings."

Her precious evenings. Only two in the month and much coveted in the summer when it was possible to get out of doors and walk in the fields or down by the river.

8

"Yes, Miss Tucker," she said, outwardly meek, inwardly seething.

Aunt Linnie's letter had been much underlined.

'Dear Caroline,

I pen this in haste. It is most *urgent* that you be here between the hours of two and four o'clock tomorrow, Wednesday. A lady, Mrs Sanderson, is to call. She has *particularly* asked to meet *you and Adele*. She once had an acquaintance with your papa and mamma. It may be she can be of assistance in helping you to *improve your situation*. I write separately to Miss Tucker that she may give you leave.

Yr. affcte aunt, C. O'Hara'

As she hurried through Cheetham village in the afternoon heat, Carrie realised how the visit of this Mrs Sanderson must have brought a desperate hope to her aunt. The lady would come, she would instantly be captivated by the two girls fallen upon hard times and for the sake of their dead parents would become their benefactor. Carrie had no such illusions. She no longer believed in fairy tales.

Though she was already late – Miss Tucker, from spite, having dawdled over dinner – she paused when she came to the corner of Smedley Lane, pressing her hand to the stitch in her side, glad of the shade of the clustering elms and the cool dampness coming from the ferns and grasses growing on the sandy bank. She looked down the hill, past the low whitewashed cottages clustered round the Eagle & Child, its signboard motionless, over the soft greenness of Temple fields and the hedgerows and pastures spreading towards town. Manchester lay two miles to the south, a dirty smudge of chimneys and smoke.

It was Aunt Linnie's constant fear that her husband would decide to remove them all to some cheap rooms in town. "I

9

think I should quite wilt away in that dirty atmosphere," she would whisper to Carrie. "This cottage is modest, but I treasure my garden and the view of the fields and river. But George thinks there may be more work for him . . ." Or, "George has heard of rooms to let in Redbank. We are behind again with the rent here, you understand . . ."

Carrie, who had taken George O'Hara's measure from the start, always tried to reassure her aunt. But it was little use. Her aunt continued to fret and worry.

Carrie knew it suited George O'Hara to live where he did, taking work here and there, enough to keep him in ale money; enough to keep them above the level of poverty, yet so finely balanced as to keep Aunt Linnie's already weakened nerves constantly quivering. There was work in plenty for a craftsman such as he in a district that was becoming more fashionable each year. Cheetham was close enough to the city for merchants and bankers and other businessmen to travel by day into town, yet it was a green and airy place, its sandy hills healthily clear of the smoke that showered soot upon the buildings of the ever-spreading town. Many of these wealthy persons building fine houses in the district would have welcomed the services of a man skilled in carving and able to fashion a chair or table so elegant that it would not have disgraced the drawing room of a titled gentleman. But George O'Hara chose not to work more than was absolutely necessary.

She also suspected that he had made a miscalculation when he had married Aunt Linnie. He had doubtless assumed that Aunt Linnie's capital and her nieces' small inheritance would keep him many years in comfortable idleness. That he had run through it all in eighteen months — despite economising on the matters of the girls' education and the laundry woman and the gardener — piqued him. And because someone must be blamed, he settled upon Aunt Linnie. She had tempted him with her good cooking, her charming cottage and her appearance of gentility and therefore she must be punished. Not that he had ever struck a blow. But there were ways. There were always ways.

Carrie clenched her fists. She had watched his methods for five years or more. She wished, fiercely, that the swaggering, good-looking George O'Hara had stayed in the south where he'd come from and Aunt Linnie had never clapped eyes on him, let alone allowed herself to be taken in by his tales of a master who had gone bankrupt and put him out of work and a sick mother whom he had nursed, the doctor's fees taking all his savings . . .

She walked on. The lane turned and dipped to the valley and the Irk lay a distant pale thread winding among its water meadows. She turned into the track that led to the cottage. There were no flowers blossoming now in the small front garden. The last time she had visited it had been massed with lavender and pinks and old-fashioned roses, a pleasant source of the pot pourri and lavender bags Aunt Linnie laid among the linen. Now the earth was dug over and raw, the shrubs and plants rotting in a heap. Carrie stopped at the sight, her face suddenly pinched. Then, averting her eyes, she half ran to the front door.

"Is that you, Carrie dear?"

She let herself quietly into the dim living room of the cottage. The room was empty save for the figure huddled in a shawl on an upright chair.

"How are you today?" she asked as she bent over her aunt and kissed her. Then, "Why, you look positively festive. Has Adele arranged your hair? And that dress, have I seen it before?" She heard her voice bright and false and her aunt's equally so and all the time her heart cried out in anguish.

Aunt Linnie's first marriage had been childless. Her second had resulted in a child, stillborn, nine months after her

11

wedding. The birth had been difficult and the clumsy ministrations of the midwife George had obtained had ruined any future chance Linnie O'Hara had of bearing a healthy child; Her pregnancies since had been frequent, but the subsequent miscarriages had sapped her health, her energy and her spirit. At thirty-eight she looked an old woman. Her once bright hair was lifeless, her cheeks were sunken and the colour she had inexpertly applied to her cheeks gave her a raddled air that her desperate eyes belied. Her hand lay pale on Carrie's arm as the girl sank to the stool at her feet.

"I am glad to have this word with you alone, dear," she whispered hurriedly. "Uncle George and Adele are taking a turn round the orchard, to see the – the improvements he is making. I would show you the letter, Mrs Sanderson's letter, but George has taken it and not returned it. It was addressed to me in my previous name, you understand, and he is so sensitive in these matters. Why, I declare it is quite flattering that he should still be jealous."

Carrie would not have called it jealousy but she said, merely, "Who is she, this Mrs Sanderson?"

"She wrote – oh, many years ago. After you came here. A letter of sympathy, I believe." She peered around vaguely. "I kept it. I kept them all, for a while."

The letters had gone, as well as the inlaid box that held them and the ornaments and trinkets and the gilt carriage clock and every other reminder that Aunt Linnie had once had an existence apart from George O'Hara.

"I think she was the person whom your papa once helped when she was in trouble of some sort, though I may be mistaken. I cannot remember clearly." Her glance came back to her niece. Her grip tightened. "But she is coming today. I thought . . . I thought George might find some way to prevent her – that is," she corrected herself, "he might have thought the visit would be too much for me in my poor health and with

12

Adele liable to become ill from excitement. But he came to the conclusion that there would be no harm in it."

And perhaps some pickings to be had himself from the visit, Carrie thought grimly.

"She spoke in the letter of some news that would be of interest to you girls and she particularly wished you both, if it was convenient, to be present. I . . . I feel, dear, that this lady's visit might be an opportunity for you." Her eyes glinted feverishly. "I have thought about nothing else since the note came from her. If she could be persuaded to raise you from your present low station . . . She may be in need of a companion or a governess. A person like that might impress George. Might make him understand that you were born to better things."

Carrie put her rough hand over her aunt's cold one, stifling a sigh. It was quite as she guessed. Her aunt's imaginings had led her to indulge in unreasonable hopes.

"Suppose Mrs Sanderson did offer me a position," she said quietly. "Do you think I could go somewhere far away from you and Adele?"

"I should miss you unbearably. You are grown so like my dear sister in your quiet ways and your ability to cope. She was always the more practical one . . . but your life is just beginning. I should not like to think of you destined to spend it at the beck and call of those disagreeable spinster ladies. No, I beg you, take the chance if it is offered."

"It is hardly likely, Aunt Linnie," Carrie said, smiling to soothe the sting of her words. "Mrs Sanderson is a lady making a polite call on children of old acquaintances."

"But she speaks of news . . ."

Carrie shrugged. "News of mutual friends? News of happenings in Malacca which is a place I can scarcely remember? I fear that is of little consequence to me now." She could hardly bear the look of disappointment on her aunt's face. She pressed

13

her hand. "If the opportunity does arise I promise I shall give it consideration."

The door to the kitchen swung open and Aunt Linnie jerked her hand guiltily from Carrie's and said in a high, quick voice. "I am so pleased Miss Tucker keeps well. This hot weather is most fatiguing. Adele, dear, you should not have gone out in the sun without a hat."

"Carrie! I did not hear you come," Adele cried. She made to rush forward to greet her sister, but the heavy hand on her shoulder restrained her. Adele glanced up uncertainly at the bland smiling face of the man whose bulk blocked the low doorway, and Carrie, watching them together, had a moment of fear so sharp that it took the words of greeting from her lips. A wordless fear, that somehow had to do with that hand – lying powerful and possessive – against Adele's thin white neck, the clubbed fingers curled into the muslin of her dress. Carrie thought of the business of the cats now all of a sudden banished to the outbuildings and the recent generosity in the matter of Adele's new clothes and the fear blossomed and unfurled like a sickly flower in her stomach.

Then Adele was released. But she did not move at once, like an imprisoned bird that does not immediately know that its cage door is open and it may fly away.

"Well, don't sisters kiss now when they meet? Or has it gone out of fashion?" He spoke jovially. He always spoke jovially. Even at his cruellest he spoke in the manner of a man who sees humour in everything, as perhaps he did.

Awkwardly now the girls greeted each other and Carrie, tight-lipped, curtseyed to him, keeping her eyes on his boots. He took a watch from the pocket of his moleskin waistcoat.

"Our fine visitor is late," he said. "Still, I suppose it is the privilege of the upper classes to keep us ordinary mortals waiting." Nobody spoke as he walked heavily across the room, seated himself in his chair and took up his churchwarden.

"Perhaps it might be better, dear," Aunt Linnie ventured, "if you did not light your pipe yet. Some ladies have an objection to – not that it displeases me, of course, but the smoke – she might not like it."

George lit his pipe, puffed on it reflectively then turned his cold, pale eyes on his wife and stared at her unblinking until her small protest faded. The silence lasted until they heard the faint clatter of hooves and harness and after a moment or two, with a flutter of apologies, Mrs Sanderson swept into the room.

Carrie had imagined some stout elderly woman, bent on a duty call because she was in the district. There was nothing dutiful, elderly or stout about Mrs Sanderson.

She perched on a chair like an exotic bird come to rest. Even the modish cut and flare of her green silk gown and the ribbons in her bonnet seemed to dispel the dimness of the room, bringing to it something vital and alive. She was tall and slender, a black-haired woman in her mid-forties who must have been a beauty in her day, and was even now so striking that the lines about her mouth and eyes were overlooked in the overall dazzle of her appearance. Her complexion had the sallow tint of one who has spent much time in a hot climate, but her fine eyes were large and dark and her skin clear.

"So these are Robert's girls," she said after the polite formalities were over. She looked from Adele to Carrie and back to Adele. "I thought of you from time to time," she said. "Wondered how you were and what life had brought you to. How old are you now?"

"I shall be seventeen come October, ma'am," said Carrie. "Adele is just turned fifteen."

"And you keep in good health?"

"Please, yes, ma'am, though Adele has the asthma."

"How tiresome. Does it trouble you much, my dear?"

"Very little now, ma'am," Adele said in her soft voice. "Not since the cats are kept out."

15

"Cats?" Mrs Sanderson raised her eyebrows. "What, please, have cats to do with your health, child?"

"It is, I am afraid, a feminine whim," Uncle George broke in with his frank laugh. "The nurse who attends my wife in her distressingly frequent illnesses has put this silly notion into their heads. An old wives' tale, merely, I'm afraid, but it pleases me to humour them."

Ah, yes, thought Carrie, you do humour us – but for what devious purpose of your own?

"Do tell me," said Mrs Sanderson, raising her clear eyes to Uncle George. "I confess I am intrigued. What is this old wives' tale? And how has it cured Adele?"

"Some nonsense about the cats' presence provoking the attacks . . ."

"It was not nonsense." Carrie could not help herself. "It was only after you got the cats in to get rid of the mice in the scullery that Adele started to have the attacks and it was Mrs Walker, who is the nurse, ma'am, and something of a herbalist, who told us of a similar case. And," she added low and quick, "because you would not listen, uncle, Adele had to suffer for three years and is now only free of it because the cats don't come indoors any more."

"Why, Carrie, you must not indulge in fancy." Uncle George's voice was hearty. "You will have our visitor believing you to be a silly goose. You know that the physician himself could give no explanation for the onset of her illness except that she was outgrowing her strength. It has been a great worry to us," he added, shaking his head, "as you might imagine."

"You need say no more," Mrs Sanderson said with a sigh. "My own son is a semi-invalid at present. He took a bad bout of fever on the ship. We are only recently returned from the East Indies you understand, and we were forced to stay in Liverpool for some weeks while he recovered. He is still weak, though." She raised her hands and shoulders in a charming, almost foreign way. "I have brought him along with me thinking the drive would brighten him but he did not feel strong enough to leave the carriage." She beseeched George O'Hara with her eyes. "The tribulations these children give us can only be known to others similarly placed."

Uncle George bowed his head in mute agreement so he did not notice the way Mrs Sanderson's glance went round the circle of faces and it was not the melting look that she had bestowed upon him, but one sharp and shrewd.

"But children give great pleasure, too," Aunt Linnie ventured. "At least . . . my nieces have always been especially dear . . ."

"But a responsibility," her husband put in. "A responsibility that I have taken upon myself gladly, though the care of growing girls is not a light duty."

"So true, Mr O'Hara, and I am sure Adele and Caroline are suitably grateful."

George O'Hara thought he heard an odd intonation in Mrs Sanderson's voice, but she was smiling at him so charmingly that he found himself standing straighter, lifting his chin, turning his head a little so that she might remark his strong profile. She had, he thought, magnificent eyes and had she not been so much a lady he might have thought her manner rather provocative. There was no doubt at all she found him an attractive man. He preened and, in response to her next innocent question, answered almost eagerly, "Why, no, Mrs Sanderson, the girls do not go to school now."

"Do they then have tuition at home?"

"Alas," he said, "that is not possible. A working man cannot afford to indulge his family in such a way, though I wish with all my heart that it were otherwise. Mind, Adele has no head for book-learning nor the stamina for it but under my wife's tender instruction she learns the housewifely duties that will stand her in good stead in later life."

"And Caroline? How do you occupy yourself, child?"

"Ma'am, I work as—"

"My wife's poor health, you understand, is I grieve to say something of a strain on the family purse," Uncle George interrupted smoothly. "Carrie lightens this burden by taking employment outside the home. A most respectable position, of course, as a companion to two elderly ladies and their bedridden mother."

Her uncle's effrontery rendered Carrie speechless. By the time she'd found words, Mrs Sanderson was plying him with questions about the garden and he was explaining about the uselessness of flowers in a working man's garden and how he was proposing to plant more potatoes. All the while, Aunt Linnie, whose joy had been the flowers, sat mutely with clasped hands and downcast eyes. Carrie burned with suppressed anger. She hated the dazzling Mrs Sanderson for being taken in so readily by Uncle George. She hung on to his every word as though each was a gem of wisdom. Just as Aunt Linnie had done all those years ago when he had called asking for work about the house and ended up master of it. It was his looks, of course, his air of capability and strength. In a few years his square, somewhat florid face would sag to fat, but now his even features and smoothly waving sandy hair and breadth of shoulder seemed an irresistible attraction to gullible women.

"Perhaps you would care to take tea," Aunt Linnie whispered when her husband and the visitor had exhausted the topic of the garden.

"I cannot. I am sorry. My poor boy will be quite wilting away in the carriage and here am I gossiping on so pleasantly and I have not come to the reason for my visit. Now, girls, come here to me."

She held out her hands and Adele and Carrie moved to stand in front of her, Carrie refusing to meet Mrs Sanderson's lustrous gaze.

"I have just this to say," she said quietly. "Once, many years ago in Penang, your papa was kind to me at a time when I was in great distress and quite without friends. When my first husband, Tom Bellamy, died leaving his affairs in a sorry mess, it was your papa, Robert Linton, who rescued me from a ruinous situation. It is something I have never forgotten."

Despite her resolve, Carrie looked up. There was a note in Mrs Sanderson's voice that had not been there previously. It was something far removed from the way she had addressed Uncle George.

"He was a clerk, you see, in Tom's offices. He had only been in the position for a few months and it came as much a shock to him as to me to find the extent and manner of my husband's debts. Tom . . . was involved in several schemes that could only be viewed as doubtful in the extreme. The details are of no interest to you – or to me, now. I have put all that behind me. But can you imagine me young, alone and helpless, faced with debts and ultimate scandal?"

Carrie could not imagine this self-assured woman ever being at a loss, but she was fascinated to have this glimpse of her papa, of whom she knew so little.

She said, half in reverie, "I seem to remember Mamma speaking of the time before she and Papa met. Tales of his travels. He had gone to India, then China, to seek his fortune. We had little mementoes once, trinkets he had picked up. We played with them as children." And brought them home and saw the last of them when Uncle George had thrown them out as rubbish.

"Ah, so many young men saw then – and still do – the East as a place of instant wealth and adventure. I think your papa did not ever make his fortune, but he was young when I knew him and loved the travel and excitement of new places. It was chance that brought him to Penang when he was returning to Europe from Canton. He viewed the island and liked it and took a temporary position in my late husband's offices in order that he might finance his stay. It was to my great benefit, because others in more trusted positions abandoned the company in a hurry when they saw which way the wind blew. He was a courteous and honourable man, your papa. He stayed and salvaged all he could from the wreckage. He worked day and night – going through books and accounts, fending off a rascally partner, protecting me from the worst of the gossip. Tom had never been popular with the English community. I had never properly understood why until the truth of his affairs came to light. I realised then that he was considered untrustworthy, something of a rogue." Her shoulders lifted; she raised one of her elegant hands expressively and let it fall to her lap. "I was so very innocent. Other people led busy social lives – parties, balls, outings to which we were never invited. I never thought to question – but I had no knowledge of the world, or of men. I married Tom Bellamy almost from the schoolroom. I was an orphan, you see, with no one to turn to for advice or to warn me that the silvery-tongued gentleman who wished to carry me off to the romantic East was not all that he seemed." She sighed deeply. "Ah, but I have no wish to trouble you with that tragic tale. It is of happier things we must speak today."

"But anything you can tell us of our papa we should like to hear," Carrie said eagerly. "It is so unexpected and brings back happy memories."

"I am sure it does, child." Mrs Sanderson's gaze went from Carrie to Adele and her brilliant eyes darkened. "Everyone liked him, for he was light-hearted, but courteous and sensible. I declare, if he had chosen to stay longer in Georgetown, some young lady would have snapped him up and your mamma would never have laid eyes on him. As it was his passage was already booked when Tom died. He was beginning to yearn for cooler climes. Once he had sorted out my affairs as best he could he took a ship for home. Before that he spoke on my behalf to several important persons on the island whom he thought might continue to advise me on business matters. So it was that Mr Miles Sanderson and I met and the happy outcome was that I made my second, very happy marriage."

"How glad I am," Uncle George put in weightily, "that all turned out so well for you. A woman alone, in a foreign place! How you must have suffered."

"Quite so," she said coolly, not removing her attention from the girls who stood so quietly before her. "I did not meet your father again. We heard he had returned to Malacca with a new bride and received a charming note from Mrs Linton for the wedding gift we sent. But as is the way of things, we lost touch. I was caught up totally in my new life – a very different one from my previous experience with Tom. I had a splendid home to run, a son to care for and as much social life as I wished for. If I were honest, I preferred to forget all that had gone before. All the same, it came as a great shock to hear that your parents had taken a fever and died within hours of each other. By the time the news reached Penang you girls were already on your way to England."

"I remember that you wrote," Aunt Linnie put in eagerly. "So many people did . . . so kind . . . enquiries as to the girls' welfare . . ."

"I owe your father a great debt," Mrs Sanderson went on. "Not only for enabling me to retain my self-respect at a difficult time but for introducing me to my dear husband. This is the first time I have been back to England since I left its shores with my first husband, and soon I shall be leaving again when I embark with my son on a Continental tour. But I was intrigued to find that Mr Sanderson's family home is within a few miles of here and, being so close, I felt the opportunity could not be missed to repay an old debt."

Carrie felt, rather than saw, Uncle George's attention sharpen. He moved a step closer.

"Naturally," Mrs Sanderson continued, "when I remarried, my husband took over my affairs. He took an especial interest in Tom's remaining investments, knowing my pride that I had not come to him penniless. They have not made a great deal of profit in the past, but they have brought in a small income which has, I understand, the likelihood of increasing. I propose that these investments be transferred to your names, girls. In this way, I can repay Robert Linton for his kindness to the distressed creature I once was. It is nothing too grand," she warned. "Perhaps a hundred pounds a year at present. But, as I say, these dividends may increase."

"For us?" Adele gasped. "A hundred pounds a year?"

All at once Mrs Sanderson seemed impatient, as though she had dawdled too long. She said, crisply. "The lawyers will see to it. They will be in touch. I have suggested that quarterly drafts would be most convenient."

Carrie closed her eyes. No more servitude. No more washing steps on freezing days or facing the black beetles in the kitchen or trudging up and down the stairs to the summons of bedridden Mrs Tucker's angry knocking. She was free! Free! Then, like a stone, her spirits sank as Uncle George rolled his big hands together and cried, "This is a fine piece of news indeed. I am quite overwhelmed, Mrs Sanderson. And so kind of you to bring it in person when a lawyer's letter would have sufficed."

"I had a notion to look in on Robert's girls and see how they fared."

"And you can see that they are well and happy and will be made all the happier by your charity."

"It is not charity, sir," Mrs Sanderson said coldly. "It is

22

repayment of an old debt. Without Robert Linton I would have been disgraced and penniless. It is right that his daughters should benefit."

"Oh, indeed, indeed."

"Now you must excuse me." She rose in a rustle of silk skirts. "Come girls," she said. "Do me the kindness of walking me to the gate. Good afternoon, Mrs O'Hara. Mr O'Hara."

With the ease of one used to having her own way she swept the girls out into the sunshine, leaving Uncle George bowing and smiling in an effusion of gratitude.

"You may put up my parasol for me, Adele. Thank you. It is almost as hot as in the tropics. I don't recall English weather being this fine before."

Carrie opened the gate and in the sandy track Mrs Sanderson looked at Adele and said, almost too casually, "You are very much like your papa, child. Has anyone told you that?"

Adele shook her head shyly. "I don't remember much of him. We had pictures in lockets once but I don't know what happened to them."

"They were sold," Carrie said flatly.

There was a pause, then Mrs Sanderson, for once apparently groping for words, said, "I understand . . . you have had a difficult time, both of you. It will perhaps be a little different . . . with the money."

Will it, Carrie thought dully? Will he allow it? We are not of age. He will take the money and use it as he thinks fit. Lawyers or no lawyers.

Mrs Sanderson shaded her face with her parasol. "If you wish ever to get in touch with me I may always be contacted through the lawyers." She walked briskly to the carriage that blocked the end of the track. The coachman leaped to open the door.

"Such a fine carriage," Adele breathed. "Oh, and to think we are rich."

Rich. Carrie stared at her sister and it seemed that she saw again that big heavy hand gripping Adele's shoulder, weighting it down; the brute strength of it crushing the delicate bones. In an instant she picked up her skirts and ran after Mrs Sanderson.

"Please, ma'am, please may I speak to you – it isn't for myself. It's for Adele."

"Good gracious," said Mrs Sanderson seating herself. "Whatever is it child?"

Carrie leaned in; in her urgency she hardly noticed the slender figure sitting in the opposite seat.

"Please, ma'am, can you not do something for Adele? Get her away from here. That is, can you find her some employment? In your household, perhaps – among your friends. She's a willing girl and nice natured – and I'm frightened for her."

"Frightened?"

Carrie said slowly, "It's Uncle George, ma'am. He looks at her sometimes. It . . . it frightens me . . . I can't explain . . ." Her voice died, knowing that she had spoken wildly and that Mrs Sanderson was eying her in a sharp, hard way, entirely new. She didn't understand. How could she? She had barely an acquaintance with Uncle George and had been quite taken in by his suaveness.

But Dorothea Sanderson knew all too well. She knew a great deal about men. She had met the likes of George O'Hara before. The bullies with smooth, lying tongues and open faces. She had not been in the cottage five minutes before she had his measure. She had noted well the frightened, pitiful wife and the two girls, the one with a beauty so promising it caught your throat and the other in her cheap print frock with her broken nails and tired shadows under her eyes that spoke of no genteel employment. The smell of hopelessness in that place had reminded her of times she preferred to forget. She did not want to be involved. She had gratified her curiosity and been generous. She wanted nothing more to do with them.

Adele wandered up the track after her sister. Mrs Sanderson's gaze was drawn, reluctantly, to her. Robert had been a handsome devil and this little one was set to be a charmer too, though she was as yet unaware of it. That innocence was a snare – a lure to a man like George O'Hara. Yet she could not do it. She could not have her in the house. She began to regret that she had not stifled that driving impulse to see Robert's girls.

Carrie noted the hesitation.

"I'm sorry. I had no right to bother you." She retreated from the carriage step and the coachman closed the door.

The girls stood in the sunshine, the breeze that had arisen billowing their skirts and stirring the branches of the old ash tree that threw shade over the carriage. Elliot Sanderson, lounging listlessly against the soft leather cushions found his glance drawn, as his mother's had been, to the golden-haired girl in the white muslin dress. He narrowed his eyes against the glare and through his lashes it seemed the outlines of the enchanting, smiling creature blurred so that she looked ethereal. He moved, frowned, pressed nearer to the glass, feeling the stirrings of interest and curiosity. The girl caught his look and dropped a curtsey, just as his mother opened the window and called, uncomprehendingly, "Write to the lawyers if there are difficulties. There is nothing more I can do."

The carriage drew away. The girls watched it out of sight, then Adele said, "Did you see him? That would be her son, wouldn't it? Wasn't he handsome? Didn't you think so, Carrie?"

Carrie sighed and said absently, "I had no right to ask – to expect her to do more than she has already. It was kind of her to come."

"But did you see him?" Adele persisted. "The young man in the carriage?"

Carrie blinked. "Yes, I saw there was someone. I didn't take much notice."

"Oh, he was *beautiful*."

Her sister smiled. "You cannot call a young man beautiful. Girls are beautiful."

Adele pressed her hands together. "But he *was*. Much more than merely handsome. Like a painting. Or a statue of a Greek god or . . . or a prince. Yes, that's it, a prince out of a fairy tale."

Carrie only half heard. She was wondering how the precious money could be kept from her uncle. There was so much the money could do. Comforts for Aunt Linnie, good food, new clothes. Carefully managed it could lift them all back to the easier life they had once known. If only there was some way to keep its control from her uncle.

"A prince," Adele murmured dreamily. "Out of a fairy tale . . ."

In the carriage bowling towards Crumpsall, Elliot Sanderson turned the name over in his mind. Adele. *Adele*. A charming name for a charming child. Aloud, he said a trifle pettishly, "I wish you had let me go in with you. You see how hot it has become in here. I was beginning to feel quite smothered. It would have been interesting to have met some new people."

His mother leaned forward and rested her hand on his knee. "My dear, it would not have done. It was perfectly dull, and only a duty call on people not at all our style."

"But less tedious than sitting staring at a tree trunk for half an hour."

"You were resting, dear," his mother said gently. "I should not have forgiven myself if you had overtaxed yourself or picked up some infection in your weakened state. Besides,"

26

she added gaily, "you provided me with an excuse to leave. Now, shall we stop somewhere and take a little stroll, or would you prefer to return home for tea?"

Neither alternative appealed to him and he was not prepared to be coaxed into good humour. "As you please," he said irritably, leaning his head back and closing his eyes. Images of the golden-haired fairy creature drifted across his mind. It was an age since his thoughts had been stirred to anything but contemplation of his bodily discomforts. Indeed, since he had *wanted* to reach out beyond the apathy of spirit and flesh that had taken him since . . . since . . . No, he would not think of that. He would not think of those dreadful days after Mahmood, his friend, his brother in spirit, and Fatimah with all her brown, lithe grace, had disappeared . . . gone without trace, with the not knowing far worse than knowing why and how and for what reason they had vanished. Some awful fate had overtaken them, he was convinced, for there had been no message, and they had been so close since childhood.

He felt tension creeping into his limbs; his hands had bunched into knuckled fists on his knees. He must not slip back into the depression of mind that had blackened his last months in Penang and led to the brain fever that had so nearly carried him off on the ship. No, he must think of other things. Of the travel his mother had promised him, of the new clothes to be ordered, the glorious poems he would write. A poet must suffer in order to write great poetry, that was certain. Well, he had suffered enough.

But one came out of the vale of tragedy in time and began to notice and be taken with delectable golden-haired girls. He wished he might have spoken to her, but perhaps that would have shattered the image. She might have the accents and mind of a country clod. But it was pleasing to think she might not and, so thinking, he began to compose a poem in his head.

The tensed fists slowly uncurled and presently his pale hands lay at rest.

He would have been surprised to know that his composed and imperious mamma found the child disturbing the serenity of her thoughts. Try as she might she could not rid herself of certain images: the urgency of Carrie's appeal, the looming presence of George O'Hara, Adele's delicate, unspoiled beauty. It put her distinctly out of temper, not least because it was her own fault. It had been a weakness to seek them out, to give in to her curiosity. She was a woman who had no patience with weakness or impulse. She felt impatient with herself because, for once, she had acted irrationally.

She thought of what was to be done, what it was possible to do without causing herself inconvenience. Several times she decided that quite the most sensible procedure was to leave the wretched child to her fate, and then the memory of the sister, with her worn hands and shadowed eyes pleading for protection not for herself – though heaven knows she looked as though she needed it – but for the younger, even more defenceless one, would rebuke her.

Later that night she went as usual to sit at her husband's bedside and relate to him all the titbits of gossip and news that would amuse and entertain him. He had been sadly low since the doctors insisted his health would not stand another year in the tropics. She tried to make light of her visit to the O'Haras' cottage but Miles, always quick to sense her moods, gently probed and questioned until in exasperation she put down her embroidery and said, "Miles, it is ridiculous, but I find the predicament of these girls quite worrying. I disliked the uncle, and their aunt is a weak creature with hardly a word to say for herself. I fear they have a disagreeable life. Their father – their parents – could never have envisaged such a future for them. Yet it is not my responsibility."

"Indeed not," he agreed.

"But I cherish a memory of Robert Linton's kindness when there was money owing on every side and rogues like that partner of Tom's, Pereira, ready to pounce on the helpless mouse I was. Without him, I think I would have been tempted to fling myself into the nearest river to feed the crocodiles!"

"Which would have been a great loss to me," her husband said gravely. "And I have much to thank him for myself. Had he not come to me on your behalf, why, we might not have met."

"I fear he would have been distressed to see the way his girls have come down in the world."

"You worry too much, Dolly. You have done what you could for them. The money . . ."

She threw out her hands. "If I could be sure the money was to benefit Robert's girls I would leave for Italy with a content mind. Whatever capital was left to them has clearly been misappropriated by the aunt and uncle, for the girls have had little education and their surroundings are impoverished."

Miles Sanderson shifted his aching bones in the feather bed and ran a tired hand through his hair. He looked at the glowing face of his wife and felt an old man. The twenty years difference in their ages had not ever seemed important until lately. Now, his health undermined by recurring bouts of swamp fever and the idleness enforced by the physicians, had flung him into a deep uncharacteristic melancholy. His years weighed heavy and he was sharply aware of his own uselessness. He, who had always been so active in business and enjoyed the cut and thrust of commerce, must now be content to let managers and agents make the decisions for him. He had lived the greater part of his life in the East Indies and was a stranger in his own country, in his own house even. The change had cut his pride and spirit. He was washed up, stranded, finished. A sick animal crawling home to die. And he was much too weary to make the effort to respond to his wife's appeal. Yet habit drove him.

"Would you like me to look into the matter for you?"

Her eyes brightened hopefully. "You are not strong enough, my love. You need to rest."

"You know how this illness runs. In a few days – a week – I shall be up and about again. It will do me no harm to drive into town to see Fogarty. Perhaps a trust of some sort. Fogarty will advise me."

"If you are quite certain."

He smiled. "You may go to Italy with an untroubled mind."

How little changed she was. He saw her, all those years ago, receiving him in the stuffy, shuttered room that had been Bellamy's office, stubbornness stiffening her back, her voice. No, she did not wish to return to England. She had no relatives or friends. There was nothing for her there. She had rather stay in Penang and build something out of what she had left of her husband's business. He remembered Robert Linton's quiet persuasion. It was no place for a woman alone, would not Mr Sanderson agree? He did. He added his arguments to Linton's, half irritated by her obstinacy, half admiring. She had listened, eyes downcast, then had said with calm determination "I shall be better here, I know it. With your help, sir, I shall manage." She had turned her dark beseeching eyes upon him and he had seen the fear that glinted behind the veneer of self-assurance. He noticed, then, that she was a handsome woman, that she gave elegance to the cheap mourning she wore. "Will you not help me, Mr Sanderson? Mr Linton already has his passage booked. I shall be quite without support when he has gone."

"If you are determined." He had seen that she was and was touched at her courage, her foolishness. And, so quickly, the feelings she had stirred at that first meeting became something very different.

She leaned forward now and kissed him on the cheek.

"You are good to me, Miles," she said softly. "You have always been good to me. I thank God that we met when we did and that we have had so many years of happiness together."

"I, too, my dear." He touched the shining coils of her hair. He had never blinded himself to the fact that she had married him for security. The adoration had been all on his side. Yet their marriage had been good for all that. Strong and satisfying. They had differed only in the matter of the rearing of their son, but in that he had given in gracefully enough. He understood her fears. There were great hazards to raising children in such an unhealthy climate and Elliot was, sadly, to be their only child. If she had overprotected, overcosseted the boy, it was understandable. Though, with hindsight, a trifle more masculine discipline, a little less pampering, might have prepared the boy better to take his place in the world.

She sighed. "I should not be leaving you to chase across Europe."

"Elliot needs the company of young people and new sights to distract him." As you do, he thought. You need company and gaiety still. All I wish is to be left to vegetate, to grow used to the idea of being an old man. "I shall meet you in London later in the year."

He had been glad when a cousin of his had suggested they join a family party travelling to Italy and Switzerland. He could urge Dolly to go knowing she was in safe company. He had no desire to make any more tiresome journeys to foreign places, sleeping in flea-ridden beds and eating unsuitable food. Dolly was anxious to see Elliot launched into society, to have him accepted into the houses of the best people, so that one day he might choose a wife from a wide circle of aristocratic young ladies. This would be a start for him.

He smiled. "You may perhaps during your wanderings be able to turn Elliot's mind towards more practical matters

31

than penning sonnets or collecting botanical specimens or haranguing the tailor over the cut of his jackets."

"Give him time, Miles. He is only a boy and not strong. The alpine air should improve his health. When we are all together in London he will perhaps be more receptive to your wishes."

It was his one disappointment that his son should show a total disinterest in the commercial empire he had built up throughout his life. The estates, the mines, the shipping interests were all now in the hands of managers. It was his hope that the boy would someday return to take up the reins of management.

He eased his legs to a less uncomfortable position. "I shall speak to him then. And seriously, mind, Dolly." He smiled to ease the sting of his words. "But enjoy your holiday, my love. You deserve it for caring so well for a crotchety old man like me. I shall look to the welfare of the Linton girls. You need not give them another thought."

Dorothea Sanderson went to bed that night, her conscience eased. Miles would make the necessary arrangements. The lawyers would ensure that the money was used wisely until the sisters were of an age to be entrusted with their own affairs. She would never have to bother her head about them again. It was a mistake to have visited them at all. She could see that now. For a few hours the calm surface of her existence had been ruffled, bringing dark images and forgotten fears to the surface, like silt from the bed of a pond that swirls upward to the light when the water is stirred with a stick. Well, she would think no more of it. There was no reason to do so. She closed her eyes and, being a determined woman, fell to a dreamless, soothing sleep.

Down in the stews of Angel Meadow George O'Hara was soddenly drunk. He had thought it politic not to celebrate at the Eagle & Child, his usual haunt, where there were too many tattling tongues. After all, with a hundred pounds a year to look forward to and the prospects of an increase in his fortunes in the coming years, he could consider himself a man of substance. He would have to look to appearances now. He would become a man to be respected.

"Buy us another gin then, Georgie-boy," the harlot at his side screeched in his ear to make herself heard above the clamour in the tavern. "Come on now, Georgie. Gin for me and another brandy for yerself."

He flung a scatter of coins among the slops on the table and fumbled drunkenly at the tattered ribbons on her bodice.

"Be a rich man one day," he mumbled. "Just you wait and see."

The girl clawed greedily at the money.

"Another drink, Georgie. Then you come upstairs with me. Nice little room I got. Give you a good time."

"Goo' time." He slurred at her and waveringly took the glass she offered. He downed the brandy. "Goo' time wi' you. Like 'em young an' plump. Not like tha' saggin' lump I wed . . ." He screwed up his eyes. "How old're you?"

The girl ran her black-rimmed fingers up his solid thigh, "Fourteen," she tittered. "Leastways, I think that's the right of it. Me mam was never too sure."

His grin was plastered to his scarlet, leering face. "Jus' nice," he said. "Young and plump." Then, slowly, he toppled forward into the mess of spilled ale and spirits on the table top.

The girl grinned. Nice easy pickings. She skilfully rifled his pockets and was rising from the bench when someone pressed her back into the seat.

The woman standing over her was grinning too and the glint in her eye made the girl's smile waver. "Now, now," she said. "Nasty that, robbin' a poor drunk. Constables wouldn't like to hear about that Biddy."

"Aw, Sal," the girl protested. "It's fair enough. He's had me company all evening. Why shouldn't he pay for it. A girl has ter live."

Sally Quick gazed down at the ruffled head on the table.

"I seen him down here before," she said. "Quite took me fancy, he did. Well-set-up feller. A sturdy girl like me needs a good strong chap to mind her." She laughed throatily.

"Well, you have him, Sal," the girl said hastily, moving from her seat. "I done wi' 'im. I'm off to try me luck down Deansgate."

The brown, hard fingers took her wrist, shaking the hand gently until Biddy's clenched fingers opened to release the shower of coins onto the table.

"Tut, tut," said Sally shaking her head. "You want to watch those quick fingers o' yours, Biddy. "Get you into trouble they will."

"Don't tell me you never picked nobody's pocket," said the girl a trifle shrilly, "because I wouldn't believe it."

"Neither would I," Sally laughed. "But wi' customers now, that's a different kettle of fish. Customers have memories. Full of drink they may be, but they might just remember that they had a purse full of money when they came to visit and an empty one afterwards – beyond what they paid out for services rendered. And they might also remember your pretty face and next time they sees it kick up a stink enough to raise the dead. No, you watch yourself, Biddy Harbottle. You're too young to rot away in the New Bailey or be transported to some plaguey colony."

The girl sniffed and flounced away. Sally lowered herself into the seat beside George. With a heave of her strong brown arms, bare to the shoulder in a scarlet flounced dress, she heaved him upright. He blinked blearily.

"By," she said, "you've had a skinful, lad. And nearly lost all your spare cash to boot." She scooped the money from the table and tipped it back into his pocket. He wagged his head at her. "Nice and plump," he said owlishly. "Differen' though. Wheresh the other . . . ?"

"Gone and best rid of," Sally said. "You'll do far better wi' me, lad. You come along o' Sal."

She hoisted him to his feet and looped his arm over her shoulder. "A fine figure of a man," she told him, her black eyes gleaming in her gypsy-brown face. "Took me eye you have. Georgie, she called you. Well, you come on George. That's it, keep your legs goin'. 'Tisn't far."

Staggering and stumbling the two of them made their way from the tavern.

At about the same time that George O'Hara was tipped unceremoniously onto Sally Quick's bed, dawn was already well up in Singapore. The island lay in a green hump on the pearly water, the first fingers of sun firing the raw red gashes of newly cleared land.

The *Esperance* lay at rest on her own reflection. After the filthy trip, the calm and quiet seemed like a good omen. The mate leaned over the rail and spat into the still water, running a thick hand over the stubble on his chin. Bad weather, sickness, shifting cargo – jinxed they'd been. Jinxed, aye, by that scrubby Malay tyke they'd taken on board in Canton. And now that he was to be shipped off, even the weather showed that luck was back with them. In his years at sea the mate had known a few Jonahs. Trailing trouble after 'em like a tart trailing a cloud of cheap scent. He should've trusted his instincts from the start, but they'd been short-handed and Mahmood had been desperate to work his passage back to Penang. There was something too soft and helpless about him. And he was too pretty for his own good, for all that he was a half-starved bag of bones. There'd been squabbles over him in the fo'c'sle before they'd cleared the Pearl River, with two of the hands flaunting bruises and bloody noses in consequence. Aye, he should've booted him ashore there and then.

The canvas-wrapped bundle on the deck stirred and muttered. The mate hurled an oath in the direction of the men unlashing the boat. Slow bastards. Quicker they got the heathen off, better he'd be pleased. The poor sod, he thought without pity. The jinx had fixed him good and proper that day when the typhoon hit them and the great cross piece had split with a crack like thunder and crashed to the deck in a mess of rope and splintered wood, torn canvas and human flesh. He'd bought it good and proper. Two dead there'd been and this one crushed to a pulp. By rights he should never have lasted an hour, something so damaged as that had no business bein' alive at all. But somehow he'd survived. Clung to life with a surprising grip as the ship limped down the wild length of the South China Sea.

With his foot the mate pushed aside the loose canvas over Mahmood's face.

"Not so pretty now, me darlin'," he grinned. "No one'll fight over your favours any more."

In the puffed, torn flesh one eye opened and rolled slowly upwards. It fixed itself on the mate's seamed and stubbled face. The swollen lips moved.

"Water is it? You'll get no more water from me. Mebbe you'll find some mates ashore to see to you, for that's where you're going pretty smartish. Singapore, that is. Can't afford the likes of you on board longer than can be helped. When you're on your feet – if you ever get back on 'em – let some other poor bugger take you on to Penang. I want no more of your cursed bad luck."

The mate watched the rhythmic dipping of the oars as the boat with its inert bundle made for the sliver of beach with its leaning palms. The drips of water from the oars caught the low sunlight and turned to diamonds. He breathed deeply of the familiar smell of tarred rope and salt-damp wood. He felt as though a burden had been lifted from the slow-dipping decks of the *Esperance*, and almost as at a signal, a cat's-paw of breeze stirred the surface of the sea. He grinned with relief. The weather would buck up now. It'd be fair winds all the way.

"Good riddance," he breathed through his teeth. "And good luck to you, matey. By God you'll need it."

Then he turned his back and put Mahmood from his mind.

The night was thick and heavy. At the cottage Linnie O'Hara dozed fitfully in the big double bed, conscious of its emptiness. In the next room Adele dreamed of sunny meadows and a vague, princely figure who came towards her bearing flowers. Half a mile away, Jem Walker lay awake staring into the darkness of the tiny room he shared with his old grandfather and his widowed sister's two young sons. He heard nothing of the familiar sounds – his grandfather's wheezy snores, the soft breathing of the boys who shared his mattress, the unceasing burble of the Irk running below the window. His head was filled with the tale Adele had poured out to him. "Papa helped this lady once with some investments and she is to give them to us. We are to have an *income* – grand ladies we shall be with a hundred pounds a year! And there will be more later."

He had stood there with the jar of liniment his mother had sent in his hand. His first reaction had been joy. He was glad that something good had happened to his Carrie. His second reaction was less pleasurable.

Mrs O'Hara said flatly, "Don't dance about so, Adele, you will bring on your cough. And it is time you were in bed. Be off with you now."

Then when Adele had gone to her room she had said, "Adele is too young to comprehend, but I had hoped that Mrs Sanderson might have benefited the girls in other ways.

Taken them away from here, away from . . . that is, given them a fresh start elsewhere." Even though Jem had chosen a time when he knew George O'Hara would be out drinking with his cronies, she whispered as though the very walls were listening and might repeat her hurried phrases to less sympathetic ears. "I hope – I pray – that Mr O'Hara will look more kindly upon the girls. He can be a difficult man. He has strong opinions. Their education, for instance, and Carrie so clever at school. Miss Browning was deeply upset when I had to remove her – but George insisted. He said there was no sense in educating females, filling their heads with nonsense." She turned her desperate, haggard face up to Jem. "It will make a difference, won't it? The money I mean. He is kinder to Adele of late. He will treat Carrie less harshly now, will he not? She cannot possibly stay where she is now employed, not with an independent income." She spoke as though to convince herself.

Jem felt an unaccustomed surge of irritation. He wanted to shout at her, 'For heaven's sake, woman, you brought trouble down on yourself and on those you were supposed to be caring for by marrying the man. Couldn't you see the kind of man he was? My Carrie has had to suffer because of your weakness.' Then he was immediately washed with shame. The poor soul was ill and had suffered more than any of them. He said instead gruffly, "I'm sure it'll turn out for the best," and he could see how she brightened at his words, clinging to this little scrap of comfort.

"Yes, it will be for the best," she repeated hopefully. "You are right, Jem. We must give it time."

The boy beside him kicked and cried out in his sleep. Automatically Jem reached out a soothing hand and pressed it against the rough head. The boy burrowed to Jem's side seeking security against the nightmare and Jem let him stay, though it was too hot and sticky a night for the warmth to be comfortable.

He thought of the money. He thought of it as a pile of golden sovereigns. He had never seen a hundred of them in his life, not even Carter Smith, he was sure, had so many in his counting house at the back of the stables where bills were drawn up and accounts rendered. Yet Carrie was to have this money, by right, each year. And each year the amount would increase and perhaps one day she would be a rich lady. One day, whatever George O'Hara did now, she would be of an age to manage her own affairs and she would be able to do what she liked with her money.

He felt the knot of unhappiness tighten in his stomach. He should be happy for Carrie, but somehow the insidious thought came that the possession of a fortune was going to take her away from him. He had nothing to offer her. He worked long hours and willingly for Carter Smith. He studied his letters every day and was planning to attend evening classes for working men. His family was poor, but respectable, and his mother's accomplishments as a nurse gave her a certain standing. But these achievements were pitifully sparse to set against the possession of an independent income.

No, the money would, inevitably, lead Carrie away into another world. A different world. Back into the kind of life she had known when she was a child. Away from him.

He felt the sweat breaking out down his side and along the length of his muscular legs where the boy's flesh touched his. His longing for Carrie possessed him like a fever. He stifled a groan and buried his face in the pillow. He couldn't let her go from him so easily. He must think. Plan.

The river gurgled on into the dark, close night and presently its faint cadences lulled him into the sleep of total exhaustion.

Carrie was still awake. The heat was stifling in the attic. The sun had burned down on the roof all day and the clouds that had slowly blotted out the stars at dusk seemed to press down, making the air thick and unbreathable.

She stood at the window that stubbornly refused to open more than two inches and pressed her forehead to the warm glass. If it hadn't been for the black beetles she would have sneaked down to the kitchen by the back stairs and stretched herself out on the cool stone flags, but she knew that the scuttling creatures would be in possession.

Her hair clung limply to her forehead and her cotton nightdress to her back though she was scarcely aware of it. She was remembering her one flash of rebellion against her uncle. How old had she been? Just thirteen and two weeks of scrubbing floors and cooking meals and cleaning furniture and emptying slops and carrying trays for sixteen hours a day had reduced her to numb defiance.

"I won't go back there! You can't make me. I want to go back to school."

He had stood over her, fixed her with his cold eyes. She had stiffened her jaw and stared straight back at him, hating him, challenging him. And sick inside when his answer came soft and agreeable and poisoned.

"Of course you may leave whenever you wish, Carrie. You may return home and look after the cottage and cook my dinners." He paused. "You might even return to your schooling. It would mean, however, some sacrifices on the part of others if you choose to be selfish. I had thought Adele should remain at school a little longer, but I can't find the fees for both of you. And though your aunt has never been used to working outside the home – indeed, she has complained that she finds even washing and ironing fatiguing now I have had to economise by putting off the laundry woman – I hear that the landlord at the Eagle & Child is looking for help. It would not pay well but it would help to keep you in idleness."

"You wouldn't, you couldn't make Aunt Linnie – she is ill!"

But she had known that George was capable even of that. He would set his wife, white and trembling from her latest miscarriage, to some skivvying job and take Adele from school in order to humiliate them all.

She had not defied him again. She had sought to relieve her aunt's distress in small ways. She submitted to her uncle's will for Aunt Linnie's sake. And for Adele's. But one day . . . one day she would escape and take her aunt and her sister from his dominance.

A distant clock struck two. She dragged herself wearily to her bed and flung herself down. If only she could take control of the money she would get them away tomorrow. How she hated him. Hated him!

Sleep would not come. Presently she heard the soft patter of rain and the room lit luridly as lightning flickered.

Out at Crumpsall the Sandersons slept soundly in their pleasantly cool house. In far less salubrious surroundings George O'Hara thought his head would split at the first crack of thunder. He moaned and burrowed his head into Sally Quick's shoulder and presently dozed again. His wife slept undisturbed in her double bed, and nearby Adele dreamed peacefully. Down in Hendham Vale Jem was oblivious in exhausted slumber.

Only Carrie was awake to hear the rumblings of the approaching storm.

Chapter Two

"Just smell the soot," Adele said, spreading her skirts carefully over the carriage seat and settling back gently in consideration of her new lavender merino. She wrinkled her nose. "I had quite forgot how the air reeks in Manchester."

Grey wet buildings went briskly past the windows. The carriage wheels splashing through puddles as they made the turn from Market Street into Market Place sent showers of muddy water over pedestrians straying too close to the traffic. They hurried on through the narrow thoroughfares leading to York Street, when the pace of the horses slowed on account of the long pull up to Cheetham Hill. The buildings diminished into rows of newly built, close-packed terraces with the occasional tall chimney of a mill or factory looming upwards, then they petered out into the fields and hedges and ponds of Strangeways and Cheetwood which lay dismal and dun-coloured under the weeping January skies.

"And everywhere looks so dirty," Carrie murmured.

"It is the rain, I expect," Adele said. "Nowhere looks well on such a day. Malvern was excessively dismal when the weather was wet, yet there was no pleasanter place when the sun shone."

Carrie sighed softly and rubbed the misting glass with her glove. "I never minded the rain at Malvern. The hills looked so splendid whatever the season. I could walk and walk and take no heed of the weather."

"Well, that is all behind us now. We shall not have Mrs Clare fussing at our heels again, kind old soul that she was."

Carrie smiled. "She deserves retirement after a lifetime of looking after unruly girls."

"I, for one, am glad to be done with schooldays," Adele declared. "It was all very well for you, Carrie. You liked nothing better than to have your nose in some dreary history book or volume of French verbs. I have no head for such things."

Good years, Carrie thought. More than two of them. I had not expected to be so happy and content there. I felt so free, unshackled. Already I feel the bonds beginning to tighten. Yet I shall be glad to see Aunt Linnie again and everything, now, is altered.

"It was kind of Mr Sanderson to send the carriage to meet us," Adele said. "He is the soul of kindness. I could wish that Aunt Linnie had married a man like Mr Sanderson rather than Uncle George, though I dare say he has mellowed. After all, he allowed us to go to Mrs Clare's to complete our education with scarce a word of protest."

Carrie had wondered often why Uncle George had given his permission so easily. But she had come to respect Mr Sanderson. He had not accumulated a fortune in the East Indies without shrewdness and effort. He had never explained how he had persuaded Uncle George to allow them to leave for Malvern. It seemed, to Carrie, something of a miracle. He had achieved even more than that – he had arranged for Uncle George and Aunt Linnie to move into the lodge of his own house, Beech Place, and given Uncle George employment.

It seemed an age ago since he had come to interview her in Miss Tucker's cheerless parlour. The elderly ladies were agog with curiosity – flattered at the visit of such a gentleman, disgruntled and suspicious because he had wished to speak to their maid in private. And the questions! Courteous but persistent, sometimes seemingly irrelevant, the quiet voice had probed. Out of loyalty to her aunt Carrie had been unwilling at first to speak, but Mr Sanderson's sympathetic manner, his obvious integrity, had won her over. She had poured out her account of their lives since they had returned to England; her fears, her hopes, to the man who sat on Miss Tucker's best chair, his hands clasped about the carved handle of his Malacca cane.

When she had finished he had taken her hand and patted it. "Something will be done," he murmured. "Something will be done."

She had tried not to be too hopeful. She could not imagine Uncle George giving an inch in the matter of anyone's welfare but his own. There had been questions about him, too. 'What did you know of your uncle before he came to Manchester?' 'How did your aunt meet him?' 'Where did he come from?' 'What is his background?'

She had to confess that George O'Hara had divulged little about his previous life beyond vague hints of a decent upbringing and education and later misfortunes. "He mentioned Bristol and Warwick, but he has travelled about England a great deal. He was last, I believe, in Stafford before he came to Manchester."

Mr Sanderson had gone away then, but not long afterwards he had sent for Uncle George to call upon him at Beech Place. What had transpired at that interview no one knew. "He came back very quiet," Aunt Linnie whispered. "Said not a word to me."

The next day Uncle George told Carrie to give in her notice for she and Adele were to go away to school.

There were no loopholes.

"I cannot leave Aunt Linnie," Carrie had protested. "She is sick."

"Your aunt will be cared for," Mr Sanderson had said. "Mr

O'Hara has agreed to enter my employ. There is a fine lodge building at Beech Place. Your aunt and uncle will take up residence there. In return, Mr O'Hara has agreed to assist with the restoration work on my house. I have seen some of his carpentry and it is excellent. Mrs Sanderson and my son will be away a good deal, as I shall myself from time to time. My housekeeper will keep an eye on your aunt, and Mrs Walker, who seems a sensible woman, will visit regularly. Seven pounds a year can be managed, I think, out of your income to secure a maidservant."

Her protests were stifled. The arrangements were made. The lawyer visited. Carrie had insisted that part of their money should be set aside for Mrs Walker's services, and for refurbishing the lodge.

"My dear girl," Mr Sanderson said, "there will be nothing left to pay your school fees."

"It is what I wish," Carrie said stubbornly.

Mr Sanderson sighed. "Very well. It is fortunate I foresaw this possibility. Mrs Clare specialises at her establishment in the care of girls whose parents are in the colonies. She was spoken of most highly by friends I had in Penang. However, she is getting on in years and when I wrote to her mentioning your age and circumstances, she advised me that she was looking for someone to help with the little ones. See them over their homesickness and that sort of thing. There would be some adjustment of the fees if you would be willing to undertake these duties. With your background you would doubtless be sympathetic to those suddenly bereft of loving parents." He paused. "It would mean, of course, that you would be required to stay at the school during the holidays."

"But I could not leave Aunt Linnie for so long."

"Your aunt is agreeable," he said mildly. "She feels it will be best for you both to stay for an extended period in such a healthful spot." His eyes were sharp and knowledgeable. "For myself I would consider that the journey from Malvern two or three times a year would be fatiguing for Adele."

So she could go with a clear conscience, though she wondered secretly if she was exchanging one kind of drudgery for another. But Mr Sanderson had been as searching in his investigations of the school as in everything else. Mrs Clare planned to retire in a few years and had consequently reduced the number of pupils at her academy for young ladies. There was a homely atmosphere about the place. Mrs Clare did most of the teaching, with the aid of a visiting mademoiselle and a dancing master. Carrie's duties were scarcely more than she would have undertaken voluntarily when she saw the small, frightened girls, newly arrived. Under Mrs Clare's motherly and shrewd eye the holidays were times of great pleasure with long walks and games of croquet and tennis in the summer, or cards and books and singing around a roaring fire in winter.

Carrie had learned again to be happy. The remembrance of her days of servitude at Miss Tucker's fell away like a banished nightmare.

Mr Sanderson had paid a visit to Malvern to take the waters after one of his regular bouts of fever.

"I cannot thank you enough," Carrie told him when he called at the school. "Adele has never been so well or I so full of energy. The days are not long enough to accomplish all that I want to do." Then she added shyly, "You have been kind beyond the ordinary. Without your help I doubt I should ever have escaped from Miss Tucker's. But may I ask you why you bothered yourself with our problems?"

"Why? A duty, my dear." His eyes twinkled. "I thought so at first, for I was full of self-pity and low in spirits. I was quite put out when my wife hinted that it would ease her mind if I saw a lawyer on your behalf."

"Why, then, did you not leave us to the mercies of lawyers?"

"Because I felt bound to see these girls that I was asked to help. Before I knew it, I was enamoured of you both and determined to do all in my power to assist you. I have never been one to do things by halves."

"Adele and I owe you – and Mrs Sanderson – a great debt of gratitude."

"On the contrary. I should thank you for preventing me from rusticating into decrepit old age. Having to deal with your small matters prodded my atrophying brain into life. I have since gone on to start up a few schemes on my own account in Manchester. Nothing too taxing, but enough to amuse me in retirement."

"Oh, look Carrie!" Adele's voice snapped the thread of her thoughts. "See, there is the Eagle & Child looking as tumbledown as ever. I wonder, does Uncle George still visit there? It seems odd not to be turning down Smedley Lane. I should like to see the cottage again. Perhaps we may walk there when the weather improves."

The carriage bowled on through Cheetham village. There was little traffic here, only a man leading a panniered donkey, a few swaddled pedestrians, a wagon splashing past. Carrie pressed to the window. Not one of Carter Smith's, so the driver, anonymous under his wrappings and broad brimmed hat, could not be Jem Walker.

She leaned back, thinking of the letters received in the last two years from Aunt Linnie and Jem. Aunt Linnie's, long and excitable at first in the euphoria of her newly secure state – when the lodge was so pretty and convenient and the girl so willing and George so settled and well-thought of – fell, eventually, to somewhat fretful catalogues of domestic trivia. The girl did not suit and was replaced with others who were briefly regarded as paragons but, too, soon fell short of expectations and had to go. Her health continued poor and there were days when she could not raise her head from the sofa, let alone get out into the fresh air as Carrie urged. Mrs Walker was kind to call but she was not versed in genteel conversation and the days were lonely, the lodge being so much out of the way and Beech Place shut up for most of the time . . .

Carrie replied with bracing letters, but she felt troubled. Was Uncle George still unkind to Aunt Linnie despite Mr Sanderson's assurances? Was it right that she should be enjoying herself at Malvern when her aunt was without companions? Adele's healthy smiling face reassured her, but she grew to feel apprehensive when Aunt Linnie's letters arrived.

Not so with Jem's. They were brief and misspelled at first but, as his penmanship improved, so the letters grew longer. They told of small matters: a horse nursed through a bout of colic; a walk along the bank of the Irk with his sister to collect primroses; an unusual load to be carried to some part of the town he had not visited before. They were little yet vivid pen pictures that brought surprising nostalgia. She imagined him, long frame hunched over the table, blue eyes narrowed in concentration, the light from the candle falling yellow across the paper and the scratching quill, and the big hand pushing impatiently through the black tangle of his hair when a word eluded him. She had seen him like that many an evening when she had taught him his letters and it was a recollection that had somehow stayed with her, seeming more intense in retrospect than all the miserable and uncomfortable times she had experienced.

He had written, too, of deeper things – the death of his grandfather, an outbreak of scarlet fever, his own hopes and ambitions. She, in turn, had confided her doubts about Aunt Linnie. '. . . You mustn't fret about her,' he had written. 'I have looked in and she is as comfortable as can be. Ma says she has too much time to dwell on her health and would do better if she would make some effort to go about. As for your uncle, he puts himself out to be agreeable, so do not worry on that score.'

It was a relief to have sensible advice, to know that she had a friend she could rely on to be honest. She was touched too that he remembered her birthday and Adele's. He sent small tokens. A length of ribbon, a handkerchief and, latterly, a book of Shakespeare's verse. She and Adele had each taken a verse and written it out in fine script on white card. Adele, because she had a pretty knack with watercolours, had painted an edging of pansies. Carrie, being less skilful with the paintbrush, had arranged a border of pressed and dried wild flowers. They had sent them to him at Christmas and had read the delight behind his carefully worded thanks.

She looked out at the quiet fields and woodlands of Crumpsall. Yes, she had missed Jem in the way she had not missed Aunt Linnie – and certainly not Uncle George! Jem was the elder brother she'd never had. Someone to talk to, to confide in. She was looking forward to seeing him again.

But not today. The carriage had turned into a narrow lane with a high wall to one side and a thick, old copse of trees on the other. Presently it turned in between high iron gates and stopped.

The lodge was a welcoming place after the windy, wet outdoors. A great fire crackled in the parlour hearth, there were flowers everywhere, vases of unseasonable blossoms Mr Sanderson had sent from the hothouses. "And why not," he declared, "Mrs Sanderson is away on one of her jaunts to Elliot's future in-laws and there is no one at the house to appreciate them. It seems an appropriate way to welcome you home."

Strange to call this lodge home when she had only been in it once before and the memories of Malvern were so strong. But it was pleasant. Surprisingly spacious for, as Mr Sanderson had once explained, this had been the dower house of the original estate, much of which had been sold off by Mr Sanderson's grandfather. 'He had a mania for altering and rebuilding. He had the old house remodelled – it was a rambling half-timbered affair – on classical lines. To pay for it he sold off much of the land which then extended down to the Irk and beyond. He built the new boundary wall and incorporated part of the old dower house as the lodge – after he had hacked it about well, of course.'

They had been large low-ceilinged rooms once; now they were divided up to give a parlour and dining room, a kitchen and a scullery with a room for the girl to sleep in, and a cluster of outbuildings and stores. And upstairs there were three good bedrooms and an attic.

And even had the house been poor and bare – which it was not, because Carrie had seen to it before she left that Mr Sanderson should select good items of furniture, piece by piece, as the money became available – the welcome would have been enough to warm them both.

Aunt Linnie wept over them. "How you have grown . . . become young ladies . . . I never thought . . . Oh, I am so pleased to see you, my dearest girls." She was greatly changed from the hollow-eyed wraith she had been. Though her hair was greying and, once she had greeted them, she moved slowly and painfully back to the sofa, two years of good food and comfortable living had swelled out her figure and plumped her cheeks. Mrs Sanderson stood smiling and benevolent by the fire and Mrs Walker was there to bustle about with the maid, bringing tea and cakes and tiny sandwiches to the weary travellers. Even the girl, Jane, the most recent, and, Carrie thought, surely the smallest of the succession of maids, smiled at them toothily, her eyes like saucers in her bony little face as she took in every detail of the new arrivals.

After a while Mrs Walker excused herself. She was a big raw-boned woman with a strong, almost severe expression, daunting to a stranger, but as the many people she had nursed and dosed with her potions could testify, possessed of a kindly and practical nature. She made her farewells saying cheerfully, "I'm glad to see you looking so bonny, the both of you, but I must be on my way. I've people to call on. Our Jem'll be looking in on you. 'Tis a pity he's had to go off on an overnight trip. He was really disappointed . . ."

Carrie too, but no matter. There was plenty of time. Time to adjust to living in these new quiet surroundings without the chatter of girls and the clamour of the young children she had mothered; time to enjoy being with Aunt Linnie again; time to take in Mr Sanderson's talk of plans for them.

Yes, it was good to be back even though she had been sad to leave Malvern. And it was good, too, she thought with relief, that Uncle George had chosen not to be present at their homecoming.

He was one person she did not miss at all.

It was dark by the time George O'Hara left his workshop at the back of the big house. He should have gone earlier. It had been expected of him, but he had his small moments of rebellion. There were times when he liked to show that long-nosed bastard Sanderson that underneath the obliging mask he wore there was still an independent spirit.

He moved with his purposeful slow tread down the gravel path that skirted the lawns. It had stopped raining and a few frosty stars pierced the thinning clouds. He did not look up. He kept his eyes fixed on the small puddle of light from the lantern as the path dipped into the shrubbery, and avoided fallen leaves which made the way slippery.

He'd played his part well. Worked steadily most of the time. Kept his nose clean. Made himself agreeable to those who were able to make life more comfortable. Like cook, who bridled at his appearance as though she was young again and not a great ageing jelly bag; and Mrs Price, the housekeeper, who had too much delicacy to say outright how dreadful it was for a lusty good-looking man like himself to be married to an invalid wife, but the hearty snacks she brought round to the workshop – half a boiled fowl, a melting slice of beef fillet, a hot mutton pie swimming in gravy – spoke for her.

She always had some excuse to visit. Could he come and attend to a window that was sticking, or were the new bookshelves for the library ready? The lowliest maid could have brought the message but no, madam herself must make the journey with the basket on her arm, the contents hidden under a white napkin. Then, after they had discussed at length the window or the bookshelves, she would exclaim over whatever piece of work lay on his bench.

"You are so skilled, Mr O'Hara. Why, only last week Mrs Dawes remarked most flatteringly about the carving over the drawing room mantel. I myself think it is as fine as any I've seen . . ." Before she left she would take the dish from the basket and whisk away the napkin. "Just a snack for you, Mr O'Hara. It must be hungry work sawing and planing and hammering all day." Then she would add hurriedly. "Oh, I sent Jones down to the lodge with the first peaches. I trust Mrs O'Hara finds an appetite for them."

"Mrs Price, I am overwhelmed at such generosity," he would say huskily. "You are so very thoughtful." And he would watch the unbecoming flush rise above the high, tight neck of her black dress and flood her long plain face.

Silly bitch, he thought, automatically swinging the lantern high as he ducked under an arch of leafless rambling roses. Silly deluded bitch. How she'd trembled when, occasionally, out of an excess of gratitude he'd clasped her hand. How her breathing quickened when he pressed close to point out some particularly fine feature on a piece of furniture on his bench.

He grinned in the darkness. He hadn't done too badly in that direction. Cook and Mrs Price kept him well fed and appreciated the need for a craftsman not to rush himself in any job he did. For his other urgent needs there was Sal down in Angel Meadow. A fine strong girl, well versed in tricks to slake a man's more earthy appetites.

Aye, he'd made the best of things. But if Sanderson, God rot him, thought he'd turned into a forelock-tugging toady, he was much mistaken. When the bastard had cornered him, he'd had to make a quick decision. Clear out and make a fresh start somewhere else or stay and make the best of what was offered. It hadn't been too difficult to make up his mind. Better the devil you knew . . . Better to wait and watch and make a move at a more auspicious time.

He could see the lights of the lodge when he came out of the shrubbery. His steps slowed and he swore under his breath. That whining bitch he'd married was in the lodge, and those two girls and Sanderson. He hated them with all the pent-up resentment of a man who'd had a long time to nurture his grievances. Things had been going very nicely for him until Sanderson had put his oar in. That money should have been his, every last farthing of it, instead of which all he saw was an account presented to him each quarter showing how and where it had been spent. So much for schooling and clothes, so much for Linnie and for the upkeep of the lodge, so much reinvested. Nothing for him. Nothing. Every shilling he needed he was forced to work for. Aye, Sanderson had tied him up very neatly and it had been politic then to submit with an appearance of humility. But he did not intend it to be a permanent arrangement.

He opened the lantern and blew out the candle. For more than two years he'd suffered and kept quiet. But his day would come. He'd take revenge on the lot of them.

He trod carefully across the last stretch of lawn and stopped just beyond the light that spilled from the lodge window. The people within were framed as though on a stage. They moved, stood, nodded their heads and mouthed speech, though only the faintest of sounds came to him. A puppet show, he thought. A roomful of puppets jerking on strings.

His gaze went round the group. Linnie was a shapeless hump on the sofa. He passed over her quickly. Sanderson stood by the fire, one elbow on the mantelpiece. George turned his head and spat before he resumed his scrutiny. The old man looked like a heron, all thin and angular with his hunched shoulders and slight stoop. His face was as yellow as a Chinaman's It was to do with the fever that took him from time to time. Real bad they said he was. Sweated so that the sheets had to be changed every hour and shook so much that the bed rattled. Pity the ague hadn't carried him off altogether.

His stage slid past the great vase of hothouse flowers and his eyes narrowed when he came to the girl in the blue dress trimmed with coffee-coloured lace. So, he thought, quite the lady you've turned into, Miss Caroline Linton. She sat, neat and attentive, her brown hair bunched into soft curls either side of cheeks that were rounder and pinker than he remembered. No better looking, though. Still an ordinary creature compared with her sister.

Adele! Now he'd had some hopes of Adele. She'd been malleable. Not irritating and stubborn like Carrie. Pretty, too. Pretty was not the word for her now.

She was on her feet, speaking to her aunt, her movements quick and lively. And, by the Devil, what a woman she'd become. What was she now? Coming up to eighteen? The wolves would soon come howling round after that one. She was a beauty, from her pale shining hair to her neat ankles glimpsed beneath full lavender skirts. She was full-bosomed and small waisted and as she turned her head in conversation, his eyes lingered on the delicate curve of her cheek, the vivid violet-blue of her eyes and the creamy-soft skin. He exhaled slowly. She was handsomer than any of the frilly misses who'd visited Beech Place, and beside her that sharp-nosed wench

Elliot Sanderson had engaged himself to would look a dowdy mess for all she was related to some lord or other.

Thoughtfully he tapped the lantern against his corduroy breeches, his eyes still fixed on the lamplit scene beyond the glass. They all looked happy, innocent and unaware. Puppets all of them. He stood there in the cold, dank air and felt hate curdle in his belly and spread tingling warmth along every nerve, sharpening his brain, nudging his wits awake. Puppets. His cold smile widened. They thought themselves very comfortable and secure. But he'd think of some way to make them dance. Before long he'd be pulling the strings and then they'd jig to his tune.

Still smiling, he left the window and went into the house.

Thinking of it later as she sat at the dressing table of the bedroom that was to be hers and Adele's, Carrie strove to be charitable about Uncle George. He had been pleasant, questioning them about Malvern and their journey, listening with apparent interest to their answers. He had been deferential to Mr Sanderson and jovial with Aunt Linnie. Why, then, had all the spontaneity, the laughter, become a touch forced? Why had an air of awkwardness invaded the parlour? Mr Sanderson had not stayed long. The maid, Jane, had hastily begun clearing away and, when accidentally she clattered some plates together she sent a scared look towards Uncle George and quickly removed herself to the kitchen.

Carrie brushed her hair with slow strokes, listening to the crackle as it curled against the bristles. She thought, I must not judge too soon. I must not allow myself to be influenced by what has happened in the past. This is a new beginning, a slate wiped clean. He has lived for some time with Aunt Linnie in apparent amity. It may be that he is a man I shall never like or wholly trust but I must keep my own counsel and try to think the best of him.

Adele, already snuggling into the feather bed, said on a yawn, "It will be delicious to share a room with you instead of five other girls – two of them snoring louder than a hurdy-gurdy."

Carrie laughed. "Perhaps you will find I snore, then what will you do?"

"Banish you to the attic where you may entertain the spiders." Then she sighed. "I shall miss the girls all the same. It is hard to lose so many friends all at once."

"You will soon make more." She looked fondly at Adele, who had been popular at school and always surrounded by a cluster of chattering girls. Her beauty might have been a barrier, drawing envy and malice, but her unselfconscious acceptance of her looks, her ability to see the best in others and to ignore their faults, her lack of sharpness or cattiness, even drew close those whose nature it was to criticise and carp. Somehow Adele had managed to steer a sunny course through these rapids. Though she had remained incapable of absorbing anything beyond the simplest arithmetical or grammatical principles, and a historical date never stayed in her head more than five minutes together, she had come in for few scoldings, and there were many damp handkerchiefs waved at her departure.

Carrie occasionally envied her unquestioning acceptance of other people's good natures. How simple life must seem to one who took words and attitudes at face value, who trusted so completely. At other times she felt uneasy. The secure world of school was a deal different from the adult one on which they would now embark. Yet how could anyone be with her for long and not like her for her artlessness, admire her for her beauty, feel happy because Adele's smiles were infectious?

"Yes, you will soon make friends," she repeated, laying down the brush because she was too weary to continue. "Mr

Sanderson seems intent on introducing us to young company, as he calls it."

"His friends sound very *worthy*," Adele said doubtfully. "Do you suppose mill owners and bankers and manufacturers dance or attend theatres and soirées?"

"You were not listening properly. He spoke warmly of a Mrs Dawes who has daughters about our age. I gather they lead busy social lives."

"Really?" Sleep momentarily forgotten, Adele said, "Are we to meet them soon?"

"I think so. In any case we are to have luncheon with Mr Sanderson in two days' time to talk over our financial affairs. He will tell us then, I dare say."

Adele wrinkled her nose "How dull. Still, I shall bear it with the greatest fortitude knowing that the delights of Mrs Dawes and her daughters await us."

Carrie climbed into bed and settled into the blissful softness. "Heavens, I ache in every bone. I feel as though we spent a month on that coach."

"And what about young men? I think it a pity that we do not possess an elder brother, for it makes it so much easier to encounter persons of the opposite sex. Brothers, after all, have friends and friends are often attentive to younger sisters. Several girls at school—"

"Had Mrs Clare overheard some of your conversations she would have despaired of ever educating you, except in the matter of the latest dance steps, gowns and fashions and the merits or otherwise of every young man you set eyes upon – be it the baker's boy or the unfortunate dancing master!"

"Ah, now, *he* was handsome," Adele said dreamily. "Quite the Mediterranean type – those melting eyes, the perfect white teeth. Jessie Cardew said he must be an Italian count fallen upon hard times."

"With a name like Briggs?"

"It was not his real name, we were all agreed upon that. We think he fell in love with Mrs Briggs against parental wishes and fled with her to England."

Carrie chuckled. "Did you ever see Mrs Briggs? She weighed twenty stone if she was an ounce and was possessed of the finest moustache I have ever seen on a lady."

"Italian women run to fat very quickly. When she was young she must have been a beauty. Jessie Cardew said they both spoke with a marked Tuscany accent."

"Both Mr and Mrs Briggs were born in Penzance. His father was a grocer; you know that perfectly well."

"That is what he *said*. What he wished everyone to believe."

"Piffle."

"Your trouble, sister dear, is that you are not in the least romantic."

"And you have a head stuffed full of nonsense. Now settle down, do."

Unabashed, Adele said blithely, "I believe even my dreams must be more interesting than yours. Do you dream of verbs and adjectives and multiplication sums? Or even Pythagoras' theorem, whatever that might be. Mrs Clare spoke highly of it, though I never cared to delve too closely. Maybe you could set a fashion in Manchester circles by discussing such matters at the very first entertainment we grace with our presence. You may become the rage . . ." She dissolved into giggles as Carrie threatened her with the pillow. But after the candle was snuffed and they lay listening to the wind rustling round the eaves she said, sleepily, "Jessie Cardew said the baker's boy had a mystery about him, too. He looked too distinguished to be the son of a tradesman. She wondered if gypsies had stolen him as a baby and sold him to the baker's wife who could not have a child of her own."

Carrie smiled into the darkness. "Go to sleep, you goose." And cling to your fairy tales, she thought. Dream of frog

58

princes and gypsy kidnappings and enchanted princesses who must be wakened with a kiss from the handsome prince on a white charger. For real life must surely soon intrude and childish fantasies be left behind.

But not too soon, she thought on the very edge of sleep. For Adele . . . let her not lose her illusions, her dreams, too soon . . .

The first day back at the lodge was a day of adjustment to a new routine, of renewing acquaintance with Aunt Linnie, almost of establishing a new relationship, for she had changed as people must — as she and Adele had also grown and altered.

Uncle George had risen early, breakfasted alone and gone to his work. His room was at the end of the small landing. Carrie had listened to his heavy footsteps pass their door and move on down the stairs, and to the faint rumble of his voice as he spoke to Jane in the kitchen. She had heard the back door close behind him and only then had she realised she had been lying tensely, as she had as a child, hoping, praying he would leave the house and leave them in peace.

There was no need for that now. No need at all. But it was an old habit, hard to break. She found herself at odd moments in the day alert for the sound of that heavy tread and relieved when it did not come. Uncle George preferred to eat his midday bread and cheese in his workshop and this evening, being Wednesday, he went out to meet a friend for an hour or two. This same gentleman he saw at weekends, sometimes staying in Manchester overnight. Carrie gleaned all this in snippets from Aunt Linnie, along with gentle sighs of, "It is hard for a man to be so bound to an invalid." Or, "He does so enjoy his hours with his friend." Or, with a long-suffering expression and a glint of something sharper in her eyes, "I trust Caroline dear, you will forget such differences you and Uncle George may have experienced in the past. We are very comfortable now. I could not bear to think of any friction, my health being so delicate."

"Why should I wish to be at loggerheads with Uncle George?" Carrie answered softly. "Circumstances are very different now, Aunt. Pray do not give it another thought."

Aunt Linnie had, Carrie concluded, rather too much time for thinking. Her routine was one of stultifying dullness. She rose late after breakfasting substantially in her room. Jane helped her to dress but Carrie and Adele were permitted to assist her downstairs, a painful matter judging from the many quick intakes of breath and constant wincings. Once into the parlour she subsided onto the sofa calling breathlessly for a glass of sherry wine to revive her. "It is good that you young people cannot possibly know what pain and suffering may lie ahead," she said with a faint, brave smile. "I trust you will never bear the burden of ill health." The wine disposed of she promptly fell to a doze until luncheon, when the manner of serving, the content and preparation of the meal was criticised, though the food itself was quickly consumed. The afternoon was long. Aunt Linnie picked up her embroidery but complained that the colours dazzled her eyes. She rang the bell at her side frequently for Jane to rearrange a cushion or stoke up the fire or pass her one of the many bottles of medicine that cluttered a corner table.

"Aunt," cried Adele, "you must allow us to help you now. We want to do everything for your comfort, as we used to."

"I would not wish to put upon you young people," she said tremulously, but submitted gracefully then to Adele's attentions and less was heard of the impatient bell.

Had the weather been better Carrie would have gone for a walk. At Malvern only the most severe of storms had denied the girls their daily outing, for Mrs Clare was a firm believer in fresh air and exercise. Aunt Linnie had been alarmed at the thought. "It is pouring down. No! I forbid it, for you would catch cold." So Carrie contented herself with conversation and embarking upon some patchwork.

Uncle George came home, affably, for his dinner and left soon after. Aunt Linnie who had been bright and loquacious in his presence, began yawning and sighing when he was gone. It was as well, Carrie thought, that she and Adele were back, for it could surely do no good for Aunt Linnie to spend so comatose a life without mental or physical stimulation. Aunt Linnie, it seemed, had settled herself firmly into the role of a permanent invalid, though apart from her indoor pallor, her ailments seemed of a vague nature.

She suggested cards, which Aunt Linnie had once enjoyed. After a considerable amount of persuasion and rearrangement of footstool, cushions and shawls and grumblings of having forgotten the rules, she and Adele set about two-handed whist. Carrie was amused to see that in a little while the ribbons on Aunt Linnie's cap began to bob quite animatedly and the fretful tone, which unfortunately coloured her voice so often, disappeared altogether as she became involved in tricks and trumps.

Carrie slipped unnoticed into the kitchen, closing the door softly upon the players. A startled Jane, coming from the scullery and staggering under the weight of a tray of newly washed dinner dishes, was torn between putting down the tray and bobbing a curtsey.

Carrie said, "Sit down, Jane. I should like to talk to you."

"Me, Miss?" She perched nervously on the edge of a stool, twining her hands in the sacking apron she had put over her print frock to protect it from splashes. It was rare that Mrs O'Hara made her way into the kitchen and Mr O'Hara passed through only once or twice a day. She had come to feel the kitchen and scullery and the tiny room where she slept was her kingdom. She loved everything in it. The uneven flagged floor she must scrub every day, the old rag rugs, the dresser with its rows of plates and jugs, her room with the previously unimaginable luxury of a bed, a chest of drawers and a candle to herself. For a few horrible minutes her security rocked. She must've done something amiss . . . serving girls was ten a penny . . . they'd fill her place easy as easy. Was it that tea she'd spilt on the lace cloth yesterday? Her eyes slid uneasily to the fire that flared up far too brightly. She shouldn't have put on that last shovelful, but she did like a warm last thing and the kitchen looked so grand when the firelight made everything cosy and sparkling.

"I am not come to scold, so do not look so frightened. I merely wished to know a little about you and your duties here. You have been here for almost three months, I think?"

"Please, Miss, yes. Twelfth of October, Miss." It was engraved for ever on her heart. The day when she had marched out of the foundling home. The forbidding doors had closed behind her with a joyous clang, her new clumsy boots had squeaked and tapped a tattoo of praise; even the parting lecture by the overseer warning of the evils and temptations to be found in the outside world couldn't quell the enormous delight that threatened to engulf her.

Carrie said, "Why, that is my birthday. Perhaps it is a sign that you are to be happy with us."

"Oh, yes, Miss," she breathed, "I am happy here. I can't tell you how much. Me nice room, this kitchen, it's lovely and warm and comfy." She sent a guilty look at the fire, but Miss Carrie seemed quite oblivious of its crackling splendour.

"You do not find the work too much for you? Mrs O'Hara, being an invalid, requires a lot of attention."

"Oh, no, Miss," Jane said, surprised. Never in her short life did she remember anyone asking such a question or even acknowledging that she might have feelings at all. People in authority had loud, hard voices that dealt out commands; they wielded canes that came down painfully on tender knuckles;

they loomed powerful and threatening over every activity, so that laughter died stillborn.

"And Mr O'Hara?" Carrie asked casually. "Does he treat you well?"

Mr O'Hara. She'd seen the previous maid briefly. A plump girl who'd tossed her head and whispered, "I'm glad I'm goin'. She's a nagging bitch – and as for him, well, you watch out!"

"What d'you mean?"

"Takes liberties, *he* does." "Don't let him come up on you quiet-like, or he'll have his hands where he's no business to." Then she grinned nastily. "Not that you've got much on you to get hold of. Right scrawny chicken you are." Later she'd gone off, thrusting her bold, bouncing bosom forward and leaving Jane nervous ever after of the big, soft-footed man who had the same air of watchful power as the overseer at the home. But he'd not touched her. Maybe the other girl had been right and she was too ugly and skinny. Or maybe it was that with Miss Carrie and Miss Adele coming back he was being careful. All the same she took care not to provoke him, or to be caught alone in the same room with him more often than need be.

But she could say none of this to Miss Carrie, for she was a lady and ladies couldn't know about such things.

She said, stoutly, "Mr O'Hara's a good master."

"And it appears you are a good servant, Jane." Carrie glanced about at the speckless kitchen and back to the tiny, upright figure on the stool. She had the pale thinness of undernourishment and her gingery hair was scraped back into a knot so that the skin over her bony forehead was shiny and tight. Her face coloured extravagantly at the unexpected praise.

"I tries, Miss," she said. "I likes to see everywhere nice. We was trained at the home in washing and cleaning and plain cooking." She looked anxious. "I don't 'zackly suit Mrs O'Hara in that direction."

"Well, I have learnt some fancy cooking at school, so I dare say between us we shall learn to please my aunt."

Jane's eyes rounded in surprise. Carrie smiled. "How old are you, Jane?"

"Nearly thirteen, Miss."

"And what time do you get up in the mornings?"

"Six, Miss."

"And do you wait up for Mr O'Hara?"

"Mrs O'Hara said not to, for he's often late." And drunk, sometimes, she thought. She'd heard him staggering about the kitchen. That was when she lay holding her breath and was glad of the bolt on her door.

"You look tired and no wonder, with extra work to do now my sister and I are here. When you have put away those dishes you may have an early night, Jane."

"But the supper tray . . ."

"I shall see to that. Does Mrs O'Hara take chocolate still before retiring?"

There was nothing to do but obey. She put away the dishes and cutlery, had a last blissful warm at the fire as Miss Carrie laid out the tray, then slipped off to her room. She scrambled into her flannel nightdress, snuffed the candle and hunched down under the sheets. She discovered she was grinning into the darkness like a daftie. October the twelfth, fancy that being Miss Carrie's birthday. Eh, but it was a true sign. She was going to be happy here, for ever and ever, amen. Then she dropped like a log into dreamless sleep.

The sudden rush of noise as the outside door opened made Carrie jump. Her fingers froze over the bread she was buttering and in the instant it took to turn her head she was back through the years to another kitchen, hearing lurching footsteps and slurred, raucous singing. Her stomach plunged sickeningly even as common sense took over and told her that this tall, rain-soaked stranger standing uncertainly in the doorway was not Uncle George.

He said, "I knocked, but the wind and rain's making a rare old noise." A pause then softly, almost shyly, "Hello Carrie."

There was an instant's non-recognition, for this lean, hard man was not the gangling youth she had pictured, but a matured and toughened image of the boy she had once taught at this same table. But the untidy dark hair was the same, his eyes the same direct honest blue under lashes too long and generous for a man.

"Jem!"

She flew across the room, holding out her hands. "Jem, how good to see you!" Her smile lit her eyes, her face, transforming it from ordinariness to beauty. He stared down at her in silence, gripping her warm hands with his own cold and calloused ones, his gaze so intense that after a moment she was forced to ask timidly, "Am I changed, Jem? Do you find me very different?"

Abruptly he released her. "No . . . yes," he said gruffly.

She laughed. "You cannot have it both ways. Which is it to be?" Then, more soberly. "It is a little of each, perhaps, for you have changed, Jem, yet I can still see something of the boy you were."

He nodded. "Aye, that is the truth of it."

She became aware of the wind and rain sweeping in at them. "Close the door, do, and come to the fire for you are soaked through."

"I can't stop, it's too late to come calling. I just wanted . . . that is, I was passing near . . . I've been working late. We're short handed at the yard."

"You cannot rush off without a hot drink and a bite to eat," she said firmly.

"I shall drip mud all over your clean floor . . ."

But she was fetching a stool to the fire, pouring steaming

chocolate into a mug and cutting a wedge of cake with the quick, neat movements he remembered, so that he was compelled to tiptoe awkwardly in his clogs across the flags and seat himself.

"What a night to come visiting," she said, "and you have another wet walk home."

"I'm used to being out in all weathers. I shall come to no harm."

He could not tell the truth, that he had lived for this moment for so long that he would have come through fire and flood to be here.

She drew up a stool facing him, her hands neat in the lap of her blue dress. The cake stuck to his dry mouth and he swilled it down with the scalding chocolate. There was so much he longed to say, so much he had rehearsed saying, and now here, with the flesh and blood Carrie looking at him with her smokey-grey eyes, he found himself tongue-tied. Writing was easy and talking to her in his head was easy but now he could think of nothing to say.

"I always enjoyed your letters, Jem," she said. "Thank you for writing so often."

He cleared his throat. "It was good practice."

All her precious letters. Read and reread. Folded and refolded so that they threatened to split. He kept them in a linen bag under a loose plank by his bed, like buried treasure. And on the wall, so that it met his eyes when waking, the card with its border of pressed flowers and leaves and the words written in fine script,

> 'Who doth ambition shun,
> And loves to live i' th' sun,
> Seeking the food he eats,
> And pleas'd with what he gets,
> Come hither, come hither, come hither.

Here shall he see
No enemy
But winter and rough weather.'

It seemed that her new-found contentment was summed up in that simple verse and the reading of it brought her gentle presence closer.

"I am pleased that Aunt Linnie is settled and Uncle George so amenable."

"Aye," he agreed. "It's a bit different to when you were in Manchester before." Different. The word sounded a warning bell that tolled deep in his mind.

"They were sad times." She stared reflectively into the fire. "I sometimes think we shall never quite escape them. At least Uncle George seems to have turned over a new leaf."

Jem did not answer. He'd never liked George O'Hara. He'd often wondered what business he had in Angel Meadow. More than once he'd seen him down there – and no good ever came out of that filthy haunt of whores and gaolbirds.

Carrie went on, more cheerfully, "We have Mr Sanderson as a friend now, though, and I cannot tell you Jem how kind he has been. I had not imagined he would look after us so thoroughly. He even has plans to introduce us to his friends. Adele imagines we shall be caught up in a social whirl, though I think it will not be so easy for us."

Suddenly the chocolate seemed tasteless, the last mouthful of cake merely sawdust. The wind rattled the back door sending a draught to ruffle the rug laid before the fire, then it died, and in the lull they heard Adele laughing in the parlour. He jerked his head, his voice harsh, "They'll be wanting their supper. I've held you up."

"Yes, I suppose I had best take it in. Will you come through, Jem and say hello to Adele?"

"Some other time. I'm not dressed for company."

He stood up and rid himself of the mug and plate. She did not move. She sat there, the fire glowing rosily on her skin, her hair in glossy curls against her cheeks.

He had imagined her like this for so long and now all he could feel was the fear kicking him in the gut. He had pretended to himself that she would still be his Carrie when she returned. That she would be the same girl who had skivvied for the Misses Tucker, who'd spent her precious free evenings teaching him to read and write, whose smile had made him feel a giant among men and whom he had longed to protect and cherish. Now he knew the chill of reality as pretence shrivelled away.

She was different. Of course she was different. He had been a fool to imagine otherwise. There was nothing left of that skinny waif with the tired eyes and roughened hands. Miss Caroline Linton could have been any of the genteel young ladies he saw driving by in private carriages or glimpsed at the piano through the parlour windows of the big houses he called at or strolling at leisure with beautifully groomed gentlemen in well-tended gardens. Her dress was of a quality his mother or his sister could never hope to possess. She had the assurance of a well-bred lady. Even her voice was changed. No longer did she speak with the flat local accent but smoothly, the vowels rounded and musical.

He was aware, sharply, that he stank of wet corduroy and of horse. There was a clod of dungy straw stuck to the side of his clogs and some of it had fallen to the clean flags. Humiliation and anger knotted his stomach. He could not look at her. He should never have looked at her. Her destiny lay elsewhere among people of Mr Sanderson's sort. He'd go home and burn those hoarded letters. Wipe her from his mind, his heart, his hopes.

"I must be off." He snatched open the door and the rain and wind flew in at him. He welcomed the cold cleanness.

The long walk home would wash away every thought of her. Purge him of his dreams.

She said, hesitant, puzzled, "Oh . . . yes. Well, goodnight, Jem. I am so very pleased you called. Next time you must stay longer."

"Goodnight," he muttered. He would not see her again. Must not. He took one more, final, glance.

She was smiling at him, that same, heart-piercing smile that he would never be able to forget as long as he drew breath. He wrenched his gaze away and went from her, head bent, into the stormy darkness.

Carrie closed the door quietly and leaned against it. She felt a curious sense of anticlimax. She had looked forward to seeing Jem. She had felt all this time that they shared a special sort of friendship. They had always been able to talk so easily and freely.

She walked slowly back to the table. The truth was, she thought sadly, his letters had not prepared her for the change in him. All the old easiness had quite gone. A bond had been broken. They had both grown up and, perhaps inevitably, grown apart, for certainly an awkwardness that had never been there before had clouded their meeting. She shook her head, as though to clear the feeling of having lost something valuable, then carefully lifted the tray and carried it through to the parlour.

Luncheon with Mr Sanderson proved more of a social occasion than the girls expected. They arrived at Beech Place fully expecting to share a simple meal with their benefactor, only to find other company assembled in the drawing room.

"I knew I should have put on my lavender merino," Adele wailed under her breath.

"You look perfectly well in your pink," Carrie said, with an assurance she did not wholly feel.

"Just a few friends I happened to run into," Mr Sanderson said, stooping over them benevolently. "I wanted you to meet Charlotte Dawes and her girls, so it seemed fortuitous that they were free today. Now, take a glass of wine before tiffin and allow me to make the introductions."

Carrie found herself trying frantically to remember Mrs Clare's precepts on the art of conversation, and failing somewhat. She had reassured Adele over the matter of her pink dress but she saw clearly that what had been pronounced highly suitable in Malvern would not do in Manchester. Mrs Dawes and her daughters moved in a rich rustle of beaded silk velvet and brocade. Even the gentlemen – Mr Henry Dawes and a Mr Edmund Brook – were expensively tailored. Indeed, Mr Brook's yellow silk waistcoat and ruffled white stock were quite dandified. She began to feel herself young and gauche in this confident company.

Fortunately, Mrs Dawes was a garrulous lady who took possession of Carrie almost at once. She was placed beside Carrie at luncheon while Mr Brook sat on her other side. The conversation washed about her as the various courses were removed and she was relieved that nothing seemed expected of her beyond the simplest remarks.

The meal drew on. Mrs Dawes ladled a great spoonful of yellow cream onto her apple tart. "Is it next week that you expect your wife and son – and of course his dear fiancée – to return from Preston, Miles?" she enquired. "You will be pleased to see them returning from their travels."

Mr Sanderson nodded. "Ever since the engagement was announced, they have been pressed to visit every far-flung branch of Margaret's family."

"They are with Lord Delayne at his country residence are they not?" Mrs Dawes queried reverently.

"It sounds very grand but his lordship lives modestly enough, I understand."

Carrie caught his eye and suppressed a smile. That was not quite how he had put it to her. "Poor as church mice the lot of them," he'd growled. "And Delayne – a cousin of Margaret's – has the bluest blood and the most rundown estates of them all. Dolly's complained of nothing but the food and the draughts since she's been there. But duty's to be done and she is happy that Elliot is to marry into a family who can trace their line back to Norman William's time. And if Dolly's satisfied and Elliot's happy that's all that matters to me." He smiled dryly. "I understand that Margaret's mamma was not averse to the match. She is a sensible lady who is pleased that Elliot's family has more than aristocratic blood to support it."

There was a burst of laughter from the Dawes twins who had been chattering happily to Adele.

"The young people are getting on splendidly," Mrs Dawes said. "Joan and Maud have been looking forward to meeting you both, Mr Sanderson having spoken of you so often – Ah, yes, I do think I might try a little wine jelly. Do take some, Edmund, I recommend it highly."

"Thank you, but no," Mr Brook said. "I have to put in a few hours down at the works this afternoon. I shall have no inclination for industry if I eat any more. May I pass you something more, Miss Linton?"

Carrie declined and presently the puddings were removed and dessert brought. Mrs Dawes allowed herself to be persuaded to take an orange and Mr Brook selected a few choice black grapes for Carrie.

"They will slip down easily," he murmured. "It is a shame you did not enjoy the rest of the meal so well."

She coloured. "I regret I was not hungry."

His eyes were amused but not unkind. "These occasions can be an ordeal when you are young and barely out of the schoolroom."

"Oh, dear. Was it so obvious?"

71

"Not obvious at all. You have behaved perfectly. Even the lack of appetite could be taken as a sign of an excess of sensibility. So suitable in a young lady . . . ah, that is better. I was afraid I might never coax a smile from you."

It was easier after that. She learned that Mr Brook owned a dye works down by the Irk, that Mr Dawes was a cotton manufacturer, that Joan and Maud were the youngest of the Dawes' five children, the elder daughters and a son being married. In no time at all, it seemed, they were back in the drawing room, the gentlemen preferring to take coffee with the ladies rather than lingering over their port in the middle of a working day. Once there the men engaged themselves in a political discussion, while Mrs Dawes drew Carrie determinedly to a sofa.

"You and your sister must visit us at the earliest opportunity," she announced. "Perhaps you would care to join us on Saturday evening. We are holding a musical evening at our home. That is, of course, if your aunt should be agreeable. I am sorry that her health confines her indoors."

"I feel sure she will appreciate your kindness," Carrie said, wondering how much Mrs Dawes knew of their circumstances. She felt she must speak, but it was not easy to find words. She said, quietly, "Mr Sanderson is a dear man, but I fear perhaps he does not quite understand. There are aspects of . . . of our position that are ambiguous. You see, Mr Sanderson allows us to live in the lodge here and employs our uncle as a carpenter." She looked frankly at the older woman. "Adele and I are possessed of a small private income that has only come to us in recent years. It has given us the opportunity to finish our schooling and we shall be able to live in a modest fashion from now on. However, before we went to Malvern we were very poor. So poor that I was compelled to work as a housemaid. I understand that you . . . that other people . . . might not consider Adele and I suitable company . . ."

"My child do not speak another word." Mrs Dawes laid

her plump, beringed hand on Carrie's and pressed it warmly. "Your sensibility and honesty does you credit. I can see why Miles was so taken with you – and he has spoken to me of your background so you need not fear on that score." Her round face folded into a smile. "Rest assured, I should not have invited you to my musical evening, had I not liked you both. Now I have embarrassed you, but it is the truth. You will visit us, will you not?"

"Indeed, yes."

"Then I shall find ten minutes tomorrow to call upon your aunt."

"It would please her very much," Carrie said, adding doubtfully, "but you must not trouble yourself too much on our behalf."

"You must meet the right people," Mrs Dawes said firmly. "Your income may be small, but that is not too much of a disadvantage. You are intelligent and educated. Your sister is uncommonly pretty. Above all, you have the patronage of Miles Sanderson whose family, like my husband's, has lived for several generations in this district and therefore has a certain standing in the community." She nodded, her eyes shrewd and bright. "There should be no difficulty in finding husbands for you both."

"Oh, but—"

Mrs Dawes trilled with laughter. "You look quite dismayed. Does my outspokenness shock you? You should not be shocked, Caroline, for is not a good marriage the ambition of all young ladies?" She shook her head. "You girls are all the same. You dream of romantic attachments, of falling in love with some dashing young man, but give no thought at all to the practical aspects. We mammas have to make sure that the right kind of gentlemen meet their daughters and that the less suitable kind are not admitted to the privileged circle. The best marriages, you know, are those which are soundly based on mutual respect and tolerance and not on some ephemeral emotion."

"But I had given no thought to marriage," Carrie said honestly.

"Then it is high time you did," Mrs Dawes said. "What are you – nineteen? You must not delay or you will be left on the shelf and that is a disagreeable position indeed. Why Joan and Maud already have had offers. Adele has time, of course, but she will be eighteen in the spring and many a girl is engaged at that age, if not married. I myself was married at seventeen and I soon mended my giddy ways with the responsibility of home and family."

"I cannot think that Adele is yet ready for such responsibilities . . . that either of us wishes to be rushed . . ."

"Yes, Adele needs a firm, kind hand to control her high spirits," Mrs Dawes went on, as though Carrie had not spoken. "Young girls of her temperament and looks can soon become high-flown and wayward, and no sensible family would wish its sons to become entangled with a puffed-up conceited miss. It might be that a more mature gentleman would be a good match for Adele. As for yourself, Caroline, your plain character and quiet demeanour will be a recommendation to any gentleman in need of an industrious helpmate."

Carrie was torn between laughter and dismay. Mrs Dawes's assessment of their character and prospects would have been amusing had she not been so obviously sincere and serious. She was clearly trying to be helpful and Carrie knew she should appear suitably grateful, for her head told her that Mrs Dawes spoke sense. She and Adele should submit gracefully to a round of visits and tea parties with the object of being introduced to and approved of by young gentlemen and their mammas. Aunt Linnie was certainly in no position to make such introductions and she knew Adele would be delighted at the prospect. Yet it was all too blunt and, quite frankly, rather depressing. As though, she thought, we were some species of dumb beast brought to market to find a buyer. Oh, she had none of Adele's silly notions of fairy tale princes, but surely there must be more to marriage than mutual respect and tolerance. What of love? How was it possible to endure a lifetime with another person without the warmth of love?

She looked at Adele, sitting between Maud and Joan and even in her plain pink gown managing to overshadow them both though they were expensively and fashionably dressed. They were all three smiling, absorbed in their doubtless frivolous conversation. She could not ever imagine Adele becoming proud and conceited – and the thought of her bright spirit subdued and dulled in a marriage of convenience made Carrie go cold.

She said, quietly, "My sister is a gentle girl, Mrs Dawes, and amenable. She has seen little of life. I should not at all like her to be hurried or pressed into any attachment, however suitable it may appear to others. She needs time to look about her, to mature and learn judgement. As I do myself." She met Mrs Dawes's gaze squarely. "We should both be happy to visit your home and join in any social occasions to which you might care to invite us, but I would not wish you to look upon us as . . . as mere fodder for the marriage market."

Mrs Dawes's eyebrows disappeared under the copious lace of her cap. "That is a most unfortunate turn of phrase, Caroline," she said with a touch of ice in her voice.

"But apt," said a voice that held laughter. Edmund Brook had strolled close and now bowed politely. "I came to make my farewells and I could not help overhearing your remarks, Miss Linton."

Carrie flushed and lowered her eyes, feeling under Mrs Dawes's chilly stare that she had perhaps been hasty and ungrateful.

"I find your attitude somewhat impertinent," Mrs Dawes said.

"I did not wish to offend you, for you mean to be kind. I just wished you to understand my feelings."

"As one who has been the subject of much – er – speculation and manipulation in the matrimonial market place," Mr Brook remarked, "I can readily realise Miss Linton's apprehensions, Charlotte."

"Edmund, that is no way to talk!" Mrs Dawes exclaimed.

"It is the truth," he said mildly and smiled. "But I am sure Miss Linton meant no offence. She was merely perturbed. It must be overwhelming, you understand, for a girl scarcely a week from the schoolroom to be faced with the ordeal of husband hunting. I think it is to Miss Linton's credit that she keeps a cool head." He spoke soothingly, but a hint of mockery lurked in his tone. When Mrs Dawes opened her mouth to scold again, he said quickly, "But, Charlotte, I wished to speak to you of more pleasant matters. I had a mind to accept your invitation for next Saturday if that should be agreeable to you. I know I intimated earlier that I had a previous engagement but I find I mistook the date."

Mrs Dawes's expression changed swiftly. She cried, "I am gratified to hear that, Edmund. It is time you showed yourself to be sociable instead of worrying over business and never meeting a soul apart from other gentlemen who are equally slaves to their factories and mills."

"My workers are grateful that I keep the factory in full production at a time when business is in the doldrums."

"All work and no play make for a dull life. You would realise that if you mixed in gayer company."

"Perhaps you will convert me yet, Charlotte," he said. Carrie noticed the ironic note in his voice but it seemed quite to pass by Mrs Dawes who bade him a smiling farewell, then informed Carrie that this time she would be indulgent and forgive the small lapse but she must guard her tongue in future and not speak out of turn, as it was most unseemly for a young unmarried person to do so.

As she spoke her glance went speculatively after Mr Brook as he made his exit, then to the three chattering girls. A pleased glow suffused her face.

"Well, well," she said. "It is the first time in an age that Edmund Brook has accepted an invitation to any social function. How delighted Joan will be. She and Edmund got on so splendidly when they met at a friend's home at Christmas, and today, before luncheon, they were engaged for a long time in a most animated conversation." She smiled smugly. "I should not be at all surprised if his decision did not have something to do with Joan. She is a charming girl and so talented musically. She will certainly show off to advantage on Saturday. Do you play an instrument, Caroline? No? Such a pity. Doubtless you will be able to render a song or give a recitation." She sighed happily. "Edmund Brook is one of the most eligible men in the district. He has a thriving business and his wife, who died tragically young, brought a substantial portion to the marriage."

"Mr Brook is a widower?"

"For these last ten years or more. It is ridiculous for a man so young to remain faithful to a memory. He should remarry and have children to inherit his fortune."

Carrie, remembering Edmund Brook's remarks, had no doubt that every mamma round about had sought to tempt and trap him into matrimony. She felt it was to his credit that he had evaded any entanglement and suppressed a smile as Mrs Dawes happily rambled on about his worthiness and eligibility.

When the Dawes had left in a flurry of instructions about their next meeting, Mr Sanderson took Carrie and Adele on a tour of the house. They walked through empty corridors and peeped into beautiful, silent rooms. The house felt still and cold now that the other visitors had gone. Not even the thick Chinese carpets and the curtains made from silk woven in Siam, or the many curiosities – the masks, the statues, the carved chests and ivory figurines, that Mr Sanderson had collected during his years in the East – made the rooms welcoming. It is all like an exquisite showpiece, Carrie thought. To be looked at and admired, but not touched.

"My wife has good taste," Mr Sanderson said. "I am afraid that as long as I have a comfortable chair, a fire to warm me and a few books about me, I tend to ignore my surroundings. But she will have none of that. She has had the place done over since we returned and, as she says, we could ask royalty here without shame."

"It is certainly very handsome," Adele breathed, awed.

"You will find my study untidy and old-fashioned," he said, smiling. "Still it is the best place to talk business."

It was a room that overflowed with books. In great glass-fronted cupboards, on shelves and chairs. Untidy heaps spilled across the desk and formed little towers on the Turkey red carpet. But it was warm and welcoming. A fire snapped in the wide hearth and dark curtains shut out the winter dusk.

Mr Sanderson ushered them into shabby armchairs before the blaze. "Now, we must talk of money and investments, a subject that young ladies find dull in the extreme, but I will try to be brief." He extracted a paper from the muddle on his desk and put on his spectacles. "The latest information to hand indicates increased profits for the coming year. I estimate you will have above £200 between you, clear, to invest after all necessary expenses have been deducted. Naturally, now you are no longer schoolchildren your personal allowances will be increased."

"So much!" Carrie gasped. "Why, that is splendid. It eases

my mind considerably for I have been thinking our girl, Jane, needs help now we are four at home. I shall engage a woman to do the laundry, most certainly."

Mr Sanderson said, gently, "I was thinking more of clothes and fripperies. You will need them now, you know."

Adele's eyes sparkled. "Do you suppose I shall be able to have a dress in yellow striped gauze? Mrs Clare was so against gauze as being too frivolous, and the dressmaker there was obsessed with things to last and never had a good word to say for anything beyond serge and merino. She would have had us fitted out in hessian sacking for its cheap and lasting qualities. Joan Dawes says their dressmaker is very modish and has all the latest London patterns. I am sure she would be *very* enthusiastic about yellow gauze."

"Your allowance," said Mr Sanderson gravely, "will certainly stretch to such a garment. You must discuss it with Caroline or the Dawes girls. You got on well with them I noticed."

"They were exceedingly friendly," said Adele. "We struck it off right away."

"And you, Caroline, did you find Mrs Dawes agreeable?"

"Most agreeable." She hesitated, not knowing whether to speak of the doubts that had assailed her but the moment was lost as Mr Sanderson nodded and said, "Good. Good. I thought she would be the right person. Do as she advises and you will neither of you go far wrong. She is a level-headed woman and her daughters enjoy a delightful round of engagements and frivolities. She is well placed to guide two inexperienced girls fresh from school."

Carrie saw then that the casual invitation to luncheon had not been casual at all. It was another example of Mr Sanderson's careful planning. It had all been arranged beforehand. The negotiations with Mrs Dawes – doubtless a consultation with Aunt Linnie – and then she and Adele had been brought out for inspection. Mrs Dawes had looked them over and marked them fit for circulation in polite society.

She stared into the fire and told herself she was an ungrateful hussy to feel again that spark of rebellion that had made her speak her mind to Mrs Dawes. Mr Sanderson was their benefactor. Without his aid they would not have gone to Malvern. She might still be drudging in some menial position, with Uncle George living fatly on their income. She admired him and had appreciated all that he had done – was doing – for them. Why, then, this wish to protest? To declare that she had ideas and opinions of her own? That she might have liked to be consulted about the plans for her future?

Somewhere distantly there was a crunching of hooves on gravel. Mr Sanderson, oblivious, regarded them benevolently and smoothed the paper between his fingers.

"That is settled, then," he said. "Leave everything to me. I shall ensure that the money will be invested soundly. Do not worry about it. Such pretty heads were not meant to be troubled with percentages and profits. Enjoy yourselves under Mrs Dawes's chaperonage. Your affairs are safe with me."

Carrie gripped her hands together. "May I ask, Mr Sanderson," she said carefully, "how you were proposing to invest our capital?"

"I had thought property or land," he said vaguely. "In a growing town that is always a wise move."

Carrie stared at him. "Have you money in property, Sir?"

"Yes. Yes, I have. Why do you ask?"

"Because I am interested."

"You must not worry yourself," began Mr Sanderson, "you will not be the loser . . ."

"I am not worried, sir. I have absolute faith in your integrity. But I am interested to know what percentage we might expect on an investment of £200."

"If we bought an established property with the money, say

some tenement in a poor district, then perhaps an immediate income of 5 to 7 per cent – at the outside 10 per cent – might be expected. If we purchased a piece of land in the suburbs, then we might have to wait longer for a return. Until the land was needed for building, or to make a new road or railway. Then, of course, the profit might be considerable – but that profit would have to be set against the possibility that it might be years before any such development took place."

"I see." Carrie thought for a moment, then said, "There has been much building in the years we have been away, I saw that as we came through Manchester. Houses need bricks. Indeed, there must be a great demand for building materials. Are there possibilities for investment in that quarter?"

Mr Sanderson's glance sharpened. "Why, yes," he said slowly. "I myself bought a piece of land at Greenhill not long since and the sand from it is sold as fast as it can be dug out. As to bricks – my dear, you might have been looking into my own mind for I have lately been toying with the idea of taking over a claypit and brickyard that has come onto the market."

"Then perhaps our money might see a better return put into bricks or sand," Carrie ventured to suggest.

Mr Sanderson's sallow face crinkled into an amused smile. "Bricks and sand and percentages. Dear me, what odd preoccupations for a young lady. You had best, I think, concern yourself with yellow striped gauze like your sister and leave such dreary things to me."

"I do not find it dreary," she persisted. "And I should like to ask a favour of you."

"A favour?"

"That before you make any decision about our investment, you explain it all clearly to me. I am ignorant of these matters but I should like to learn more; in fact, if it would not put you to a great deal of trouble I should wish to visit either the property you intend to buy on our behalf – or the land – or even the claypit or brickworks in which we might have a share . . ."

"You cannot mean that, Carrie," Adele broke in. "Visit a brickworks! It would not be at all the thing, would it Mr Sanderson?"

"Unusual, certainly," he said, shaking his head.

"But not impossible," said Carrie. Emboldened by his hesitation, she added, firmly, "I have quite set my mind on it, sir."

He looked at her from under his shaggy brows. Eventually he said, in the manner of one who humours an awkward child, "Very well. I shall see what can be arranged."

"Thank you," Carrie said, meekly, trying to subdue an impish sense of having triumphed in a small way over authority.

Mr Sanderson put away the paper and as the girls rose to make their departure there was an urgent rap at the door and a maid burst in.

"Sir, it's Mrs Sanderson returned unexpected."

"Something is wrong?"

"No, Sir," the maid stammered, "leastways not as I know of. They've just come back sudden-like. Mr Elliot and Miss Gordon . . ."

He was past her and out into the hall. Carrie asked the maid to fetch their cloaks, then stood with Adele, a touch awkwardly at the study door.

". . . It was too dreadful, Miles," Mrs Sanderson was saying in her clear carrying voice. "There had been a case a week ago which made me very uneasy, but when Lord Delayne announced yesterday that three more people on the estate had succumbed to the smallpox, I knew it would be foolish to stay a moment longer. Lord Delayne understood my anxiety and quite agreed that we should leave at once."

"Are you sure you have not been exposed to the contagion?" Mr Sanderson asked anxiously.

"The persons affected were merely a labouring family on one of his farms," Mrs Sanderson assured him, "but I could not take any risk with the health of dear Margaret or Elliot."

Mrs Sanderson was still a striking woman. Despite the fatigue of the journey she stood straight and tall in deep crimson velvet, her matching bonnet trimmed with dramatic white plumes.

She has style, Carrie thought. In the chilly elegance of the lamplit hall she was a dominating figure, overshadowing the other members of the family group like a showy gold-finch among a cluster of sparrows. And sparrow was not an inapt description of Margaret Gordon who, though clothed in expensive quilted snuff-brown silk trimmed with dark fur, seemed devoid of any style at all. She turned her pale face towards the girls, dismissed them with a glance from her round gooseberry-green eyes then, to Mr Sanderson's query said in a languid voice, "The journey was abominable but I think poor Elliot feels the more exhausted for he had too much of cousin Delayne's cognac after dinner last night and has suffered all day from a sore head."

"That is unfair," Elliot Sanderson said sulkily. "I took it because Delayne swore it to be a specific against infection and he would have me take an extra glass or two."

"Two only? I should have thought you had drunk a bottle to yourself judging by your pallor this morning."

"It was deucedly strong stuff," Elliot protested. "He did not warn me . . ."

"Children! Children!" Mrs Sanderson cried, "Pray do not be tetchy. You are both tired, as I am myself, but when we have rested and dined we shall be able to laugh at the discomforts we have suffered."

Elliot erased the frown that disfigured his handsome face but did not quite manage to return the appeasing smile that his fiancée bestowed on him.

83

Carrie thought it a pity that his mouth had such a soft, sulky look to it, for the rest of his features were nicely arranged and proportioned. He had a classically straight nose, a high noble brow set in an oval face. Soft brown hair fell in waves about his ears and his slender body was garbed in a fawn-coloured full-sleeved coat, cut away to show an embroidered gold satin waistcoat above white nankeen trousers. His cravat was carelessly knotted and he held his round chin high as though to show off his splendid profile. He was very like his mother, though his features seemed to have been cast in a softer, weaker mould.

"Your cloaks, Miss," the maid whispered in Carrie's ear and as the girls quickly put them on, Mrs Sanderson caught sight of them.

"Who have we here?" she asked pleasantly. "I did not know that you entertained visitors, Miles."

"The Daweses have been to luncheon, and Edmund Brook. I wished them to meet Caroline and Adele Linton. You remember them, my dear? They are lately out of school and I kept them a while to discuss their finances. They were just about to leave." He beckoned them. "My wife you will remember. My son and his fiancée you have not yet met." He made the introductions. The girls curtseyed. Margaret Gordon inclined her head coolly. Elliot Sanderson bowed slightly to each in turn, straightened and stared, somewhat puzzled at Adele as though he recognised, but could not quite place, her.

Pleasantries were exchanged, but when Carrie began to express her gratitude towards the woman who had heralded their good fortune, her words were brushed aside. "Do not speak of it, pray," she said lightly. "It is all done with. I am not a person who wishes to be reminded of the past." She cast a proud, possessive glance at her son and Miss Gordon. "Especially when it is the happy future we must contemplate."

Her tone was dismissive. Carrie said, quietly, "Our aunt will be anxious for our return. Would you excuse us? Thank you for the luncheon Mr Sanderson, it was delightful."

Adele, unusually, had remained silent all the while. After glancing from one face to another, she had taken a sudden and absorbing interest in a glossy-leafed plant standing stiffly in a white porcelain urn. Now, Elliot Sanderson said suddenly, "Forgive me, but I am here so seldom that I am not in touch – is it your aunt who lives in the lodge? And you used to live in that cottage in Smedley?" Carrie assured him that he remembered correctly. "Ah, I have you placed, now. You benefited by way of investments Mamma once made, and Papa looks to your affairs." He looked across to Adele. "It comes back to me."

Mrs Sanderson gave a light laugh. "You have a prodigious memory, Elliot, for I had almost forgotten such a trifling matter myself. But pray, dear, do not delay these young people. They are anxious to be off."

Elliot had moved across to Adele where she stood in rapt contemplation of the urn. "You are interested in the gardenia, Miss Linton? They grew like weeds in our Penang compound. Here they have to be grown most carefully. Have you seen the collection in the glasshouses here?"

"No. No I have not."

"Come, Elliot, you must rest." Mrs Sanderson's clear tones rang across the hall.

"Coming, Mamma," he answered a touch impatiently, his attention still on Adele who was apparently so bemused by the plant that she could not wrench her gaze from it.

"You must get the gardener to show you over the glasshouses. There are some fine specimens there. Many tropical plants and a variety of orchids, in which I take an interest myself."

"Oh . . . yes."

"Fascinating things. Unusual method of culture. They grow on trees in tropical latitudes."

"Like mistletoe?"

"Something similar, yes. They have to be treated with enormous care when cultivating them in the artificial surroundings of a hothouse."

"Elliot, if Miss Linton is the slightest bit taken with orchids she can obtain all the information she needs from the gardener. Can you not see that the poor girl is fretting to be away and you are boring her with your nonsense."

"But I was not—" Adele broke off as she met Mrs Sanderson's cool glance, and her colour deepened. She said in a voice scarcely above a whisper, "Yes, I must go. But I was not bored. It was most . . . most entertaining." Slowly she raised her head and looked fully at Elliot Sanderson. "I shall, most certainly, take time to visit the glasshouses."

Carrie, who had taken possession of the lantern glanced round to see why her sister delayed.

The people in the hall stood as in a tableau, as sculpted as the white marble statues set in alcoves along the walls. Mr Sanderson, tall and stooped, leaned solicitously in conversation over the brown-clad plumpness of Margaret Gordon. Mrs Sanderson stood a little apart, very straight, very commanding a brilliant, showy figure in red velvet. But not smiling now. Not smiling at all as she waited for her son to leave off his conversation with Adele. And somehow, now, the lamplight was less kind. It cast dark shadows under her eyes and in the hollow of her cheeks; revealed a slackness of flesh beneath the smooth chin, as though the façade of youth and beauty had momentarily blurred.

The lamplight falling soft and golden about Adele revealed no flaws, only the perfection of smooth young flesh over shapely bone. Beside her, the poetic classical handsomeness of Elliot Sanderson, whom Adele herself had once called

86

beautiful, made a perfect foil for her graceful delicacy. They stared at each other, these two young people, and the seconds ticked soundlessly away.

It was Mrs Sanderson who broke the spell. She stepped forward, half raising her hand, the fingers bent inwards as though she might clutch at her son's coat-tails. She said, "Elliot! Come!" It was no longer a request but a command.

Adele blinked, turned her head and took a long breath before crossing to Carrie's side. Elliot remained still for a second or two then he, too, turned away and walked slowly back across the hall to his mother.

Adele did not look after him and with unaccustomed discourtesy, she did not pause to thank her host. She went straight out into the windy, dark night.

Carrie followed her. Afterwards she would remember that innocent scene. It would be burnt onto her memory as though etched with vitriol.

Chapter Three

There was a company of about thirty gathered for the musical evening in the old panelled gallery that ran the length of the Dawes' house. 'Not a large house, but of considerable age,' Mrs Dawes had informed Aunt Linnie when she had called upon her. 'It has been in my husband's family for years.' It had not been modernised in the elegant way of Beech Place, but retained all its mature dignity, with its low ceilings and uneven floors and heavy oak doors. The gallery was warmed by two generous fires and flooded with light from clusters of candles. A pianoforte, a harp and an assortment of music stands stood to one end and chairs were grouped to give a good view of the performance.

Mrs Dawes, majestic in violet satin with a turban of white blonde over violet crêpe set on her grey curls, bore down on Carrie and Adele. "How well you look, girls," she cried, dismissing the handiwork of the Malvern dressmaker with one disparaging glance. "And how is your aunt? Well, I trust. Good. I found her a most genteel person. Come, come." With the skill of the successful hostess she whisked them around several groups of people, covered their initial hesitation in a waterfall of small talk, before leaving them to engage herself with other guests.

Carrie was left with an elderly military man, whose name had escaped her. She glanced about her for conversational inspiration, wishing that Adele had not been borne off by

Maud Dawes. She saw the Sandersons and the haughty Miss Gordon, and the gallery seemed filled with the swish of opulent gowns and the sounds of conversation and laughter. How could she stand with Adele before all these people and sing? These assured and wealthy persons must be used to talented performances from ladies and gentlemen of great accomplishment.

So distracted, she gave quite the wrong answer to some remark of the military man and then made it worse by trying to make light of her gaffe. The Colonel frowned frostily and all Mrs Clare's training was forgotten under that discouraging stare. She knew she must present a gauche picture indeed. After a polite interval the military man excused himself and moved away to find more congenial company. To her horror Carrie found herself standing alone.

Her fingers tightened about her fan. She glanced about as though taking an interest in the pictures ranged on the walls, but seeking some refuge where she would be unnoticed. Strangers had closed about her in animated groups. She was as isolated as a small island in an unfriendly sea. In an agony of embarrassment she felt all eyes upon her, mocking her solitary state. She could almost hear the sniggers behind gloved hands and raised fans.

"Good evening, Miss Linton."

"Oh! Mr Brook."

She swung round eagerly, her sudden wide, sweet smile lighting her face. "How very pleasant to meet you again." She was overjoyed at being rescued.

Mr Brook looked into her glowing face. There was a small silence before he said softly, "It is my pleasure entirely. May I say how charming you look?"

"That is kind, Mr Brook. I fear Adele and I are somewhat the country mice in this assembly."

"If you are a country mouse, Miss Linton," he said gallantly, "then all the ladies here would do well to fashion themselves upon your style. Some of them are wonderfully overdressed."

She laughed. "You are balm to my spirit, Mr Brook, which has recently been much bruised." She told him of her encounter with the Colonel, quite at her ease now and able to poke fun at herself. "I felt every eye in the room was upon me as I stood there alone. Now I am composed, I can see that my moment of embarrassment went by totally unmarked."

"The Colonel's a bore," Mr Brook said, abruptly. "At least I always found him so. He is discourteous, too, if he left you unattended."

"Do not blame him. Every precept regarding the art of conversation quite forsook me."

"You are recovered now?"

"Perfectly."

He crooked his arm. "Then allow me to escort you to a seat. On these occasions I always find it best to be seated to the rear of the assembly and to one side, preferably with some item of statuary or a potted palm close by where one may lurk unnoticed."

"Lurk, Mr Brook?"

"Lurk, Miss Linton. Then if one shuts one's eyes in an excess of emotion due to the music's effect upon the senses and if by some mischance one falls asleep, then a tasteful array of greenery or a marble nymph upon a stand provides splendid cover. I have often had cause to commend the hostess who is generous with the shrubbery in her drawing room and mean with candles. It is then quite possible to slip away unobserved and savour a cigar in some quiet room well away from the wailings and scrapings."

Carrie raised her fan to hide her smiling face.

"It is no laughing matter," he said severely, yet there was a twinkle in his eye. "I have known men stronger than I turn pale and run at the sound of a violin being tuned or some middle-aged matron, convinced that she has A Voice, practising her high notes."

"Then you had best find yourself a particularly shady corner this evening, sir, for Adele and I have been pressed to sing a duet and we are not very accomplished." She glanced at him ruefully. "I find the prospect nerve-racking. I shall not enjoy the evening until we have done our piece and reseated ourselves – and I am afraid we are placed quite late in the programme."

He patted the hand lying on his coat sleeve. "By which time, it may comfort you to know that most of the older gentlemen will be nodding off, the young people will be too busy making sheep's eyes at one another to notice the music at all, and their mammas will be satisfactorily engaged in weighing up the fashions."

"Do you not sing or play an instrument yourself, sir?"

"Unfortunately, I shall be called upon to perform," he said dryly. "It is the penalty for accepting the invitation, and as I have not played in public for some time, it will be just as much an ordeal for me as for you."

Before she could ask more Mrs Dawes was upon them with Joan blushing and bridling in her wake.

"How striking you look, Charlotte," Mr Brook said easily, bowing over her hand. "And Joan, too. You grow more like your mother each time I set eyes upon you."

Carrie, beginning to understand Edmund Brook's somewhat ironic humour, felt that the remark was not the compliment the other women obviously took it to be. Joan, like her mother, was in satin but of a strong turquoise shade that went ill with her high colouring. A spray of blue and yellow feathers sprang from the fat sausage curls that framed her round cheeks. A few more years of good living would swell her to the same stout proportions as her mamma.

Edmund gestured towards the dais. "You will be playing the harp for us this evening, Joan?"

"She will, indeed," Mrs Dawes cried. "She has been practising hard for an age – some French piece, is it not, dear? Most intricate and difficult."

"Not the solo arrangement of the Boieldieu concerto?" he enquired faintly.

"You remembered! We spoke of it at Christmas," Joan said.

Edmund closed his eyes and nodded, as though carried away at the thought of the treat to come.

"And you will doubtless give us some delightful rendering, Charlotte." He caught Carrie's eye. "Mrs Dawes," he said gravely, "is possessed of A Voice. A contralto Voice."

"How . . . how delightful," Carrie said, swallowing.

"I shall be singing two items from Schumann's 'Winterreise' song cycle," Mrs Dawes said proudly.

"Most suitable," Edmund murmured.

"I am so glad you agree. Your taste is impeccable in these matters. But poor Caroline, you must be so bored listening to talk of music when you are not accomplished in that direction." She laughed merrily. "Now, do come with me. There are other guests to meet before the entertainment begins and these two young people, who have so much talent, will have much to discuss." She bore Carrie away, scolding her gently as they went. "You really should not have monopolised Mr Brook's attention for so long. Of course, you have not the experience to know when a gentleman wishes to disengage himself from a conversation – and Edmund Brook has such perfect manners that he would never show that he was becoming wearied. It was fortunate that I saw his predicament and came to his rescue. I have known him, you see, for many years and am conversant with his likes and dislikes."

Carrie rather thought that Mrs Dawes knew Edmund Brook's

character less well than she imagined. She said, meekly, "I am sorry. I shall try not to commit such an offence again."

Mrs Dawes eyed her sharply, but Carrie's apologetic smile reassured her.

"You will learn in time," she said. "One cannot expect miracles overnight. Now I shall introduce you to a Miss Prince and her brother, a banker . . ."

They were two dour grey middle-aged persons. They peered at Carrie through their similar round eyeglasses, asked her a few sharp questions and, scarcely waiting for her answers, began a detailed duologue about the state of their health and the ailments they were prone to, due to the dampness of the winter.

Carrie was grateful when a general move was made to the chairs and she could seek out Adele, who detached herself from an admiring circle of young men to sit beside her sister and whisper excitedly of the people she had met and the invitations they might well receive.

The music struck up and as item followed item Carrie realised with relief that some of the contributions were more ambitious than talented. She and Adele at least had the ability to sing in tune and provided they were not overcome with nerves, they would not disgrace themselves.

She glanced around for Mr Brook. She spied him near the front, sandwiched between Joan and Mrs Dawes. Alas, he had not managed to find a potted palm to shelter behind and she hoped that he had not nodded off to sleep so bastioned by the Dawes family.

Joan mounted the dais and beamed upon her captive audience before plunging into the Boieldieu. Carrie clenched her teeth against laughter as wayward twangs of the harp punctuated the melodic phrases. After that, even Mrs Dawes's performance was restful. A Voice she certainly had and Carrie could well understand Mr Brook's dry approval of her choice of songs. They would be sombre airs at any time. Rendered in Mrs Dawes's mooing contralto they reached the nadir of mournfulness.

The moment came when she and Adele were summoned. They had chosen to sing an old air, 'Greensleeves', without accompaniament. They made a hesitant start before Adele's light, true soprano strengthened and Carrie settled to the harmony in her deeper, softer voice.

> '. . . And I have loved you so long
> Delighting in your company . . .'

She saw that Edmund Brook was not sleeping but watching her with grave attention. Behind him, Mrs Sanderson sat handsome and unsmiling, obviously less enamoured of their performance than her husband, who smiled and nodded his head to the tune. Next to him Elliot sat very still, listening intently, while his fiancée fanned herself and gazed round in evident boredom at finding herself in such provincial company.

Adele looked at no one. She was rapt, lost in the song, her hands clasped loosely before her, her slender throat revealed above the modest neck of her white dress, chin uplifted, her eyes luminous in the candlelight and the colour of violets, fixed on some far distance.

> 'If you intend thus to disdain
> It does the more entrapture me.
> And even so, I shall remain
> A lover in captivity . . .'

The last notes faded down the antique gallery like a ghostly echo from some distant century. Then the silence was broken by loud applause.

Adele smiled and curtseyed modestly. As they returned to their seats Carrie saw that her eyes had an unfocused, dreamy look as though the music had swept her to a faraway place of the imagination.

It was almost over. Edmund Brook sat at the pianoforte, waited for silence and began to play.

He did not make an imposing figure. He was slight in build, with a somewhat scholarly air. The light caught his high, pale forehead and the receding fair hair. But there was nothing slight about his playing. Bach's 'Fantasia' rang out crisp, assured, exciting in its mathematical precision. A small pause and straight into a Scarlatti sonata. He finished with a complete switch of mood to one of the modern Viennese waltzes that had everyone swaying to the compulsive rhythm.

The applause was tremendous when he finished and there were shouts of 'Encore! Encore'. But he declined and Mrs Dawes, rising and beaming as supper was announced had, everyone agreed, been skilful in reserving Mr Brook's performance until last, so providing a fitting climax.

"Had it been an occupation for a gentleman, he might have made a name in the concert hall . . ."

". . . His wife was gifted, too. Sad that she died so young . . ."

"I am surprised that he should agree to play in public after such a long interval . . ."

"Had you not heard? Joan Dawes is the attraction. I have it on the most reliable authority that it is only a matter of time before an announcement . . ."

Carrie heard the whispers as she went into supper. She was still bemused by Mr Brook's splendid recital and it struck an odd note that someone possessed of such musical talent, someone so intelligent and cultured, should have much in common with a girl who, although agreeable enough, had neither a musical gift nor was possessed of any great intellect.

95

Love, perhaps? Love, she had heard, was no great respecter of intellect. Love, the poets said, was blind to practical matters. Soul appealed to soul, heart to heart. Yet even to her inexperienced eye, Mr Brook did not seem a soulmate to Joan Dawes.

The dour Mr Prince appeared by her side at the buffet table, a narrow smile half concealing his long yellow teeth.

"Pray take a seat, Miss Linton. I shall fetch your refreshments. Should you like the lobster patties or the ham? I am afraid my digestion will not take such rich fare – but perhaps a little of the cold mutton? There. May I congratulate you on your performance? You and your sister sang admirably. You must introduce Miss Adele to us. Miss Prince was most taken by the way she sang."

She did not see Edmund Brook for what remained of the evening. Only in the last minutes did she spy him striding towards her down the gallery. He bowed.

"I regret that our conversation earlier was interrupted. Perhaps we may continue it on some other occasion. You have enjoyed your evening?"

"It has been most pleasant," she said, honestly Even the time spent with Mr and Miss Prince had been, in a macabre way, interesting.

"Then I shall not hesitate to send you an invitation to one of my own evenings."

"But I did not think that you . . . that is, I heard . . ."

"That I did not entertain at all?" He smiled wryly. "It is true. But I feel that the time has come for me to make an effort in that direction."

She said, "If there is to be music then I pray you not to ask me to make a contribution. You played so splendidly Mr Brook, that I should be forever comparing the ineptness of my own performance."

"You could not have done better than you did tonight. You

and Miss Adele sang without pretension, without affectation. It was simple and in its way quite charming."

"I was not seeking flattery . . ."

"Nor do I give it. You shall not be asked to sing if that is your wish, but I should still be honoured if I might be permitted to send you an invitation?"

She smiled, a little shyly, because he seemed suddenly so serious and not at all mocking or flippant. "Thank you," she said. "I see no reason why not."

Charlotte Dawes said the last farewell to the final departing guest, sighed, linked her arm comfortably with her husband's and said, "Well, a successful evening, I think."

Henry Dawes stifled a yawn. "Splendid. Splendid. You organised everything beautifully, as usual."

They stood in the hall for a few moments, speaking of their guests – who had said what to whom – then Charlotte said, thoughtfully, "Those girls, the Lintons, do you suppose I have taken on too much? I wonder if they will truly fit in – their background is not quite the thing. I know dear Miles has a foolish hope that his protégées will emerge as society belles, but really, the elder girl is plain and a deal too prickly in her manner than is seemly, while the younger one is decidedly precocious. Did you see the way she was flirting with young Mark Hughes?"

"Flirting, dear? I thought it was merely high spirits. She seemed to get on well with everyone. Pretty little thing."

"Pretty, undoubtedly, but in a showy kind of way. I always think that yellow hair a touch vulgar. Of course men are so easily taken in by flamboyant looks. I fear such girls create trouble for themselves and a nuisance for others by their high-flown ways. I do wonder if I did the right thing, Henry, obliging Miles so readily."

"Give it a little time," he said easily. "I am fond of old

Miles and I may say he was a deuced good friend last year
when I overstretched myself financially due to the purchase of
those new looms. I should not have come out so well had the
bankers got their claws in deeper." He patted the plump hand
on his arm. "He is not a well man. I should like to think we
could oblige him in this."

"*We*, Henry?"

"You, of course, Charlotte. You must agree you are emi-
nently suitable, having such experience with our elder girls."

"You men," Charlotte said, testily, "have no idea of the
effort involved. The moral and physical welfare of gently
reared girls such as our daughters is a heavy enough burden
to any mother without the extra responsibility of strangers."

Her husband would not be drawn further. He smiled at her
encouragingly and said he would take a last brandy and cigar
in his study before retiring. She was not best pleased as she
made her way to her bedroom. Henry, who should support
her in this, was clearly in Miles Sanderson's camp. But she
knew who would take the responsibility if the young Linton
girl caused a scandal and the elder proved a social disaster.
Not Henry for sure!

She entered her bedroom and the sleepy maid began to help
her out of her clothes. Even the relief of being out of her
new stays did not dispel the disagreeable picture of Adele
Linton attracting stares and attention. Young Mark Hughes,
for one, had hung about her all evening – and this winter
at every function, he had been so very attentive to Maud.
. . . She snatched at the hairbrush her maid was wielding so
clumsily and rapped the girl on the knuckles. Was it her lot
to be surrounded by dolts?

Once in bed and the candle snuffed she made up her mind.
Miles or no Miles she would not be burdened with those girls
for longer than was necessary. It would be too wearing on her
nerves – and she needed all her robust health to steer her own

dear daughters through the stormy channels of courtship to the safe haven of a good marriage. She must of course *try* – put on an appearance of doing her best – at least for a little while.

Comforted by this decision she gave herself up to the pleasurable thoughts of Edmund Brook on his knees proposing marriage to Joan. A June wedding would be delightful and mousseline-de-soie so suitable for a summer bride . . .

As the Dawes' carriage rattled them homewards, Adele and Carrie relived the evening. Adele still bubbled over with high spirits. Carrie leaned back against the smooth leather upholstery and listened as her sister giggled over Mark Hughes – "Like a sheep with eyeglasses – I quite expected him to 'baa' at me" – spoke of the fashionable dresses, declared herself to be still in favour of yellow striped gauze, as there had not been one garment of that material or colour, and recounted all the conversations she had engaged in.

"I gather you enjoyed yourself," Carrie said when Adele at last paused for breath, "with all those dull mill owners and manufacturers."

"They were not so stuffy as I had supposed," Adele declared.

"You have a knack of drawing smiles from the most sombre," Carrie said. "Even from Miss Prince and her brother."

Adele rolled her eyes. "Can you imagine what they are like at home as they vie with each other to present the most morbid and horrid symptoms? Why, when Mr Prince knew that I had once been subject to asthmatic attacks he urged me to take everything from Congreve's compound petroleum pills to Church's cough drops – though I protested that I hardly, if ever, suffered an attack these days."

"You should not have mentioned the subject at all. I do believe you deliberately led him on."

"But he grew quite animated when he was presenting me with advice. I had picked upon the one subject bound to give him gratification. You should yourself have confessed to megrims or weak ankles or such and you would have risen considerably in Mr Prince's estimation."

Carrie chuckled, then said, "I must tell you that my evening was not entirely without success. Mr Sanderson is to take me to look at a brickworks – among other places – next week. And you need not look so horrified. The invitation did not include you."

"A brickworks! How vastly dreary. I think I had rather listen to Miss Prince detailing the workings of her digestion."

They smiled at each other in complete understanding. Adele, at last beginning to feel the effects of the late hour, smothered a yawn.

"I did not speak to the others of the Sanderson party," Carrie said. "Mrs Sanderson nodded to me, very coolly, and Miss Gordon contrived not to see me at all. Did you have conversation with them?"

Adele stared out at the blackness beyond the window. "No, none of them. But there were so many other people to talk to."

"I have the feeling that Mrs Sanderson has no wish to know us socially. Perhaps now her son is to marry the cousin of a lord she feels she should be moving in more gracious circles, for whenever I saw her she had a haughty look upon her face."

"I did not notice," Adele said vaguely. "But Mr Sanderson is agreeable to us and it is he who manages our affairs, so I dare say that is all that matters."

The carriage turned into the lane that led to the lodge. It dipped and lurched over the ruts and Adele continued to stare at her dim reflection in the darkened glass, but her thoughts had winged away, seeing that other face. *His.* So many people there, so many faces. She had listened and laughed and teased, and the dull, smooth, ordinary people had circled her and moved on and all the while she had looked for him. It was extraordinary how so often, lifting her eyes, searching, she had met his glance; and how the cadences of his voice had come to her through other conversations. Extraordinary and exciting. From that first moment at Beech Place she had known. And it was something that made all the romantic yearnings of Jessie Cardew's stories pale to nothing. For something more beautiful, more thrilling, more awesome had happened when he had looked at her and spoken then, than imagination had prepared her for.

She had sung for him tonight. The notes, the words, had been drawn from her effortlessly, uncontrollably from her heart. She had caught, unguarded, in his eyes the same entrancement she kept close to her own heart and, afterwards, as she had known he must, he had found a brief moment to speak to her.

She had not been honest with Carrie. But it was a secret too deep, too vulnerable to share. Carrie, with her common sense, would have trodden roughly on her golden dream, broken the delicate threads of enchantment.

But now they would meet. She and Elliot. Scarcely an assignation, for they would be where other people could remark them. Yet, in a way, hidden because of its openness and innocence. And nothing so definite as a time. A mere hint that at certain hours he might be there, a breathless confirmation that she, too, could find a free moment . . .

The carriage drew up at the gates; the sisters descended and the carriage rattled away. Carrie moved briskly from the cold night air to the welcome of the lodge's warmth. Adele, slower, lingered to gaze up the drive to where the lighted windows of the big house glinted into the darkness. Then, clutching her dreams about her like a cloak, she floated quietly after her sister.

Carter Smith was a man of worries. He took his worries to bed with him at nights and it was a rare day when he awoke with a free mind and a light heart. He worried all the time about his horses falling sick or being mistreated by the drivers (less on humane grounds than that the horses were the heart and mainstay of his business and an ailing or damaged animal meant a reduction in profits). He worried that his stablemen or drivers might cheat him and that customers might not meet their accounts. He had worried that each of his four daughters might not find suitable husbands and now that they were safely off his hands and the weddings paid for, he worried that his wife's constant nagging was about to force him into further expenditure.

He stood at the door of the counting house staring through the dusty glass into the stable yard, as he had stood every Thursday since he was big enough to accompany his father. 'Never slack, lad' his father had told him. 'Allus lets them as works for you know you've a keen eye and you'll stand no nonsense. You'll be respected then. A lazy master makes for lazy men.'

It was the precept on which he'd built his business. Whiners and slackers got short shrift. Hard luck tales fell on deaf ears. Anyone who couldn't keep up with the job was out. Even now he was thinking of getting rid of old Spencer who was scratching away with his quill in a fever of activity as though to show he still had plenty of fire and enthusiasm left in him. But Spencer was getting negligent. Twice this morning he'd found mistakes in the accounts – and one was in a bill to his biggest contractor who had been undercharged by no less than £5 6s 4d. One more mistake like that and Spencer would have to go for all he might plead that his wife ailed and he was too old to find fresh employment.

Carter Smith enjoyed Thursdays as a rule. Thursday was his day for the accounts. He went meticulously through the ledgers. He checked the petty cash. He scrutinised every incoming and outgoing bill. He reckoned the week's profits.

He was usually finished by midday, by which time he had stationed himself by the door or by the window or, on warm days, wandered casually into the yard to get a better view of Sally Quick when she came to visit her grandmother.

Today, even the promise of Sally Quick flaunting herself through the yard was not in the front of his mind, though he had prudently stationed himself by the door in good time. He was still hearing the grind of his wife's complaints. "It isn't right, Albert, that we should be living in this place. Every year the district gets worse. We're scarce a stone's throw from Angel Meadow – and as for living on top of your work, well, it may be convenient for you but I'm ashamed to ask anyone to visit." By 'anyone' she meant the wives of the small businessmen and respectable tradesmen who made up their social circle and who, one by one, had moved out from the town to greener suburbs. "Besides you have a position to maintain, now that you are a pew-holder at St Ann's. It ill behoves a God-fearing man to rub shoulders daily with the riff-raff who live round about. Look at that slut Sally Quick!" He had started at the name, but she was angrily twitching an ornament straight on the mantelshelf and did not notice. "She had the gall to speak to me the other day when we passed in the street. Brazen hussy! A good-living woman shouldn't have to put up with meeting the likes of her. No, I tell you Albert, it won't do." She had then gone on, in less carping tones, to mention the new villas being built at Ardwick Green and Broughton. "Both good addresses," she'd wheedled. "It'll do no harm to go out and have a look."

For the sake of peace he'd promised a ride out to view on his next free afternoon. It was a prospect he'd contemplated with gloom. Such a house as his wife had set her heart on wouldn't be leased for under forty guineas a year, a ridiculous expense when they owned a perfectly sound house. The house he'd been born and raised in, adjacent to the stable and very convenient for a master who liked to keep his men on their toes. But he had to admit the truth of her case. Times changed. The slums were creeping up on them and he could do nothing to stop them. He fingered his chin, and the wrinkles that all the years of worry had written on his face deepened. Whatever else, business was good. It expanded every year and, dammit, he could do with more space.

His property stood on three sides of the yard. The fourth side was occupied by a tenement that fell steadily more ramshackle. He had once hoped that the owner of the tenement might come round to selling or leasing him the building, but the property made a fat income as, year by year, more partitions divided up the once large rooms into smaller and smaller cubicles to accommodate more people. Carter Smith had gloomily accepted the fact that he would never be able to expand the stables in that direction. Once the yard had been the back entrance for all the respectable houses that stood about it. Now, these houses were turned into stables and haylofts and sheds for the carts. Only his own narrow, three-storeyed house, which stood beside the archway giving sole access to the street, and the tenement, remained. It was part of his wife's complaints that the impoverished tenants who lived in the rear of the tenement had no access to their damp cells except through the archway and across the yard, so offending her eyes when she glanced from the back windows.

He gnawed his lower lip, and his small sharp eyes contemplated the lace-curtained windows of his house. He had a certain fondness for it. He'd be sorry if he had to move out, and there were complications in living away from one's business. The men might take advantage. Yet it might not be an inopportune moment to consider the prospect. With his house empty and a wall or two knocked down he could have direct entry from the stables. There were possibilities there indeed. This present counting house left much to be desired. It had served well in his father's day when he and his father had only two men to help them and competition was fierce for every scrap of business. Now it was too small, too shabby and too cluttered and the agents of the larger manufactories that he so much wished to encourage, could hardly be impressed by it. If he had a new office in the upper part of the house with a large desk and comfortable chairs so that he could invite important customers to take a glass of wine while future arrangements and contracts were discussed, why that would surely be to his advantage.

He stood for a few moments longer, rocking on his short, bowed legs, lost in thought. He was a cautious man. It would not do to become carried away with this tempting vision. Still, it would do no harm to see a builder and get quotations for the work. He'd say nowt to his wife, though. Not until he was quite satisfied that the expense was justified. He pulled on his beaver hat and went out across the yard. He had forgotten about Sally Quick and was more than a little disconcerted when he came face to face with her in the dank cobbled archway leading to the street.

"G'morning Carter Smith, sir," she said, grinning to show her big gappy teeth. "Cold mornin'."

He nodded brusquely, composing his face into what he hoped was a stern authoritarian mask suitable for a pew-holder at St Ann's. His eyes, however, accustomed as they were to take a necessarily covert or distant view of her, did not miss this opportunity to take a fulfilling look at Sally's splendid body.

She had been strolling along with her slow, hip-swaying stride, but now she halted, blocking his path, letting her black shawl slide from her shoulders. She was a big girl, a head taller than Carter Smith and bonny in proportion. The day was bitter but she was of hardy stock – some said of travelling gypsy folk – and took no heed of the weather. She wore a green skirt, indecently short, so that her sturdy white-stockinged ankles showed almost to the calf. Her bodice was laced low so that the creamy mounds of her bosom quivered within inches of his nose.

"Seen anything of Gran, have you sir?" she asked, swinging her basket idly in one brown hand. "She weren't too good when I come last week. Winter's a bad time for old folk."

Carter Smith cared nothing for the bent bundle of filthy black garments who was Sally Quick's grandmother. The old crone seldom ventured out of doors and when she did it was to curse and rail in her senile way at anyone working in the yard. Yet he said, "A bad time, indeed," his voice coming somewhat strangulated as his eyes irresistibly fastened on the swell of flesh above her bodice. His brain sounded a warning. It was madness to be seen in conversation with a whore. But something held him: the lust that gripped him whenever he had seen her about the yard; the close-locked fantasies he had woven about her to strengthen himself during the dutiful couplings with his wife. These now swarmed unbidden into his head, causing his breath to quicken and a dew of sweat to break out on his forehead despite the chill of the day. He could smell the warm musky odour of her body, overlaid with some cheap flowery scent, quite unlike the prim smell of starched linen and common soap that hung about his wife.

"But you're looking well, sir" she said, swaying closer. "Seems to me as you look younger'n ever you did. Said to Gran only last week, 'Carter Smith must be a few years less in age than his good wife, for her hair's quite grey and he's scarcely a white hair on his head and a good high colour in his face.' I expect it comes of the outdoor life you leads, sir, in your way of business. Meself, I always gets out into the fresh air whenever I can. Folk do say my complexion's the better for it." She lowered her voice to a husky whisper. "Don't you think I've a fine complexion, Carter Smith, sir?"

She raised her hand to her cheek. Fascinated, he watched her fingers as they smoothed the pinky brown flesh. He clenched his own tingling fingers, and said, weakly, "I have business to attend to. Kindly step aside, madam."

She made no move. "A gentleman such as you must have little time to spare." Her bold eyes sparkled wickedly. "But a man needs to take his ease sometimes and I've ways, sir, of soothing a man and pleasuring him . . ."

"I'll not listen . . ."

"I've a fine room of me own, all hid away and reached from an entry, so's after dark no one need ever know who it is that calls upon me."

"Be off with you," he choked. "I'm a respectable man. I'll have the constables set on you . . ."

"Coney Alley off Angel Street. Remember it, sir, if you're ever in need of . . . comfort."

He thrust past her. Her skirts swept around his legs so that he stumbled. He scurried off over the worn cobbles, not daring to look back, and the sound of her throaty laughter followed him, burning his ears, lingering in his mind as he made his way through the warren of streets towards the Old Shambles. His feet carried him automatically towards the tavern where a builder of his acquaintance took a pint of porter and a chop at this time of the day. His mind was entirely given to thoughts lewd and sinful. He kept reminding himself that he was a churchman, respectably married. It did no good at all. Sally's hints of the forbidden joys to be bought in Coney Alley consumed him.

He paused to mop his face with his handkerchief and the sight of one of his own carts rumbling up Long Millgate towards him made him recollect himself. He drew a deep calming breath, aware all at once, of the people pushing past

him and the carriages and drays clattering along the road. Jem
Walker on the cart raised his whip in acknowledgement. Carter
Smith impulsively signalled him to stop and in a voice that
sounded a touch breathless told him of a small load of fents
to be picked up from a mill at Ancoats and transported to an
address near the New Bailey. "Do it after you've unloaded
those packages for the infirmary. You're on your way then."

"Aye, sir, I'll do that."

Carter Smith asked him about the progress of the morning's
deliveries and Jem answered. This small, ordinary exchange
was soothing and settling. The swollen, fevered visions blurred
and dispersed. The ordered workaday world crowded back. He
straightened his narrow shoulders and adjusted the tilt of his
hat. He was once again in command of himself. The visions
were banished to the remoteness of his lower mind. Later, in
the indulgent darkness of night when his wife was sleeping,
he might allow himself the luxury of recalling the pleasurable
torments of Sally's promises. Now he was glad he had come to
his senses and felt grateful to young Jem for being the innocent
cause of his return to sanity.

A good lad, Jem. Since he'd come to work for him at
eleven or twelve he'd been quick and willing. Never had to
be told anything twice and dependable to boot. Carter Smith
admitted he'd been doubtful when the lad had taken to book
learning. He was feared that the ability to read and write would
give him airs above his station, but his fears were unfounded.
Even now, when Jem had taken to attending lectures on such
useless subjects as astronomy and foreign languages given
by professors and such at the Mechanics' Institute, it hadn't
turned his head. In fact, of late, come to think of it, he'd been
very quiet, taking on extra work with never a murmur when
the other men grumbled and pulled long faces. Not that he'd
ever been a great talker. As a young lad he'd always taken
the men's leg-pulling and teasing good-naturedly, but there'd

always been an air of reserve about him that had cooled the wilder horseplay. Now he was grown to manhood he was respected by his workmates and his opinions valued in the stable yard arguments and debates.

"If there's nothing else, Master, I'll be off," Jem said.

"Aye, time wasted means brass lost." Carter Smith's eyes were thoughtful as he looked at the young man on the cart. Now he came to notice, Jem seemed a bit on the peaky side. The wind had nipped his nose and cheeks pink, but there was a pinched look about the mouth and a sag to his shoulders that he'd not observed before. Carter Smith wasn't given to regarding the health of his men unless it affected their work, and therefore his pocket, but he couldn't remember Jem having a day off for being poorly and he hoped, with business so good, he wasn't sickening for something now.

"Feeling all right are you, lad?"

"Me, sir?" said Jem, startled at the uncharacteristic enquiry. "Me? Right as ninepence."

"Thought you looked cold. Not surprising though, considering the weather." He patted the horse's warm rump. "You should put a muffler on or throw some of those sacks round your shoulders when the wind's as sharp as this. Don't want one of me best men going down with an ague."

Jem was too astonished to answer. The most he usually got from his master was a grudging acknowledgement when he'd completed a job in extra quick time. He'd never known that Carter Smith regarded him with any particular favour. Even now, he stepped back and swivelled his eyes away as though already regretting such an extravagant compliment.

Jem tipped his cap and flicked the reins. The obliging horse strained forward. Carter Smith watched the cart rumble away then hurried off past the grey collegiate church, known as t'owd church, and into the Shambles where the old buildings leaned top-heavy over the alleys to block out what there was of the gloomy daylight. An idea had begun to shape itself as he'd talked to Jem. A young man who knew the practical side of the business but was yet able to read and write and reckon numbers. A man with a cool head on his shoulders, trustworthy, respected by those he worked with. If . . . *if* the house-moving came about, then such a man would be ideal to put in charge of the yard.

What would he be now? Two and twenty? Young for responsibility and there were older men who might consider they had more claim. But none had Jem's intelligence and certainly none other had his scholarship. Aye, he'd soon pick up the way the counting house was run – enough to keep that old dog Spencer on his toes. He'd surely be agreeable to living on the premises if he set aside a couple of attic rooms in the house for his use, for he lived in some overcrowded hovel in Smedley and a young fellow like him must be thinking of marrying soon. It would be a good start for any young couple to have such agreeable prospects and accommodation. He'd have to be paid more, though.

His face settled to its habitual worried lines as he pushed through the throng in the tap room to where the builder sat with his tankard and plate before him. Time enough for that. First things first. If the builder's quotations were too high, be damned to his wife's ideas. He'd not move for her or anyone else.

He ordered a glass of brandy and water, seated himself and fell into conversation with the builder, giving no more thought to his wife, Sally Quick or Jem, now guiding his horse up Market Street towards the infirmary.

Jem carried the parcels into the infirmary dispensary, forcing his way through the crush of waiting people. It was hot inside and thick with the smell of stale clothes and impoverished, unwashed bodies. White faces turned to stare apathetically at

110

him then turned away, too engrossed in their ailments and in ensuring that nobody pushed their way out of turn.

He was glad to be out in the air again, sorry though he was for those inside. To be poor was bad enough. To be poor and sick and have to rely on charity for the relief of pain and distress, was worse. He knew the hopelessness of the people in there. The husband who must take the precious bottle of medicine to a wife who needed no more cure than to be removed from the cellar dwelling where the walls ran with wet and filth; the mother with the child sick because it never got food enough to sustain it or shoes to keep its feet from freezing pavements; the girl with lungs ruined from cotton fluff who must return to the mill or lose her place and become another burden to an already overburdened family; the man, old and homeless, who snatched an hour's warmth and comfort in the dispensary before he was spied and thrown out into the street as not being a suitable case for charity. Jem had a fierce compassion for them all and, in an odd way, a fear of them. As though they might have the power to pull him down to their level.

For almost a year he had taken classes at the Sunday School of a Wesleyan mission in the town, teaching adults and children their letters as Carrie had once taught him. It seemed little enough to give and he was pleased to be of use, but he sometimes felt an inward shrinking as he looked across the rows of heads bent over squeaking slates. The black-shawled careworn mothers; the fathers in their threadbare Sunday best; the children with their stick limbs and pale faces, their smiles optimistic still, unlike their parents who had long learned to exist without hope. It was the patience of them, the acceptance, that frightened him. They had given up fighting. Poverty was their lot and there was nothing much to expect of this world. They could only pray that glory would be theirs in the next. *Blessed are the meek: for they shall inherit the earth.* They had heard that text often enough from the pulpit. He wondered bitterly what comfort it gave in the face of the tyrannical landlord and slave-driving mill owner.

The ministers of the mission were good, sincere, practical men. They tried to alleviate the distress of the poor on weekdays as they fought for their souls on Sundays. There were other charitable institutions and societies thick on the ground, yet they could only graze the surface. They might educate a few female children to domestic work or provide night asylum for vagrants or dole out soup to those on the brink of starvation, but nothing really touched the deep black core of human misery that flowed like a river under the rich commercial flinty surface of the town. That dark tide frightened Jem. Frightened him because, even now, he was not so far from its treacherous brink. It only needed a stumble, an unwary step, and he and his family might begin the slide down the slippery banks.

He crossed the infirmary gardens. In summer the gravelled paths were a popular promenade. In winter with a north wind slicing across the slaty surface of the pond and rattling the black bare branches of the shrubs it was no place to linger except for those, like the crouched huddle of rags sheltering by a laurel hedge, who had nowhere else to go. The rags moved as he passed and a black claw emerged, palm upwards. Jem dug in his pocket. There was nothing much in it the day before payday, but he found a penny and dropped it into the supplicating palm. The coin was snatched back in among the rags that heaved up and shuffled sideways out of the grounds. Jem watched the creature dodge away among the traffic, then walked slowly to his cart.

The men of the mission would have gently reprimanded him for his prodigality. The money would only be spent in some gin shop. It would have been better to speak a few words about salvation to the wretch and bought him a pie with the penny so

112

that it would not have been squandered. So, with charity and kindness tempered with firmness, were sinners brought to the fold. Jem swung aboard the cart. He was not possessed of that true Christian purpose, he knew. He had rather the poor devil make his situation tolerable in his own chosen way, even if it did mean scarcely being sober from one day to the next.

He flicked the reins and the horse wove its way through the carriages and cabs on Piccadilly and turned into Lever Street.

Perhaps it was from his mother that he had inherited his horror of being swept under. He had been six when his father – a shoemaker with a respectable trade at his fingertips though dogged with ill health – had died. There had been scarcely enough money to give him a decent burial. He had heard his mother crying in the night and huddled close to his elder sister in the narrow bed, for it was a fearful thing to know that his strong capable mother was driven to tears. By day she was stony and resolute, bewilderment and grief showing in her eyes only when she thought she was unobserved. The local squire who owned all the houses round about called upon them when his agent had failed to extract the rent for the third week running. His mother, humbled, knotted her fingers in her apron and asked haltingly for his help until she could find employment.

Jem held the recollection of that day as clear in his head as if it were yesterday. The cramped kitchen with the sunlight slanting through the window. The florid man in knee breeches and gleaming leather boots, shaking his bewigged head and pursing his mouth. "Nothing I can do for you, I'm afraid, Nellie. Far too many in your position. If you can't find the rent, I have families waiting who'll be glad of a sound house like this." His voice was hearty. "There's always the poorhouse until you get on your feet. It's no time for pride."

There was a breathing silence then, slowly, his mother raised her head. She was tall, but to Jem's eye it seemed that at that moment she grew in stature. In her clean white pinafore, her black hair scraped back from her strong features, she slowly unbuttoned her cuffs and rolled the sleeves of her worn cotton dress to the elbow. She lifted up her hands, coarse and reddened from the morning's washing. She stared the squire in the face. "While I've two good arms," she said softly, "none of mine shall ever be so disgraced. I asked you for help, sir, because I can't bear to see me children wi' empty bellies and with all my grievin' over my dead husband I could see no way out for us. But I'll manage. I'll manage. And ask none again for charity."

She had turned her head away. The squire had blustered a while and then gone, putting them easily from his mind. He hadn't the time or inclination to fret over them if they chose to ignore his advice.

They gathered their possessions together. A bargain was struck with a neighbour who owned a handcart. The next day they had crossed the town, Jem and his sister, who was two years older, helping to push, and grandfather hobbling beside them on his sticks.

"We're going back to Smedley," his mother had said curtly when Jem complained that his legs ached, "so hold your noise." And when he had asked where that was she snapped, "It's where I was born. There'll be those there as knew me mam, God rest her. She helped many a one with her herbs and remedies and as I've all that she learned me tucked in my head, I shall carry on doing as she did if there's no other work to be found." She strained against the handles as the cart sagged into a rut. "Push now, lad – and you, too, Lily. The harder we push the sooner we'll be there. And if there's nowhere to lodge tonight then we shall sleep under a hedge and pretend we're gypsies."

They had been fortunate. An old neighbour took them in for the night and the next day his mother found work at a tavern and, it being haymaking time, the children were able to earn a copper or two in the fields. On her way to and from her work his mother carried her basket, detouring by hedgerows and common land to gather leaves and plants. The children often went with her, learning the plants by name: comfrey and coltsfoot, meadowsweet and tansy, shepherd's purse and dandelion . . . They gathered them carefully so as not to bruise the leaves and flowers, taking their hoard back to the room they rented, where they were hung in bunches to dry or seethed in water over the hearth so that the air of the room became pungent.

Then, gradually, people began to knock at the door. They wanted something to cure heartburn or stop fluxing of the bowels or soothe a headache and they went away with their twist of paper containing the dried herbs or an old jar with some liniment to rub the afflicted spot. The women came, glancing at Jem and Lily with knowing looks, so that their mother sent them to play out of doors while the whispered consultations took place. Some of them came furtively after dark and wept and begged for help uncaring that the children were not yet asleep on the pallet in the corner. These, too, were sent away comforted, hiding the twist of herbs in their apron pocket, praying that they worked and there would not be another mouth to feed next winter.

There were knocks at the door at all hours. 'Will Mrs Walker come, for Mary is right bad . . .' Or, '. . . the baby's had a fit and I'm that frightened . . .' Or, 'Mam's coughing is that terrible I think it's the end . . .' For lyings-in and layings-out, they came for his mother. Once or twice at these houses of birth or death, she met a physician called in out of desperation though his fees could be ill-afforded. One doctor saw her to be capable and calm and said he was in need of a nurse for a spoilt young woman expecting her first child. His mother gave up her work at the tavern and went to look after the woman and her child. The doctor put other work her way.

By this time his sister had gone into service and his mother had found Jem a place with Carter Smith. "It's an outdoor life," she told him. "Better'n working in a factory. I wasn't much for our Lily going into service, but rather that than ruinin' her health in some mill. You work hard, Jem, and learn what you can. I've heard Carter Smith's business is a growing one and he'll maybe look kindly on a willing lad." In one of her rare, tender gestures, she touched his shoulder. "You're growin', lad," she said softly. "Eh, I wish your dad could see you. He'd be proud. You've got his eyes, you know. Such a clear bright blue his were. And his quietness. He were more gentle than me. I was always a bit the fiery one." She sighed. "The strongest I suppose. He were too soft-hearted. He couldn't bear it when trade got bad. All those months of it, wi' money running out, and him getting sicker. I reckon he didn't have the heart to fight back. He just give up and let go." She dropped her hand. "Don't you never get like that, Jem. Life can be very cruel sometimes and it can be hard to see the point of fighting back. But that's just when you must." Her voice sharpened. "It's the trials of life that show what sort of stuff a person's made of. There's them that sinks under trouble and them that starts swimming and drags themselves out of it. You be one of them kind, lad."

Then she said, briskly, "That's enough talking. My time's precious. Run up Smedley Lane and take this packet to Mrs O'Hara. Tell her I'll be up to see her tomorrow. Poor soul. She's in a deal of trouble and she's no fighter. Married the wrong sort of man – a bully and no mistake. Heaven knows what'll happen to them nieces of hers. Nice well-brought-up girls – course, havin' no money when you've been used to it is worse than never havin' much to start with. Off you go. You're not too big to run errands, even though you are ready to start work."

That was how he had met Carrie.

Carrie.

He cursed softly under his breath. However careful he was his thoughts always returned to Carrie. He'd tried – and God alone knew how he'd tried – to put her out of his head. He'd taken her letters from under the loose floorboard meaning to rip them into shreds and throw them into the river, but it hadn't been possible. Her neat sloping writing had stared up at him. His name written in her hand. He'd thrust the bundle back into its hiding place and stamped viciously on the board to knock it into place. He would do it. In the future when the wound was not so raw, when her memory had dimmed. He would not read the letters again. He would abandon them and in time he would be able to take them out carelessly and toss them away. In time.

Not seeing her now was worse torment because he knew she was so near. Twice his resolve had weakened and he had gone the long way home, pausing near the lodge hoping he might catch an accidental glimpse of her, and then wrenching himself angrily away. He was ashamed of his weakness, yet to rid himself of her was like tearing himself in half. He did not think he would ever do it, yet he must try – and hope that the despair would eventually lessen.

Automatically his hands pulled and slackened the reins and the horse, knowing his touch, responded. The cart wheels made a great clattering in the quieter streets but the noise could not drown the weary round of his thoughts. She was not for him. She never had been. She was well bred. Born of gentlefolk. Born in a foreign place. Circumstances had dragged her down but she had always been that much different. She had always had dignity, even skivvying for those old bitches in Halliwell Lane. His mother had called at the lodge and reported on events. Each seeming to carry her further out of reach. New dresses were to be ordered for the social delights in prospect.

"Mrs O'Hara has secret hopes that both will make a good marriage." His mother had smiled. "It's a load off her mind to know that Mrs Dawes is seeing to them. She's been mithered as to what'd happen to the girls once they was back. And who knows they might meet some rich sprig of the gentry. Little 'un's pretty enough anyway and Carrie's got a winning way with her."

These snippets of news brought him no comfort. When he was alone he imagined the sort of man Carrie would choose. A well-to-do gentleman who would heap beautiful clothes and jewels upon her. Who would make her mistress of a fine house, waited on by respectful servants. The temptation was too great, sometimes, and he would slip into the character of that vague shadowy gentleman. It would be he, clad in fine broadcloth and crisp linen who would walk sculptured green lawns with Carrie on his arm, or raise his glass to her at some long table groaning with silver and fine china or, in a darkened, scented bedroom, take her into his arms and feel the soft trembling eagerness of her under his hands before he lifted her into the intimacy of a soft curtained bed . . .

He looked down at the reins lying easily in his big hands. Fine gentlemen, he thought, did not have rough calloused palms, seamed already with a morning's grime. There would be no soft touchings and smoothings with hands like that. A lass like Carrie would cringe at his touch and shudder at his advances. And he was a damned fool for mooning about her — more so because it was broad daylight and he'd work to do.

He guided the horse into a short narrow street. One side was entirely taken up with the high wall of a mill, the sound of the looms within clearly audible. The mill faced a terrace of slatternly houses. They had once been elegant, with broad flights of stairs to the solid front doors and lesser railed staircases to the basement kitchens. Now the railings were broken and rusted and smashed windows covered with rags or paper. The steps and the broken pavement were puddled with filth and amid the slime ragged children played, heedless of the stench from the gutter where refuse lay rotting in half-frozen heaps.

He scarcely noticed his surroundings though. He'd been here often enough, and streets like it – or worse. But the carriage at the end of the street caught his attention. It was a smart equipage and its alienness in that dingy street had drawn a crowd of urchins who knew enough to stand well back from the reach of the coachman's whip.

He caught the sound of the coachman's curses as he went into the mill yard and grinned to himself. If the gentleman who owned the equipage didn't return to it soon he'd find any removable parts of his carriage missing. The children here were light-fingered from the cradle.

He loaded the heavy packages onto the cart and the patient horse pulled the cart back to the street. Jem glanced again at the carriage and frowned. There was some kind of rumpus going on. The street had emptied as all the playing urchins had moved in a raggletailed pack to view the disturbance and one or two of their sluttish mothers had come out on the steps. He could hear a woman's voice, coarse and shrill, and see a black-shawled head amid the noisy mob. The coachman half stood on the carriage and, as Jem watched, snapped his whip at the crowd. One bold lad leapt at the leather thong and almost toppled the coachman.

The press of children swayed and laughed. The black-shawled woman moved with them and Jem saw that she was thin, drab, toothless and virulent of aspect.

And he saw someone else, the astonishing sight freezing him for a second.

Then he leapt down from the cart and thundered across the slimy cobbles. For, in the middle of that jeering rowdy crowd, white and defiant, yet obviously frightened, stood Carrie.

Chapter Four

Against the thumping noise from the mill and the catcalls from the small crowd, they did not hear his iron-nailed clogs clattering towards them. He was in among them, lifting small bodies aside by the scruff of the neck, snatching at the shoulder of the old harridan so that she screeched a curse at him.

"Hold your noise," he ordered and something in his voice, his face, silenced her and made the squalling children fall back.

"What the devil are you doing here, Carrie?"

She stood there, the colour drained from her face so that her eyes seemed enormous. He could see clearly the dark rim round the iris and the flecks of green in the slumbering grey. She looked small and defiant and, amid that ragged dirty crowd, glaringly incongruous in her good green cloak and flower-trimmed bonnet. In her hands she held a small white dove. Blood stained the feathers round its beak and dripped unnoticed onto her cream kid gloves.

"I could not bear it," she said. "The children . . . they were tormenting it so . . ."

"She's nowt but a thief." The old woman had recovered her voice. "Stealin' from them as is poor and helpless."

"Me mam give it us to play with," a small girl snivelled. "It's for us dinner. Mam'll wring its neck when she's ready for it."

"They had it by a string attached to its leg," Carrie said.

"They threw it again and again into the air and laughed every time it crashed to the ground."

"A thief!" the crone shrieked. "She snatched it off young Maggie. I saw her!"

"I wanted to pay . . . but they would not listen. I have a shilling in my purse . . ."

"A prime bird like that is worth two shillings," the old woman cried, her eyes glinting greedily.

Jem poked the dove's flaccid breast. "You'd buy two like this for sixpence," he growled, "and well you know it."

"It was probably pinched from somebody's loft, anyway," a wag from the back of the crowd shouted, to a roar of laughter. "Maggie's dad's a dab hand at spiritin' birds from their perches."

"Among other things," another called.

"Not true!" Maggie cried, forgetting to snivel, and as further argument broke out, Jem said to Carrie in an undertone. "Do you really want to keep it?"

"It is injured," she said. "I cannot just leave it to suffer." She groped with difficulty in the embroidered bag that hung from her wrist. "Here," she said, producing a shilling.

He shook his head. "It's almost dead," he said gently. "Let me wring its neck and put it out of its misery."

"Its heartbeat is strong. I can feel it through my glove. I had rather pay for it and take it with me."

He shrugged. Maggie was now pummelling a boy bigger than herself. Jem pulled her away and held up the shilling.

"Take this straight to your mother," he said sternly. "It's more than the bird's worth so you've struck a good bargain. Next time you're to have pigeon pie for supper make sure I don't ever catch you making a cruel plaything of the bird. Do you hear me? I'm down this way often and I shall find out if you don't heed what I say." The girl snatched the coin, grinning, and sidled into the crowd. "You be off too, old woman," Jem said, jerking his head. "The peep-show's over."

She made as if to protest, glanced at him and thought better of it. She went off muttering, to disappear down the nearest flight of stairs to her cellar. The rest of the children, disappointed that all had ended so tamely, wandered off to resume their games and snigger about the strange lady who had been so angry over a bird.

"Jem, I am so grateful to you." Now they were alone her defiance seemed to ebb. She looked vulnerable, not a little scared. "It was frightening. Though they were only children they were so fierce. They threw things." He saw the stain of mud on her cloak and his mouth tightened. "When the old woman came she was hateful. I thought she would strike me."

"You should not be in this sort of place," he said. "How do you come to be here?"

"Mr Sanderson brought me."

"To Ancoats? Whatever for?"

"He was merely making a call before we returned home. He owns some of these houses. It is quite my own fault that I got into a scrape. I should not have left the carriage."

"Aye, Miss," grumbled the coachman. "You'd best get back inside afore Master catches you or I shall be in trouble meself."

"Small thanks to you that the trouble was not worse," Jem said sharply. "You took care not to risk your own skin."

"Please, Jem. I will not have you blaming others for my own rashness."

"You should have had more sense!"

"You are shouting, Jem," she said softly.

With an effort he calmed himself. Her clear gaze, her concern for the dove lying helpless in her hands, moved him to an overwhelming weakening tenderness. His anger was his only defence against it.

He said, stiffly, "I had no right. I'm sorry. I'll get back to my work when I have seen you safe inside the carriage."

She did not move. She looked past him up the street at the gaggle of unkempt children. A woman screeched abuse somewhere behind the blind boarded windows. Thick smoke from the mill chimney eddied downward in the fitful wind, dropping its soot on a scabby-headed infant digging with its hands into the black filth of the gutter.

"Such a dreadful place," she whispered. "It is not right that children must grow up in such a place."

"There's far worse than this. At least here they have houses of sorts to live in. Better than sleeping rough in doorways or finding a corner out of the wind under a cart in the market or under a bridge."

She shuddered, her gaze ranging over the house fronts. "Something should be done. Mr Sanderson cannot allow his property to fall into such disrepair. I must speak to him. People should be housed decently."

"You would encourage him to improve his property?"

"Oh, yes. Perhaps he has not had time yet to do anything. I know he has only recently bought the houses . . ."

"And what do you suppose would happen if he spent his capital putting these houses to rights? He'd then have to increase the rents to pay for the improvements and the people who live here now would be forced to move because they could not pay. They'd be worse off than before."

"Surely that need not be the case. Something could be done – should be done."

"Aye, there's much that should be done, but you're in no position to alter things. Now, please get into the carriage."

Her fingers smoothed the dove's matted feathers.

"To be a woman," she said quietly, "is to be almost as

helpless as this poor bird. I am treated as though I should have no thought in my head beyond pretty dresses and the latest dance steps." She sighed. "I was looking forward so much to this morning. I had hoped Mr Sanderson would have talked to me in detail about his investments and about the places we visited. I wanted everything explained to me. I wanted to *learn*." She gave a short bitter laugh. "Oh, he took me here and there as he had promised. We viewed a sandpit where his men are excavating sand to be sold to builders. We viewed the brickworks and a few fields where houses are to be built. I was not allowed once to get out of the carriage to talk to the workpeople or the overseers. 'It would not be suitable,' he said. Yet he seemed to see nothing unsuitable in children of no more than five or six working in that brickyard. Tiny things struggling with loads of bricks on their shoulders. There were women and girls, too, doing such heavy backbreaking work. I wanted to know *why*. I wanted to know of their lives. I wanted to know about the profits on such a place, the way it is run from day to day.

"Mr Sanderson would not allow me to leave my seat and though I pressed him with questions, he kept brushing them aside. 'Don't bother your head . . . leave such matters to those who are more experienced.' How is one supposed to gain experience if one is treated like an addlehead?" Her eyes sparked. "You are no better, Jem. 'Get into the carriage,' she mocked. 'Don't ask questions. Don't get involved.' Am I then to go through life closing my eyes to injustice? Allowing others to make my decisions for me? Being protected all the time?"

"And would you have had me stand by and watch you being ridiculed and humiliated by that scummy mob? If I'd not come along you'd have had more than a gob of mud on your skirts."

"You are deliberately obtuse. It is the *principle* I speak of."

"If such principle leads you into daft actions in a place like this, then I'm against it."

"How can I make you understand?"

"Why should I have to understand? It's nothing to do with me."

They glared at each other. He understood too well what she was trying to say but he knew, too, that any display of softness, of sympathy on his part would topple his hard-won defences.

"You have changed, Jem. Once I could have talked to you."

"Everything was different then."

"Yes it was. Your letters had not led me to suppose that you had become insensitive. I am sorry to have lost your friendship, Jem."

"I have work to do," he said harshly.

"Then do not keep from it on my account." She raised her chin, but her mouth drooped disconsolately. It was almost more than he could bear. He clenched his fingers, fighting the impulse to deny her words.

He should have gone then. She had dismissed him, clear enough. Afterwards he wondered how it would all have turned out had he left her and not looked back. But some stubborn instinct held him. He would see her safe to her carriage and be damned to her dismissal.

She moved with dignity, the dove lying limp in her hands. As she was about to mount the carriage step her foot slid in the ooze accumulated in the corner of a broken flagstone. Off balance and unable to help herself because of the bird, she stumbled sideways against Jem.

Her bonnet caught his chin. Her elbow dug into his midriff. The dove, roused from its stupor, struggled feebly in her hands. But he had her safe, his arms tight about her. The faint scent of sandalwood from her clothes, the tang of warm, clean skin filled his nostrils, suffocating all his good sense. She lay still against him for a moment and he held his breath, certain she must hear the wild thudding of his heart.

"Oh, dear," she uttered, "how did that happen?" She glanced up at him in embarrassment and the movement dislodged her bonnet so that it fell to her shoulders held by the green strings. Her soft curling hair blew loose in the wind. Blindly, unthinkingly, he turned his head so that the silky strands fell across his mouth like a caress.

Somewhere a long way off his anger smouldered. He reached for it but it sank back like a coward against the violent, intoxicating surge of delight and desire. Under the thick wool of her cloak he could feel the roundness of her upper arm. He moved his hand slowly upwards over the bones of his shoulder until the back of his fingers brushed against her neck.

Far away a voice said, "Master's coming. Make haste into the carriage, Miss."

She said, "For the second time today, Jem, I have to thank you for rescuing me. I have recovered my balance so you may let me go. Perhaps you would be kind enough to hold the bird while I get into the carriage." Under the light rush of her words there was an odd uncertainty.

His throat was dry. He could no more answer her than release her. He wanted to crush her to him, to pour out all his feelings for her in a wild delcaration. He wanted to see the response in her eyes, to feel her mouth parted and eager under his. But she was not even looking at him. She had eyes only for the bird lying in her cupped hands and he silently damned the bird and damned the speech that must not be spoken and cursed himself for a fool and all the time the surging tide of tenderness shivered in his blood.

"Jem . . . ?" Her eyes lifted to his, puzzlement in them, a small frown drawing down her brows. He could not stand here any longer. Mr Sanderson was already stepping down the broken steps of the house.

Roughly he swept her up into his arms, shouldered aside the carriage door, slid her into the seat. She gasped and laughed in surprise.

"What's this?" Mr Sanderson's dry voice asked. "Jem, what are you doing here? And what is that you are holding, Caroline?"

Carrie leaned forward. "I saw this injured bird. I got out to attend to it, then I slipped and Jem, who fortunately was passing, came to help me up." She was smiling, collected. "But I am perfectly all right so do not fret, though Jem thinks I am foolish to trouble over a bird." She glanced at Jem from under her lashes, a veiled pleading look that begged him not to upset the deliberate half-truth of her story.

"And foolish you are, my dear. You are far too soft-hearted, but then it is a womanly attribute and where should we men be without the compassion of the gentler sex, eh Jem?"

Jem who wished for nothing but that all Carrie's compassion should be heaped upon him, felt heat in his face. Awkwardly he touched his cap.

"I must be off," he said. "I've a load to take to Salford."

"Then we must not detain you," Mr Sanderson said pleasantly. "My regards to your mother, Jem. And this is for your trouble. Good day to you."

Jem stared at the coin pressed into his hand. The tall but stooped man now climbing to the carriage had nicely reminded him of his place. His fingers tightened about the coin and the muscles along his jaw tightened. Through the carriage window Carrie smiled a little ruefully as though she sensed his hurt, and raised her hand in farewell.

He stood in the road until the carriage turned the corner. And he knew, with blinding clarity that flashed through him like a bolt of lightning, that he had to fight.

He had to fight for Carrie. He had to fight Mr Sanderson and his powerful influence. He had to fight every one of those shadowy suitors who would come courting his girl. He would have to fight his own pride.

His mother's words came to him. '*Your father . . . he just give up and let go . . . it's the trials of life that show what sort of stuff a person's made of . . . there's them that sinks under trouble and them that starts swimming and drags themselves out of it. You be one of them kind, lad . . .*'

By God he would be. He'd take on the lot of them. He'd not back down from the challenge. He'd work to make himself worthy of her. Somehow he'd better himself and make her take notice of him.

He went to his cart and swung himself aboard. Hope warmed his ribs. He flicked the reins and as the cart passed the rabble of children squabbling at the corner, he tossed the shilling Mr Sanderson had given him into their midst. Their screams as they fought over its possession rang in his ears like music.

When she got back to the lodge Carrie bathed the blood from the dove's feathers then put it in a deep box and watched over it until it revived enough to take a deep draught of water and to peck at the grain she scattered about it. When it began to preen its broken, disarranged feathers she knew that it would survive. It gave her a warm sense of pleasure, offsetting the frustrations of the morning: Mr Sanderson's smiling, infuriating evasions; his protectiveness that had made her feel she was cocooned in a smothering soft blanket; and that disturbing meeting with Jem, who had been so angry and stiff and unreasonable. Yet when he had lifted her into the carriage, and afterwards when she had looked back at him standing in the grey slatternly street she had glimpsed the old caring Jem in the face of the truculent stranger. And that had touched her with a subtle melancholy that lingered even now.

She knelt before the fire watching the bird in the box. Aunt Linnie lay on the sofa, grumbling gently. Carrie had given her the same edited account of the rescue of the bird as she had given to Mr Sanderson. Aunt Linnie had given her consent to the morning's excursion most reluctantly.

"I am relieved to see you returned, dear," she fretted now. "Adele thought it a joke but I have been distressed all morning to think of you in such places and I fail to see why Mr Sanderson had to encourage you in your whim. I trust you are satisfied and will take no more such foolish notions into your head."

Carrie touched the soft breast feathers of the dove and was glad when her aunt was distracted by the chiming clock, crying, "Adele is very late for luncheon. She should not be out at all in this wind but she was determined to go for a stroll. I declare I have two very self-willed young ladies about me."

At that moment the door burst open and Adele came in, rosy cheeked from the wind and holding aloft a letter.

"I met a messenger in the drive. It is addressed to us both, Carrie."

It was an invitation to a ball at the house of Mr Edmund Brook in three weeks' time.

"My yellow gauze must be ready by then." Adele was wound up tight as a spring with excitement. She flew around the room discarding cloak and bonnet, exclaiming over the bird, flinging questions and not waiting for answers. "It will be a grand affair, I know. Is it not exciting, Carrie?"

Carrie laughed. "Do sit down and calm yourself. I do not suppose it will be anything too grand. Mr Brook is not the gentleman to want too much ostentation."

"But a *ball*," Adele cried. "It will be our very first. And Mr Brook has been out of the social round for years. He is bound to make it a special occasion." She whirled to a halt on the rug before the fire.

"Do not over-excite yourself," Aunt Linnie warned. "You will bring on a breathless attack . . ."

"Oh, I am almost grown out of such things," Adele said airily.

"You look flushed, dear. Quite feverishly so. The wind is far too chilling for you to have been out so long – and now this excitement. You must take a cooling powder."

"I have not been far, truly. Only round the grounds. I was surprised to find how interesting the garden is. There is a stretch of woodland at the rear of the house and a steep knoll with a view over Lower Blackley."

"If you have been climbing hills, then you will surely have over-exerted yourself."

Adele laughed. "It was only a little hill and for much of the time I was not even out of doors. I was in the glasshouses. A fractional pause and then she rushed on, "I even looked in on Uncle George. His workshop is perfectly cosy and draught free."

Carrie rose from her knees. "You went to see the orchids that Elliot Sanderson mentioned?" she asked.

"Yes. Yes, I did," Adele said brightly. She held out her hands to the fire. "And what of your outing Carrie? Did you enjoy your trip to the brickworks?"

"It was interesting. Perhaps not quite so much as orchids. I must walk up and see them myself sometime."

"Oh, they are not very showy just now. Many of them are dormant. Later on, in the spring and summer there will be a good showing."

Aunt Linnie glanced sharply at her niece. The girl did sound breathless. She knew it! The walk in the cold had done her no good at all.

"Tell, me," Adele went on quickly, "did you decide how you wished to invest our money?"

Perhaps a glass of angelica tea, Linnie thought. That would

be warm and soothing for her chest. And an eggnog might not come amiss for Carrie. She had been quiet since she had come in. Heaven knew what infections hung about that bird – not to mention the places Mr Sanderson had taken her to. It was a lowering time of year and she must be firmer with them in future about excursions in inclement weather.

"I have one or two ideas," Carrie began, but was glad when Jane came in to announce luncheon was ready. She did not wish to say too much of the vague plan that was forming in her mind. It had come to her on the journey back to Crumpsall, and there was much work to do before it could be spoken of.

In the dining room at Beech Place Margaret Gordon toyed with her fork and remarked in her well-bred voice that she was pleased she would be able to accept Mr Edmund Brook's invitation before her aunt and uncle came to escort her back to London.

"It will make a grand finale, as it were, to your visit," Mrs Sanderson said. She dabbed at her mouth with her napkin. "When you get back to London it will be all hustle and bustle to prepare for the wedding. Such an exciting time for any bride."

She gave a small sigh as though swept by nostalgia and wished, privately, that her future daughter-in-law was not so fond of that particular shade of brown. Her complexion was not so clear that she could afford to make it look muddier. A nice light blue would work wonders for her but she had ignored every hint, and had even once drawled that she thought too much colour vulgar. She, Dorothea, had been wearing her favourite scarlet morning gown at the time and though Margaret had been talking to one of those dull Dawes girls and had perhaps not meant her remark to be overheard, the barb had struck sharp. There were times when Margaret's high-nosed manners were a trifle wearing. Not that she let it trouble her for more than a few seconds. She was too experienced, too worldly-wise for that. She had overcome more snubs and slights than the casually innocent ones of a girl scarcely twenty. Overcome a great many difficulties and travelled a thorny road to get where she was now. That knowledge often afforded her a private amusement that over the years had countered any tendency to self-doubt.

"I have been away from London so long it will be quite strange to be returning there," Margaret drawled. "One feels so out of touch in the provinces." She made it sound, Dolly Sanderson thought, that she might have been living wild with naked heathen. "I confess, Elliot, that I am happy that we shall be living close to dear Mamma and all my friends when we are married."

All those aristocratic pillars of rectitude. Those plummy-mouthed misses fancying themselves superior in every way because of their blood and lineage, paraded by their mammas at balls and entertainments in gowns and jewels that could be ill afforded, in the hopes of catching the eye of a gentleman of means. Oh, yes, Margaret would wish to be close to them in order to impress upon them her good fortune in finding so rich a husband. Disappointingly not of a titled family, but wealthy indeed, and one would soon shrug off the provincial family who had rather vulgarly made their money in trade, though in the East Indies which was more acceptable — in fact rather romantic — then if the trade had been conducted in England.

And again, Elliot had such fine looks and absolutely no interest in the family business. He had a talent for pretty verse, danced elegantly, rode a horse well and lost at cards with good humour. All such gentlemanly attributes. Against his father's pressure he had resisted any temptation to involve himself in the East India trade and there was really no need at all for him to do so. He had come into part of his fortune on his twenty-first birthday and there would be another goodly portion on his marriage. And he was the sole heir. The refined but poor Lady Gordon, her vapid son and her dutiful, shrewd daughter Margaret need never worry again about keeping up appearances on a slender and rapidly diminishing income from the late Sir Charles's mismanaged inheritance.

Mrs Sanderson knew precisely how Margaret's mind worked. Knew and was prepared to be condescended to because for Elliot, and his children, it would be very different. They would, by right of marriage, of birth, move in aristocratic circles. She wanted no more than that. Nothing for herself. Her life's purpose would be over when Elliot married. She would gracefully retire to become a comfort and a companion to Miles in his declining years. It would be painful for her, but it was a sacrifice she would gladly make. Elliot would be safe and secure as she – despite everything she had achieved for herself against what had seemed at times insurmountable odds – had never quite been.

"I do hope cousin Delayne will be well enough to attend the wedding," Margaret said. "Gout is such a painful affliction."

"Most trying," Mrs Sanderson agreed. Wretched man, she thought. Decadent, decaying like his appalling mansion, half drunk most of the time. Roistering with his equally decrepit cronies and daring to include Elliot in the nightly carousals in the squalour of the old hall. She had stayed only as long as politeness dictated and then only for the sake of the downtrodden mouse of a wife who, poorly served and friendless, had been pathetically eager for them to prolong their visit. The smallpox outbreak had been a timely excuse, sorry though she had been for Lady Delayne, who childless, neglected and frightened of her husband, was forced to spend year after dreary year in that mausoleum. Well, she had done her duty. She had known it would not be pleasant but even she had been taken aback by the dilapidation of the estates and had wondered if, after all, she had been a trifle hasty in selecting Margaret Gordon for Elliot.

But back again in her own smoothly run household common sense had reasserted itself. It was for the future she planned. She had always been a forward-looking woman. Lord Delayne, prematurely aged, suffering from gout and an affliction of the liver, would drink himself to an early grave. There were no legitimate male heirs though there had been plenty of urchins in the village bearing Lord Delayne's prominent nose and cleft chin. Lady Delayne was past childbearing. The title would pass to Margaret's brother. Then, Elliot's children would have an earl for an uncle, as well as the various minor gentry on Lady Gordon's side of the family. If she, Dorothea Sanderson, born Dorothea Grey, daughter of a whore, lived to see that day, then she would die with a smile on her face.

She looked round the table, her glance lingering with affection on Miles who had been patient and understanding these last two years while she had travelled with Elliot. But then he had always been a good, kind man. He had even resigned himself with good grace to the knowledge that his son was only interested in the comfortable life that money could buy and had neither the inclination nor, regrettably, the sharpness of mind necessary to engage himself in the manipulation of his fortune.

She felt the familiar pangs of love tinged with exasperation as her glance went to Elliot. He was so much the son she had desired him to be – handsome, cultured, elegant. He had a pretty way with a poem – some were quite good enough to be read aloud in company – and he had an interest in botany, but there was a lazy, indolent streak in him.

There was a time, when he was a child, that she had been glad he had been passively content to sit on the cool verandah or in a shaded room of the house that stood high on the slopes of Penang Hill, well above the fever-ridden air of the coastal lowlands. Given a book or a sketching pad, he would amuse himself by the hour, an amah squatting at his side to whisk away flies and mosquitoes with a palm-leaf fan. Obediently holding the amah's hand he would walk, morning and evening, in the shady compound, happy to peer at the flowers and birds: the cascades of purple and pink bougainvillea; the hibiscus bushes that guarded the deep cupped nests of the bulbuls whose bubbling song was the first thing she heard every morning; the stately canna lilies, scarlet and crimson. He knew all the birds by name. The tiny darting sunbirds, the perky black and white *murai* with his clear whistle, the flocks of gentle brown doves considered lucky by the Malays who trapped and caged them to keep luck close, the great sea eagles, *lang hindek*, circling in the air currents over the hill slopes, the brainfever bird, whose descending scales sent a superstitious shiver down her back, for the Malays named it *burong mati anak*, the dead child bird.

So many children died in the East. Those Europeans who could, sent their precious offspring home to England, preferring to let them risk the hazards of months at sea, inevitable home-sickness and the iron discipline of some boarding establishment rather than fall prey to cholera or marsh fever or the many diseases, named and unnamed, that rampaged in the thick, damp heat. By the time the children were grown they were strangers to their parents. She did not intend that to happen to Elliot. She loved him with a fierce possessive devotion that had amazed her with its intensity when he had first been laid, squalling and wrinkled into her arms, for she had neither welcomed nor wanted him. She had spent a wretched pregnancy, regretting every day the loss of her figure, and the three-day labour had been far worse than anything she had imagined. But love had sprung, unbidden and astonishingly powerful, into her soul and she was prepared to take the chance that some disease might or might not carry him off against the sudden brutal severance of banishment to England.

So she had protected, nurtured and cosseted him through every childish ailment. She had engaged an amah to devote all her waking hours to the child and another to watch over him at night. She paid a small boy to search every bush, every flower bed, every drain about the garden before Elliot took his walks and, before bedtime, every cranny and crevice in Elliot's room to ensure that no snake or poisonous centipede lurked there.

She had been glad, then, that he was a docile child who did not demand to play with other, rougher, children. She kept such meetings to the very minimum for fear of infection. She herself taught him to write and number and for a while was able to plead that Elliot was shy and delicate and must not be forced into learning. A stranger coming daily into the boy's cloistered world would mean risk of disease brought in from the less wholesome air of the town. Presently Miles in his quiet way had insisted. Tutors came, tutors went: an impoverished cleric or two come to preach the gospel and glad of a little extra income to stretch their stipend; minor clerks with the East India Company with talents in Latin or mathematics.

To them all, Elliot showed a stubbornness to learn anything that did not immediately interest him. And what interested him as he grew from childhood to gangly adolescence was lounging on a cane chair composing verses, or taking his horse on long saunters about the hill, returning with saddle bags full of botanical specimens that he replanted in the garden, or escaping down to the beach outside the town with young Mahmood, the boy once hired to seek out snakes and scorpions but now grown lithe and merry-eyed and elevated to the position of Elliot's body servant.

Dorothea realised, with growing disquiet, that Mahmood had come to fill the place of the English companions Elliot had never had. He was a friend, rather than a servant. Elliot was not a talkative boy, indeed he could be sullen when crossed, but with Mahmood he was never reticent. They laughed together, talked in the rapid Malay she had never mastered and were prone, when anyone else came within earshot, to lower their voices to a conspiratorial whisper, as though they shared secrets. Which was quite, quite ridiculous, for what sort of secrets could a poor Malay boy from a fishing *kampong* and a rich gently-reared *tuan besar*'s son have in common? She disliked the intimacy. She felt excluded by it, hurt even. Yet for the moment she tolerated it. The time was coming when Elliot would have to move in wider circles and the friendship with the Malay boy would wane of its own accord. He would make friends with people of his own sort.

On Elliot's eighteenth birthday his father took him into the family business and it was soon apparent that it was not a success. "Dearest Mamma," he complained, "can you not use your influence with Papa? I find the office tedious in the extreme and the people – agents, managers, accountants – insufferably boring. For Papa, no doubt, it is very interesting. He has the head for profits and losses and whether the price of pineapples and copra and nutmeg is better this year than last. I cannot raise any enthusiasm about such matters. There are so many in the office capable of dealing with things that I should never be missed."

"You must try, dear. For Papa's sake. He has lived for the time when you would take your place beside him."

"But I have no place. I sit at my father's side and listen to the dreary talk and before I know it my mind has drifted on to more interesting topics. Then when Papa questions me I am at a loss and though he does not lose his temper I know he is cross and the clerks all snigger because of my ignorance. It is not pleasant."

"Have patience. It is important that you learn, for one day the business will be yours."

"Then I shall sell it or put it in the hands of managers." His handsome face was flushed.

She longed to hold his head to her breast as she had when he was a child. "I shall speak to Papa," she said soothingly.

"Will you, Mamma?" She was rewarded by a glowing smile. She had never refused him anything. She had always made the way smooth for him. She would smooth over this difficulty and he need never bother himself with the tedium of business.

But Miles was adamant. He said, calmly, "He will settle in time. Let us face the fact, Dolly, that he has had a deal too much of his own way in the past." He smiled at her protests. "You meant it for the best for the boy has not been strong and every illness has posed a threat. But he cannot fritter his time away for ever. He must learn to take his place in the world."

Elliot took the news in astonishment. Then he grew sullen and withdrawn as he had done in the days when he had been forced to pore over books of arithmetic and Euclid. Dorothea was hurt that this sullenness was turned upon her. It was more than she could do to coax a smile out of him. It was unfair that she should be blamed for something beyond her control. The only time she heard his laughter was when he and Mahmood enjoyed some private joke. The sound of that laughter was wounding indeed. She realised, painfully, that her son was beginning to grow away from her. More and more there would be parts of his life she could not influence or guide. A voice inside her cried *not yet, not yet* and alongside the hurt a little anger grew. Was she to be cast aside so soon and so lightly? She, who had been the most devoted, caring and loving of mothers?

Because it was impossible that her anger should be directed against the son she loved passionately above everyone, it became channelled towards the slim brown boy who was his constant companion. She grew sharp with Mahmood. Every trifling mistake she pounced upon and the soft dark eyes turned humbly on her, the gentle apologies, were, to her, proofs of his deviousness.

Then Miles took an ague which seemed a passing thing but would not be shaken off. Immediately afterwards he had a lowering bout of marsh fever from which he had been plagued over the years. Usually he shook off the attacks quickly but this time the doctor spoke of a strain to the heart and ordered Miles, despite his protests, to rest in bed where he would be bled daily until all the noxious poisons were eliminated from his system. Dorothea, worried and distracted, was pleased that Elliot continued to go each day to the office and appeared to have reconciled himself. He grew cheerful and whistled about the house once more.

She did not learn till later that, at his father's desk, he waved away ledgers unopened. The chief clerk, a man who had served his father for years, made any decisions that had to be made and when he accompanied Elliot on courtesy calls to the captains of ships engaged in his father's trade, it was he who talked of freight and tonnage and bills of lading while Elliot sat drinking Madeira in moody silence. Presently he refused to go at all. It was not the chief clerk's place to tell him otherwise and with the *tuan besar* being so sick and not to be troubled and with the young *tuan* being a hindrance anyway, he was relieved when Elliot began to appear less and less at the office.

It was a small, closed community and little went unremarked. It did not take long before one of the many visitors who called to ask after Miles let drop the information that Elliot had been seen several times on the coast road in company with his Malay boy, Mahmood, and a pretty Malay girl. The same three had been seen bathing on a nearby beach and glimpsed out in a sampan engaged in fishing. All these activities had taken place when, surely, the young man should have been occupied in more useful pursuits.

Dorothea remembered her informant well. A sour-faced woman who had once hoped her daughter might catch Miles's eye and had never forgiven him for rushing into marriage with a person whose previous husband had been not quite the thing. Memories were long and beauty, as always, distrusted by those less favoured. Dorothea knew she was tolerated only because of Miles and his position. She said, gaily, "How very observant people are. My poor Elliot can hardly take his nose from the grindstone before all kinds of silly assumptions are made. My husband had business interests in the area. He owns land there and has certain plans for it. I expect, as young people will, Elliot was combining business with pleasure." The woman went back down the hill in her sedan chair carried by sweating coolies, feeling aggrieved, suspicious (for everyone knew that Elliot Sanderson was an idler and a fool, for all his looks) and cheated because she had expected denials and horror, instead of laughter and agreement.

Dorothea sat in shocked silence for a long time. She thought of her son with tender despair, for he was obviously being led sadly astray by evil influences. For Mahmood she felt only rage. Her jealous anger was fed now by indignation. As for that girl, Fatimah, Mahmood's sister, she had refused to have her in the house for a long time now. Once, like Mahmood, a stick of a child with big black wondering eyes, attractive like these Malay children were, she had been employed occasionally, to help in the kitchens when there was a dinner party, or some other large social function. But the girl had grown. She had reached twelve or thirteen, maturing early as these native girls did, and at one function she had moved among the guests gathering empty glasses and Dorothea had noticed how the men's eyes had followed her. The downcast eyes and modest manner gave extra allure to the budding breasts and shapely hips, as she moved with the languid, easy sway of her race.

She saw the smiles that passed between her son and this girl, blossoming ripely to womanhood. She remembered how the child Fatimah had tagged after her brother and Elliot, and even now was part of the easy intimacy the other two shared. Fatimah was never employed about the house again.

Dorothea's resolve hardened. Mahmood must go. Fatimah, this new and unsuspected threat, must also be removed. No use insisting that Mahmood was to be dismissed. Elliot would turn his wrath on her. Miles could not be troubled, sick as he was. There must be a way to get rid of the troublesome pair without Elliot suspecting she had a hand in it. Some way of discrediting them – of removing them far from Elliot. Some secret way.

She thought of Pereira.

Her first husband, Tom, had been involved in several of his more shady enterprises, with a man called Pereira. He was a Eurasion of Portuguese/Indian descent. She had never liked him. His smooth brown smiling face, the careful waves in his oiled black hair, the pink wet lips and the hooded brown eyes – there was something too soft, too smooth about him. She was reminded of one of those thin brown snakes that lay camouflaged on a branch until the tiny victim went by and, in an eye's flicker, was seized and consumed. But at the time of Tom's death he had been discreet – at a price. There was nothing to link Tom's name with the opium dens on the waterfront or the false issue of shares in a non-existent silver mine. And rumour had it that Pereira's wealth and influence had grown greatly since. The opium dens flourished. He ran a chain of gambling hells and it was said that every whore on the island paid dues to him. Above anyone, he would be the man to arrange things quietly.

Certainly, he said, for a comparatively small sum it could all be done clandestinely. How many were there? An old grandmother, her widowed daughter and the two children, Mahmood and Fatimah? Poor and without influence? Good.

"I do not wish to know the details," she said. "I just wish them to be permanently removed from the island."

"They have offended the memsahib in some way?"

She said, stonily, "The boy has become a bad influence on my son."

"Ah, yes," he said, "your son." The red mouth smiled under the dark line of the moustache he had grown since she had last seen him. He was plumper, too, and his white suit was impeccably tailored, his hands fat with gold rings. "You must be anxious to shelter him from harm, and your husband, I hear, is indisposed."

"He must know nothing," she said sharply.

"Your secret is in good hands."

They stared at each other and Dorothea's glance was the first to falter. He leaned forward. "I am a man who profits from other people's secrets," he said softly. I have, locked in my brain, many pieces of information. Some of it useless, some of it valuable. Yours is of minor importance, Mrs Sanderson, though at some future time I may find it necessary to seek some small favour. It seems unlikely at this present moment, but I trust you will consider any such request with partiality."

"Blackmail?"

His lips parted just enough to show his glossy white teeth. "An objectionable word. A favour for a favour. I think we understand each other. We are something of a kind, you and I."

"That is impertinence!"

"Do not pretend insult. The colour of our skins, our ancestry, our sex, is different. At heart we are both opportunists. We turn each situation to our advantage and we each have a ruthless streak. We are the ones who survive when kindlier natures succumb."

"I quite misunderstand you," she said in an icy voice. "I think we have little in common, Mr Pereira."

He inclined his head, knowing that the shadow in her eyes was acknowledgement enough. Then, briskly, he said, "Send the servant, Mahmood, to the market in three days' time. You obtain your fruit and vegetables from Keng Chiang. Return his chit with some query and make sure your son is occupied elsewhere for the day."

In three days' time she took a chill that confined her to bed for the day. "I should so much like it, Elliot, if you would stay at home for once," she said. "Your papa looks to me for company, but I am not up to it and he will be pleased if you sit and read to him."

Elliot amiably agreed. He prepared himself to entertain his father as Mahmood set out down the winding hill carrying the memsahib's accounts and with the message he had been given fixed in his head.

Much later she learned the whole of it, but over the next few days she had only Elliot's reports as, white-faced, he pieced together the confused accounts of how Mahmood had disappeared after a disturbance in the market. "Someone said he was caught stealing money from a woman's basket – and that was a lie for he was honest, you know that, Mamma. I would have trusted him with my life! He was hustled by the crowd into the street and after that . . ." he shrugged his shoulders hopelessly, ". . . after that it is all confusion. Everywhere I go I am met with blank stares. No one has seen him. Even his family—" He broke off and turned away, his shoulders bent.

Dorothea said, in the perfect tone of shocked sympathy, "But what did his family say?"

"I could ask nothing of them. They were gone."

He had ridden out to the house to find that, in the night, the *attap* thatch had set alight and sparks flying before the breeze had set other houses ablaze. The villagers had spent the hours of darkness damping down the flames and, standing amid black and smouldering ruination, they were dazed and disinterested in his questioning. They blamed the old grandmother who was often careless and forgetful and had probably not doused the cooking fire before she slept. But the family had gone. At daylight a man with a cart had come to fetch them and their possessions. It was understood he had come from Mahmood, who had had word of the fire and sent for his homeless family. Were they not now up at the *tuan*'s house?

"My dear," Dorothea said, soothingly, "you will make yourself ill if you continue to upset yourself. I am very distressed for you, but I think your friendship blinded you to Mahmood's faults. He had become slipshod of late. I had many occasions recently to reprimand him. Perhaps he has got himself into some mischief and could not bear to face you over it."

"Never!"

She laid a gentle hand on his arm. "He was only a servant, Elliot. A native. I shall find you another . . ."

"He was my only friend." His eyes were tragic. "I thought you would understand."

"I do, my dear," she said. "He had been with us a long time. Perhaps too long. Perhaps it is time for you to make friends among young people of your own race."

He looked at her stonily. She saw that he had drawn all his feelings within himself, shutting her out. He refused to speak to her of Mahmood again.

She fought against uncertainty in the days that followed, as Elliot grew more withdrawn, more haggard, as his search for Mahmood proved fruitless. But any doubts she held were dispelled when she went into Elliot's room one day to speak to a servant there. The woman was sweeping, the furniture disarranged. Her broom had dislodged a piece of paper that had fallen between Elliot's desk and the wall. Dorothea glanced at it, then snatched it up. It was a poem, lacking in style and form, but full of impassioned phrases. It was titled 'On Fatimah's Disappearance'. The incriminating lines burned in her mind. After that she had no regrets. None.

A few months later she met Pereira quite by chance in the circulating library. He bowed, smiled, and to any chance observer appeared to pass a few polite words with the handsome Mrs Sanderson, who was properly distant.

"The person in question will not trouble you further. He is far away in the southern seas on a ship whose master will see that he is suitably subdued."

"The family?"

"The two elder women are gone away to work as house servants. The girl, the daughter, has been taken care of." His hooded lids lowered. "A delicate flower, Fatimah. One understands why your son should be attracted as, from enquiries, I find he was. Perhaps you did not realise . . . ah, yes, I see that you did. Well, you need not worry. Make sure, that is all, that during the next few years he does not visit the House of Smiling Blossoms hard by the quay in Singapore. After that . . ." he flicked his plump fingers, "After that she will be no use to me for these Malay girls flower early and voluptuously but soon run to seed and become fat and lazy." He raised his hat. "Good day to you, Mrs Sanderson. Such a pleasant morning."

She should have been shocked. She felt only relief.

She had expected Elliot to mope for a few days, a week or two, but months slipped by and still he brooded, locking himself by the hour into his room. She grew worried, then exasperated, and was preparing to read him a homily on the advantages of mingling with the other young people on the island who were engaging themselves in parties and picnics and tiger hunts, when Miles's health suddenly worsened. The doctors said he had been too long in the sickly climate. If he stayed on he would never recover his health. If he returned to England he might continue into an active old age.

"A little more sherry trifle, Dolly?" Miles asked.

"I have eaten far too much already." She glanced at the

attendant housekeeper. "Pray thank cook, Mrs Price, luncheon was excellent."

Mrs Price bowed. The compliment would please them below stairs. Dorothea had learned the value of a little praise in the right quarter, just as she had learned the precise moment to deliver a chilling criticism. "Forgive me, Margaret, but I quite forgot to enquire about your megrim. Is it quite better?"

"Much improved."

"How sad that it prevented you from taking the air this morning. Now I fear it has started to rain."

Margaret was not the prettiest of the eligible young ladies Dorothea had met, but her character made up for the lack of looks. She had the right sort of strength and shrewdness that Elliot needed in a wife. Where he would fritter money away, Margaret would use it sensibly. She had lived too near the edge of insolvency through her growing years to wish to jeopardise her position. If she had chosen some frippery miss without a thought in her head they would go through his fortune unthinking and uncaring. No, Margaret would be good for Elliot. Her shrewdness would balance his unworldliness, her common sense his disinterest in practical matters. Dorothea thought how much easier her own young life would have been if her mamma had lived. Her mother had had plans. She had told Dolly, making no secret of her profession (proud of it even for she had dragged herself from the gutter to a life of ease and luxury purely through driving purpose and a pretty face), of all her ideas for her daughter. "You will go to a good school and, later, to a finishing establishment. Perhaps in France or Belgium. It is best that we see little of each other. Your background must be quite without reproach. You shall have the best grounding, the best education that money can buy. And there will be a handsome dowry later on. Once you are comfortably settled in marriage, you may perhaps write to me from time to time. I shall, of course, never answer. You

146

will know, however, that my prayers and hopes will be all for you, Dolly, even if I must never be acknowledged. You are an orphan, my dear, from this moment on . . ."

She could not remember weeping, for her mother had been a shadowy figure from her infancy. She was taken occasionally by the 'aunt' who fostered other children similarly placed, to a house in a grey, quiet street. Her mamma had sat, laughing, warm, scented amid crimson velvet furnishings. Once she started school the visits ceased, save for that one last occasion when she was nine or ten and she was told the way her life was planned.

Alas, Mamma's hopes had foundered, as did the carriage which overturned and threw her, a tangle of velvet and lace and crushed bone, on the icy rutted road. After that had come the dark, dark time. 'Your mother is dead,' some thin-nosed teacher had informed her. No pretence now of a 'benefactor' who paid the fees. No smiles or kind words for a girl who had suddenly become a liability. The hard years were upon her now. It had taken every scrap of will and determination to claw herself up and out. She had been forced to use her youth, her looks, her wiles, and those years had hardened her, tempered her ambition to fine steel. She had seen marriage to Tom as a step upwards to security. He was, he said, a man of some small fortune. The East Indies was a place where ambition and achievement ran neck and neck. Young, hopeful – and quickly disillusioned – she had gone to Penang. A mistake, and she had suffered for it. But it had led in the end to Miles.

There would be no mistakes for Elliot and Margaret. It was a well-balanced match and Elliot was fond of Margaret – as much as he was fond of anyone. Sometimes Dorothea thought some vital spark had left him when Mahmood had disappeared, and then rejected the notion as fanciful. It was the fever he had taken on the ship home, that had been such a shock to his system as to leave him languid and uncaring.

He was, naturally, of an indolent temperament, easily bored. Marriage would alter that. With a careful, managing wife and with children to divert him he would regain his spirits. She had chosen well.

Margaret turned her gooseberry-green eyes on her fiancé. "I find the climate up here distinctly fresher than in London and though it is healthy to spend part of the day in the open air, it is a pleasure I can easily forgo."

"But Elliot so enjoys your company on his strolls," Dorothea said. The girl had an irritating way of setting her on edge. Fresher climate indeed. She had known worse weather by far in London. Those dreadful fogs rising from the river, the bitter east wind with no hills to soften its force . . . Then, in an instant, she was alert as Margaret casually said, "You did not want for company, though, this morning, did you, Elliot?"

His face was blank of expression. "I am sorry I do not quite take you . . ."

"Come, come," Margaret laughed and there was a sharpness to it. "Do not tell me that was a wraith I saw you with. From my window I have a splendid view of the rear garden – right the way to the top of the hill. I watched you walking there, deep in conversation, so if the girl was a ghost, then she was a most conversational one."

"Yes, of course," Elliot said, as though suddenly remembering "It was the girl from the lodge. What is her name? Linton? I must have mentioned to her about the orchids. She had gone to the hothouses to look at them and then would have me show her round the gardens. It was deucedly chilly out there and you were quite right not to venture out, Margaret."

"A pushy creature." Margaret's eyes glinted under her stubby lashes. "But pretty."

Elliot shrugged. "A common sort of prettiness."

"I would disagree," Miles said mildly. "I think she is a beauty, though without the character of her sister. Caroline is the deep one, but Adele has the looks and they will take her far if she is sensible. If the admirable Charlotte Dawes guides her right, we shall find her a suitable husband."

"I can hardly understand why you bother with them," Elliot said idly. "You have so many interests. It must be tiresome to make yourself responsible for them."

"Your father has ever taken his responsibilities seriously," Dorothea said. "When I first mentioned to him about these girls, it was merely to ensure that they got the fairest possible representation through the lawyers. I was taken aback when I found on our return from that first tour of the Continent, that he had taken me so seriously. I should never have permitted it had I been here." She had been aghast when she learned of the extent of his patronge. But it was too late. By then the wretched aunt was moved into the lodge and the uncle employed in the house. Her only relief was that the girls were away at school and she did not have to clap eyes on them.

"You were not here, Dolly, and I have enjoyed looking to them."

She smiled at him. "You were ever kind, my dear, but your health was so frail when we first returned to England. Even now you overdo things, does he not, Elliot?"

Elliot smothered a yawn. "Lord, I fear I walked too far this morning. I think a little nap is called for."

His remark, as he guessed, provided a diversion.

"You have not caught a chill?" his mamma asked anxiously. "You should not have overtired yourself. Shall I have a hot tisane prepared?"

"You spoil me, Mamma," he said lightly. "I am merely fatigued. An hour in my room is all that is necessary, then I shall join you, Margaret, in the drawing room and we will continue our game of chess. Perhaps I shall succeed in beating you for once."

*　　*　　*

In his room Elliot did not lie down. He took paper and pen to the window seat. The windows were smeared with sleety rain and the grounds misty and grey. The little hill where he had stood so short a time ago with Adele was almost obscured by sweeping wet veils.

Phrases jumbled in his head. He wanted to pour out unforgettable verses, incandescent rhymes, but words seemed halting things against the reality of her beauty. It came to him as he sat there gazing out onto the winter landscape, who it was that Adele resembled. Not remotely in appearance. But in some inner quality of innocence, of freshness. Something in the clear eyes had reminded him of other eyes, sloe black, shining, slightly tilted under moth-wing eyebrows. Fatimah had once looked at him with all that lambency of budding, virginal womanhood.

He thought, with melancholy, of Mahmood. He had loved Mahmood. His brother, his friend. Once, as children, they had scratched their wrists and held them together, letting their blood mingle. 'We shall be faithful to each other,' they had sworn solemnly. 'We will fight for each other. We will die for each other. We are blood brothers.' It had been part of some game they were playing, a long-drawn-out affair that took them through childhood, involving pirates and battles and chivalry and bloody deeds. But the childish ceremony ran deeper than that. There had never been a time without Mahmood to share his secrets, to argue with, to command, or simply to sit by in companionable silence. As they grew older they had gone swimming in the great breaking rollers of the Indian Ocean or spent hours fishing from an old sampan, or wandered in the forest. Sometimes Fatimah joined them when they swam, averting her eyes modestly from their nakedness, retaining her own modesty under a sarong that, wetted by the salty spray, clung to her young body in a way that brought him an almost painful pleasure.

"You grow up and grow away from Mahmood and me," she would tease. "Your mother wishes you to mix with your own people and it is proper that you should."

"I find them boring," he cried. "Dull! Riding round in their carriages, gossiping over teacups, parading on a ballroom floor like dressed up dolls. I had rather be here with you both."

"But I shall be betrothed soon, to Suleiman," Fatimah said. "Then I must not come with you."

He had stared at her, shocked. "You are not old enough."

She giggled softly. "Of course I am old enough. Soon I shall be married. And soon you will get married to an English girl. That is how it should be. You will forget all about Mahmood and me. You'll see."

He had not forgotten them though. How could he? The sudden wrench of their disappearance had stunned him. It was like a small death. He could not believe his mother's supposition that Mahmood had committed some crime and been ashamed to face him. Not Mahmood, he was bone-sure of it. And Fatimah, what of her? All his questioning had brought him no nearer the truth, though one man had told him he thought they had fled the island. But without a word to him? Everywhere he had asked – begged – people to look for Mahmood. To find him and give him a message. That he was still his friend and must let him know why he had gone off. No message had come.

He shivered. Perhaps he had caught cold after all. He stared through the smeared window. He would never know now and for as long as he lived he must endure the emptiness of not knowing.

His thoughts returned to Adele. He would banish all his sad memories by thinking of her bright face. Then he would compose a sonnet, his favourite verse form.

So pleasantly diverted, he was soon able to rid himself of the shadows in his mind.

* * *

Dorothea Sanderson, too, retired to her room to be alone after luncheon. Her unquiet thoughts were not so easily dismissed. She could not rid herself of the picture of Elliot and that girl parading the grounds for all to see.

She paced the room for a while, then seated herself at her desk. No Pereira here to remove, discreetly, an unsuitable influence. She chided herself. She was overdramatising. Nothing could possibly go wrong now.

Yet the niggling feeling of threat persisted. She realised it had been with her since the moment she had returned from the trip to Preston and they had encountered the Linton sisters in the hall. Which was ridiculous, for what had she to fear? Adele was a chit of a girl, scarcely two steps from the schoolroom, Elliot secure in his engagement to Margaret.

All the same, it was best to be prepared – and was not attack the best form of defence?

She pondered for a long time, choosing and rejecting several possibilities. Eventually she settled on a course of action – well, hardly action. Merely a tiny move that might or might not have potential.

She drew paper towards her and began to pen a letter to Charlotte Dawes.

Chapter Five

The idea that had sprung to Carrie's mind in that street of broken-down houses had grown and developed. It was nurtured, she candidly admitted to herself, by frustration. There was something within her that struggled against the weight of Mr Sanderson's patronage. She had been – still was – grateful for all that he had done, yet the stubborn feeling persisted that she was entitled to some say in her future. The money, after all, was hers and Adele's and if she could do some good with it and still make a small profit, how satisfying that would be!

Each day as she fed the dove she thought of the dirty urchins who had tormented it. In a way they were as helpless as the bird. Trapped by poverty, by ignorance, there was little chance for them. They were condemned by the circumstances of their birth to grow up as part of the great anonymous mass of the poor. When the dove recovered she would free it to fly where it would. Few of those children would ever be free of squalour and ugliness.

There *was* something she could do, she was sure. She lay awake at night, scheming. Sometimes she lit the candle and scribbled figures on a scrap of paper. She took to scanning back numbers of Wheelers *Manchester Chronicle*, passed on to Uncle George by the housekeeper, Mrs Price, but she could not find what she wanted. She needed prices of cheap rundown properties, not gentlemen's residences and quality villas. She needed advice from a builder. She needed accurate figures.

Something solid to lay before Mr Sanderson. Anything less and he would sweep aside her ideas and she would achieve nothing.

If she could buy one of those slum houses and improve it. It would surely not be too expensive to make the roof and structure sound, to drain a damp basement and give every room a coat of whitewash. Even, perhaps, to encourage the tenants to do the work themselves if the materials were provided. Anything to bring a spark of brightness into the lives of those children, to make their surroundings less noisome.

She wished there was someone she could speak to of her plan. She could not trouble Aunt Linnie, who would beg her to do nothing to offend Mr Sanderson. Adele cared for little beyond the immediate delight of her new ballgown and a sudden enthusiasm for orchids. Carrie herself had walked with her one day to view them in the hothouses and had been disappointed. She thought them rather ungainly plants and the few that flowered in this winter season were not to her taste. Stiff and unmoving in the cloying warmth they seemed to her pallid things, the waxy flower clusters having the immobility and deathly perfection of preserved museum specimens. They gave her a sad feeling. It was only afterwards that she remembered the circle of murmuring black figures and the flowers heaped upon the two coffins in the shrivelling sunlight. Orchids of purple and tiger gold and brown and greenish-white and mauve, bound into wreaths and formal sprays and pinned about with black-edged cards. She could not look upon orchids with pleasure. They would forever be associated with loss and pain.

Adele had no such morbid recollections. She happily took her sketching pad and watercolours to the hothouse and spent many hours making delicate copies of them.

The obvious confidante was Uncle George. In his trade he often had contact with builders, but she shrank from all but

154

superficial dealings with him. She tried to think kindly of him, tried to make agreeable conversation as he sat before the fire of an evening puffing on his churchwarden. Always, hanging like a shadow, was the memory of past hurts. She could never bring the right degree of warmth to her voice when she addressed him and sometimes she fancied he understood. At those moments, smiling, the carefully smooth phrases on his lips, his eyes seemed to signal a different message. She saw amusement there and something brooding and watchful that chilled her. It would be gone in a flash and she would force herself to remember the kindnesses he had done. Unprompted he had offered to make the frames for Adele's pictures; he had repaired an old wicker birdcage to house the dove; he always returned from his outings to town with some confection of marzipan or chocolate for Aunt Linnie, and never, never did he harass her with sarcasm or criticism. But the shadow still hovered. She could not respond as Adele did to his ponderous attempts at humour. She watched Aunt Linnie flutter with pleasure at his little flatteries, but when he spoke to her in that cajoling way it was like the touch of metal on an exposed nerve, and however she tried, she knew her smile to be fixed and false and her answer reserved.

No, she would not ask his advice.

There was Jem. Once she could have poured out all her ideas to him and he would have listened, matched her enthusiasm with his own and then willingly sought out the facts and figures she wanted. But they had lost their old camaraderie. She could not approach him now.

She would have to make her enquiries alone and she found this far from easy.

The weather continued inclement. There were no sharp sunny days when she might make the excuse of a brisk walk to the village on her own. There was a biting northerly wind and days of rain. Against Aunt Linnie's warnings of chills, she and Adele braved the weather to visit the dressmaker for their final fittings. Had the woman been of a close nature she might have asked for the name of a village builder but she was a garrulous woman who dropped gossipy indiscretions about her clients as she scattered pins and pattern books and bobbins about her cluttered fitting room. She was quite likely to relate any enquiry to other customers. Mrs Dawes or her girls might come to hear of it and that was the last thing she wanted.

There were other outings. Mrs Dawes sent the carriage so that she and Adele might join her ladies' sewing circle one afternoon. This activity was of a charitable nature. The ladies gathered to make baby clothes for destitute mothers at the lying-in hospital. Another evening they had a trip to the Theatre Royal where Mr and Mrs Dawes had taken a box. Carrie was relieved to see that Miss Prince was not included in the theatre party. At the sewing circle she had placed herself squarely between Carrie and Adele and when not reading a tart lecture about the feckless women who relied upon charity and the good nature of those more provident in order to clothe their infants, noisily sucked mints to ward off the heartburn to which she was a martyr.

"I think it is a deserving cause," Carrie had said. "Not all poor people are feckless. There are many who work hard and try to better themselves."

"A few," Miss Prince sniffed. "A handful perhaps. The rest are spongers and idlers. Look how they have flocked to Manchester in recent years in search of easy pickings. We have the dross here from every county not to mention the low Irish who are thieves and vagabonds to the last man. The charge on the poor rate is beyond belief."

"Many of them come to Manchester because their livelihood is taken from them by the factories – the handloom weavers, for instance—"

"My brother read in the newspaper the other day," Miss Prince interrupted, "that persons of our class pay more than a third of income in rates and taxes. It is disgraceful." She jabbed her needle into the scrap of flannel she was hemming. "Too much of that goes in providing for the lazy. All this clothing that we sew. Do you suppose that these women are grateful for it? Not a bit of it. It is only loaned to them, you understand, for three months, after which time it must be returned to the hospital. If the clothing is in good condition and the woman of a respectable character the committee can at its discretion allow her to keep the clothing." She crunched the last of the mint. "Very few come up to that standard. Some of the clothes never reappear. Most that do are dirty, torn and unusable. They are like pigs who enjoy wallowing in their own filth."

"When you are reduced to such low circumstances," Carrie said quietly, "perhaps it becomes difficult to make the effort. Hunger and sickness can sap the will of the stoutest. When you live in a cellar with only verminous straw for a bed it must be hard to keep up any standard of decency."

"If you gave people like that the means to remove themselves, what do you suppose they would do? I can tell you, Miss Linton. Every penny would be frittered away in some gin shop or spent on cheap finery. In a week or two it would be gone and they would be back where they started and calling upon the world to see how badly placed they were." The ribbons in her cap swung indignantly about her stringy hair. "I pray for these Godless people daily, that they might turn from evil and weak ways. On my knees I go, night and morning. But they would not give a farthing for my prayers."

Adele caught Carrie's eye, but Carrie could not respond to the laughter in them. She felt saddened. She could imagine Miss Prince's comments should it come to her ears that sitting next to her was someone thinking to provide a more comfortable situation for a few poor families.

"To spend so much time on your knees," Adele said innocently, "must be a penance, your rheumatism being such a
trouble to you."

Miss Prince was pleasantly diverted by this turn in the
conversation. She filled the rest of the afternoon speaking with
the greatest enthusiasm about her rheumatism and weak chest,
with illuminating anecdotes about her dear brother's proneness
to take cold.

Carrie sat silently, working with extra care on the tiny
cotton jacket she had been given. She had some coloured
thread in her basket and she embroidered yellow-centred
daisies down the front, in defiant disregard of Mrs Dawes's
instructions that there was no need for anything but the
plainest sewing. She hoped that some distressed young woman
might take heart from the cheerful cluster of flowers on her
baby's jacket.

Fortunately they were spared Miss Prince's presence at the
theatre. It was a small cheerful party that seated itself in the
box and from the time the curtain swung up on the comedy
'John Bull' to the time it descended on the bowing row of
actors after the bucolic romp, 'The Miller's Maid' both Carrie
and Adele were entranced.

"It is your first visit to the theatre?" Edmund Brook asked
in the interval. He had extracted himself from his seat between
Joan and Maud Dawes where he had been firmly placed by
Mrs Dawes and had moved to speak to the sisters.

"Indeed it is," Adele cried, clasping her hands together
ecstatically. "I think I could attend every night and not be
in the least bored."

"Then we must arrange another visit soon. Perhaps you
would consent to be my guests at some future date." He
looked at Carrie. "You seemed to be enjoying Mr Rayner's
antics, too, Miss Linton."

"My sides still ache from laughing," she said, putting her

hand to her waist. "I never thought it would be so funny – or the scenery and costumes so splendid."

"The theatre is grand, too," Adele said. "And such a size."

"London folk would doubtless think it a poky place," he said, "but we Mancunians are proud of our Theatre Royal."

The orchestra was filing back into the pit and Mrs Dawes began to make signals with her fan for Mr Brook to return to his place. He chose, for a moment, not to notice.

"It gives me the greatest pleasure," he said gravely, toying with his cuff, "to know that you will honour me by attending the function at my house."

"We are longing to practise the steps we learned at Mrs Clare's, are we not Carrie?" Adele said artlessly. "This will be our first ball, Mr Brook and we have splendiferous new gowns. Mine is yellow and Carrie's is apricot. We do most truly thank you for inviting us."

He bowed. "It has been so long since I was at a ball myself that it will be like starting afresh. The three of us shall make our debut together – though I shall be put in the shade by the pair of you. The time when a gentleman could array himself in pink or yellow silk is long gone, alas, so I shall have to be content with dark broadcloth."

Mrs Dawes's signals were now becoming urgent, though the frown that was gathering quickly turned to a brilliant smile as Edmund looked over to her and raised his hand in acknowledgement. He still did not seem in any hurry to move.

He said, gravely, "Even in new ballgowns, you could hardly look more delightful than you do this evening."

Adele blushed prettily and Carrie said, quietly, "I fear that if you do not return to your seat, Mr Brook, Mrs Dawes will suffer apoplexy, for the orchestra is ready to strike up."

He smiled ruefully, "Then I had best go. I hope that we shall continue this conversation later."

"Mr Brook is most gallant," Adele whispered, "for we are quite outshone by Joan and Maud. But it is nice to have compliments. I begin to like him very much."

"The curtain is going up," Carrie warned. But she had to admit that she too, found Mr Brook most likeable. Just the person, she realised, she could take into her confidence over the matter of the house she wished to purchase. He was easy to talk to and would be discreet. But there was little chance that she would be able to get a word alone with him, for Mrs Dawes would keep Joan assiduously at his side. And so it proved. For the rest of the evening and at the supper they took afterwards, Mr Brook was surrounded by the Dawes family.

Perhaps she would get the chance of some private conversation at the ball – though she was beginning to fret that if she did not do something soon it would be too late. Mr Sanderson would have decided on his own account where their money was to be invested.

That sordid street was never far from her mind. Yet when help did come it was from a source she thought closed to her. For, surprisingly, it was Jem Walker who came to her aid.

Jem stood beyond the gate, hidden in the deep shadow of the trees. A full moon came fitfully from behind the racing clouds and a rime of ice was gathering on the puddles in the lane. But he bided his time, the cold striking upwards through the soles of his best boots until George O'Hara, whistling softly, had left the lodge and stridden away into the darkness. Despite the cold he felt a dew of sweat prickle his chest under the unaccustomed stiffness of his linen shirt.

"Goin' courting, our Jem?" his young nephews had called, seeing him in his Sunday finery.

He aimed a friendly cuff at their tousled heads.

"Never you mind," he'd said and avoided his mother's eye as she tweaked a cotton fluff from the shoulders of his jacket and said proudly, "You look grand, lad, and I'll not ask where you're off to because you'll tell me in your own good time. If that lass of Billy Walsh's got anything to do wi the gleam in your eye, you could go farther and fare worse." He hadn't answered, hoping his silence would be taken for bashfulness. "She'll be pleased to hear your good news, so be off with you. What with you and our Lily both walking out, I can see I shall be having the pair of you off me hands before long."

He almost laughed aloud when he thought of May Walsh and Carrie. It was like comparing a suet pudding to a champagne supper. How his ma could ever think he was taken with that giggling tease was beyond him. Still, the small deception filled his purpose. It provided a shield for his true intention.

The wind shivered the bare branches of the spreading beech trees that gave the house its name. At the same moment he heard a splintering sound, as though a foot had gone through the ice crust on a puddle. He held his breath. There were tales aplenty of the footpads who took advantage of the dark winter evenings to accost the unwary, but he breathed easier when the sound was not repeated. A hungry fox, maybe, or a rabbit.

Time to go.

He stepped from the shadow of the tree, rehearsing the words he would say to Carrie. He could spoil everything by appearing awkward. He had to win her attention, to make her look at him, not as the poor carrier's lad, but as a young man with prospects. How he wished for the gift of words that had come so easily in his letters. But maybe luck would be with him, for he was fired by the feeling of things working to his advantage. He walked briskly through the small side gate and round to the back door of the lodge. He was unaware of the other shadow that detached itself from the blackness of a tree clump and, moving in an ungainly hobble, flitted across the lane to stand by the tall double gates, now barred and bolted for the night.

The moon came out, etching in silver the hands gripping the bars, the hunched shoulders, the ragged breeches bound about with frayed rope, the broad brimmed hat pulled low. The stranger stood, immobile, staring up the long drive to the yellow glimmer of light from the house. Then the clouds covered the moon and, shivering in the bitter air, the man let his hands drop, and pulling his jacket close to his chest he turned away and shuffled off to become part of the darkness.

"I was passing," Jem began, huskily. He cleared his throat. "I was passing and I thought I would drop in to let you know my good news."

The kitchen was full of candlelight and warmth. The maid had summoned Carrie, who drew him inside. "Why did you not come to the front door?"

"Eh, back doors are more my mark," he said, grinning.

Carrie still held the patchwork she was engaged upon. She regarded him warily.

"What news is this, Jem?"

"Of my advancement. I feel – I know – that I owe it in part to you. Had you not taught me to read and write, then the post would have been offered to one of the older men. But because of my book learning Carter Smith has given me first chance."

"But what advancement is this?"

"Mrs Smith wants to move out of the Meadow and there's a house in view at Broughton. If the Smiths move, then there's need for a man – an overseer – to live close by. To look to the yard and the horses and to see that things run smooth in his absence."

Her eyes were suddenly warm. "And this new overseer is to be you, Jem? That is perfectly splendid!"

"Nothing's settled yet. I'm to start learning the way of things straight off. If I take to it and Carter Smith finds I suit then I'm to be given the job."

"Suit? Of course you'll suit!" Her obvious delight warmed him. "But you must come and tell Aunt Linnie. Now that your mother has no need to call so often she misses hearing the news of you and your family."

He told his tale again to Adele, who had grown as pretty as a rose and greeted him with genuine pleasure, and to Mrs O'Hara who seemed a touch put out at an unforeseen visitor, though she politely added her congratulations, saying, "Your mother always expected great things of you, Jem. She will be very proud."

Adele said, teasingly, "You will make your fortune yet, Jem. And you will owe it all to Carrie teaching you your letters. Shall you remember us when you are rich and famous?"

He laughed. "Indeed I shall." It was from the heart and he could not help glancing at Carrie as he spoke.

Mrs O'Hara seemed impatient to be back at her cards, but Adele cried, "We should celebrate. Aunt Linnie likes a glass of wine at this time of evening. Join us Jem, and let us toast your future."

In a moment she had the wine poured and her cheerful chatter covered any undercurrent of awkwardness. Presently she said, "Aunt you must have a hand of trumps the way you keep looking at the card table. Shall we continue our game? You do not mind, Jem? Aunt Linnie has become a fiend at whist since our return and if we were playing for money she would have had my year's allowance off me already. Now sit down by the fire and amuse Carrie for a while."

And so easily, so comfortably, did he find himself sitting opposite Carrie across the hearth. Perhaps that glimpse of himself in the mirror over the mantelpiece had something to do with the sudden rush of confidence – the glint of polished brass buttons on the smooth blue cloth of his jacket, the crisp whiteness of his shirt, the carefully combed hair. No reek of the stables, no working clothes tonight. But perhaps it was just

163

the wine. It was too heavy and sweet for his taste but it imbued him with a heady glow.

They were silent for a while, but it was a relaxed silence. He felt his inner tension ease and it was the most natural thing in the world to begin speaking of his work at the yard, of his family. How he was determined to keep his two nephews at the dame school as long as he could afford it, though the eldest was coming up to ten and his sister thought he had idled long enough. How his sister was courting a blacksmith, a widower with a grown-up family, so the problem of his nephew's schooling might not be his for much longer. There was already talk of the elder boy being apprenticed to the blacksmith's own trade.

All the while he was feasting his eyes, watching her fingers moving among the coloured cottons in her lap, treasuring the delicacy of her wrist where a vein showed blue against the white skin, the smallness of her waist, the full curve of her breast under the modest blue bodice, the tendrils of brown hair that curled against her neck. She raised her eyes from time to time, looking at him in a reflective way. Then she frowned, answered him vaguely and, apparently coming to some decision, laid her sewing in her lap.

She glanced at the absorbed card players, before saying quietly, "Jem, I do not quite know how to put this because I feel you will not approve at all of what I have to say. You made yourself perfectly clear that day when you came to my aid in the street. You find it incomprehensible that I should wish to involve myself in any way with the people there. But I must ask you a favour and I do not wish you to immediately say I should not concern myself with such matters. I should like you to think carefully before you reply. Of course, you may not be in a position to find out what it is I wish to know, and that I shall quite understand. But do not, please, treat me as though I was a nincompoop—"

"Hold hard," he stopped her, "you have me confused."

She sighed. "It is all so clear in my mind yet I have not been able to speak to anyone of it, or ask for help. Your coming here tonight is provident, Jem."

"If there is anything at all I can do for you, I shall do my best to help." His spirits soared. If she asked him to fetch down the moon he would do his damnedest to get it for her.

It was nothing so fanciful. She spilled out her plan and he saw at once why she wished to keep it to herself, for Mr Sanderson would surely never approve. But he saw the eagerness in her face and he could no more dash her spirits than kick aside a playful puppy.

"I have been so fortunate, Jem," she ended. "Things would have been different had Mr Sanderson not taken us under his wing. In my turn I should like to do something to help those less comfortably placed."

He thought of the grey ranks of the poor that he saw at the mission Sunday School and of the dedicated men of the mission who worked to save souls and bodies. Even they were hopelessly outnumbered in their task. Carrie saw her project with the enthusiasm of one who had great heart but little practical understanding. He felt she was bound to disappointment and failure.

He said, "I can see that you have worked everything out in your mind."

"But you still do not approve." The downward droop of her mouth wrenched his heart.

"I can't say I heartily agree with your scheme . . ."

"Have you no charity?" she said in exasperation. "None of that caring spirit that was such a comfort to me when I was a child?"

"Hear me out. If you are determined I'll try to find out what you want to know. Carter Smith has a builder in this week to give estimates for alterations at the yard. I'll have a word with him. And I'll make a note of any old properties that might be for sale."

There was a small silence, then she said humbly, "I apologise. You never were uncaring."

"If I could dissuade you, I would. There are plenty of charitable societies that might be more suitable for you to join."

"More ladylike? I know. I am already enrolled in one run by Mrs Dawes. But this is something I wish to do by myself. *For* myself, to prove – oh, I do not know what it is I wish to prove. Because I am a woman it is assumed that anything weightier than learning a new dance step might tax my brain. Even Mrs Clare warned me that if I studied too hard and filled my head with scholarly subjects I should get myself labelled a blue stocking." She smiled sadly. "My studies were too much interrupted for me to become a scholar, so perhaps I should thank Uncle George . . ." – he noted the faint ironic reflection as she spoke the name – ". . . for sparing me such a frightful fate. All the same I should like to stretch my poor female brain just a little now and then so that it does not diminish into complete atrophy."

He said, cautiously, "It is a large undertaking. You may find it too much for you. If it is, the ministers of the mission would be glad of help. I teach at the Sunday School. Just simple letters and numbering. You taught me so well I imagine you would be good with a class." The wives and daughters of the ministers taught in the Sunday School. They were decent, respectable souls, and would make impeccable chaperones. He would rest easier if he thought she was working alongside women like that. If this harebrained scheme of hers took shape, heaven knows what riff-raff she might associate with. "If you cared," he added diffidently, "I would take you down there one Sunday. With Mrs O'Hara's permission, of course."

"That might be interesting," she agreed, but she was abstracted. Her own plans obviously filled her head. Still, he had progressed. Hurrying home later through the dark lanes, oblivious to the frost and the ragged clouds clawing across the moon, he was elated. She had shared her secret with him and it bound them together. They were conspirators. It did not matter that he could not wholeheartedly approve of her plan. It provided him with an excuse to meet her again, and if he could persuade her to go down to the mission with him one Sunday, then there was the prospect of a whole afternoon in her company.

He lost no time in setting about the task she had given him. He took the builder aside one dinner hour at the stables and carefully wrote down prices of materials and labour. The matter of the house was not so easy. There were plenty enough for sale but it had to be the right one. She might have grand ideas of refurbishing some ramshackle tenement in the worst slum but such a district would be full of unsavoury characters. Eventually he settled on a tall house on the fringe of Ancoats. The street still contained many families struggling to keep a respectable face on their poverty and the property, divided up into rented rooms, contained a good percentage of hard-working families. He braved the sharp-nosed solicitor's clerk in King Street to obtain full particulars of the house. The clerk eyed his working clothes suspiciously. "You must tell your master to speak to me himself," he quavered, fussing with his papers. "Most irregular . . . most irregular." But Jem emerged with the printed sheet jubilantly stowed in his pocket.

By Saturday he had everything he needed and he fretted with impatience as the afternoon wore on and Carter Smith kept him busy. It had begun to snow, a fine drift blowing in the north wind, the flakes scarcely having time to settle before they were whisked over the dry, frozen ground to impact eventually against house walls and kerbstones. It was a bleak dark walk up to the lodge and by the time he got there he was chilled through.

He had the packet sealed and addressed but Jane, pink with responsibility, urged him to come in by the fire.

"Miss Carrie told me to ask you in when you come," she said, solemn with the importance of sharing a secret with Miss Carrie, who was well on the way to becoming the brightest star in her firmament. 'Should Mr Jem Walker call, I should like to have a few moments' talk with him in private. If you could signal me, discreetly, Jane, without my aunt or Miss Adele seeing, then I should be very pleased.'

Jane tiptoed upstairs to the bedroom with exaggerated steps and fortunately caught Carrie's eye before her strange frownings and mouthings were noticed by Adele and her aunt.

"Thank you, Jane," Carrie whispered, closing the bedroom door behind her.

Jane glowed. Mr Jem Walker was a handsome man. Was it, she wondered, a Hassignation? Mr Walker had looked so fine when he'd called the other night it fair made her heart beat faster. Mind you, seein' him tonight he hadn't looked so special. No more than a rough working man – and here was her Miss Carrie looking a picture in a frilly wrapper with her hair done up all pretty. It was clear Mr Walker thought so too.

"Forgive me, Jem, for appearing so," she said.

"I . . . I've come at a bad moment. I'm sorry."

"We go to Mr Brook's ball tonight. Adele insisted we prepare early so now we have ages to wait before we dare get into our new dresses for fear of crushing them. . . . But you have news for me?" She eagerly took the packet he held out and ripped it open. She scanned the pages and said, delightedly, "This is exactly what I wanted – and you have been so quick." Her eyes sparkled. "I can now put everything to Mr Sanderson as I had hoped. I might even get a chance this evening."

"I'm pleased it suits. I'll be off, then."

168

"Will you come again if I send for you, Jem? Mr Sanderson may want to know more of the house, or of the builder. And I might need you for moral support. Would you come again if I asked, Jem?"

"Gladly."

Impatiently she tugged the lacy frills on her wrapper. "If only we did not have to parade at this ball I should go this minute to Mr Sanderson."

"You'll forget all about house repairing when you start dancing," he said lightly, fighting down the jealousy that the picture of Carrie in the arms of some languid sprig aroused. "Like as not you'll be belle of the ball."

She laughed. "Not I. Adele maybe. She takes to dancing like a duck to water. I shall be content to sit and watch, for I shall be worrying about tripping or making the wrong steps and throwing my partner into a tizzy."

There was a loud rapping at the door. Jane opened it and took the box off the muffled messenger. "For you, Miss Carrie, with Mr Edmund Brook's compliments," she repeated carefully

Carrie untied the ribbons and cried, "Do look, Jem!"

Two posies of flowers nestled in a bed of damp moss. One was of pale yellow and white roses, the other of tight-curled rosebuds flushed from palest cream to dark apricot. "They could not more perfectly match our gowns. How clever of Mr Brook." She lifted the posies to her face and inhaled their fragrances. "They smell of summer when everything is green and fresh."

Above the flowers she looked at Jem and her blissful smile faltered. He was staring at her so strangely that it made her catch her breath. He looked fierce, angry, but behind that anger, something else. Something that blazed in his eyes for a few seconds and caused her to have the oddest sensation, that Jane, the snapping fire, the rows of shining pans, receded far distant, leaving them quite alone.

169

Then it was gone and he was saying quietly, "I must take my leave," and his smile was sad, his face shadowed with tiredness under the damp tangle of his dark hair. She wanted to take his arm and lead him to the fire. Ease him out of his damp coat. Dispel that pinched, chilled look.

But he was turning to the door. She said quickly, "If I speak to Mr Sanderson tonight, I should like to tell you of the outcome. I . . . we shall be at home tomorrow afternoon. Oh, but you have your classes at the mission — and there is the weather. If it snows in earnest I should not expect you to come . . ."

"If you want to see me, Carrie, I'll be here."

"I . . . yes. Should it be convenient."

"Convenient?" All the tiredness seemed to slip from his face. He said, softly, "A bit of snow won't keep me away. I'll be here tomorrow afternoon."

The door closed behind him. Carrie gazed down at the posies. Then she said absently, "Take them, Jane, will you, and put them in the scullery to keep fresh."

Reverently, Jane carried them out. She was deeply impressed. Not only a Hassignation with Mr Walker, but another admirer, too — and rich. For rich and fine he must be to give a ball and send flowers like this, prettier than anything she'd ever seen. Eh, it was all so excitin' for Miss Carrie, yet she was so calm about it. Seeming to be more concerned with the bits o' paper Mr Walker had given her, folding them carefully after she had read them, and placing them for safety in the drawer of the dresser.

Carrie went from the kitchen, leaving Jane to sit by the coals and see dream pictures in the glowing embers.

Edmund Brook stood at the foot of the sweeping staircase that led from the high entrance hall of his house. Double doors to his left stood open to a long room, the drawing room, where groups of people were gathering and the sound of fidlers tuning up heralded the start of the dancing. He greeted the guests with his pleasant smile, a slight dapper figure under the candles of the crystal chandeliers that cast a brilliant light on powdered shoulders and shimmering silks.

It was time, he thought, to sweep away dusty memories. To bring gaiety to a house that had lain too long in the shadow of mourning. Charlotte Dawes had been right. "You have grieved too long over Nora," she had told him more than once. "It was sad that she was taken so young, but you cannot go on revering her memory for ever. You should have children about you, a good wife to run your home and to be a comfort as you grow older."

He had been amused at her transparent efforts to bring her daughters to his attention and perhaps it had been a trifle cowardly to encourage her to believe that he found Joan interesting. He had thought it tactful to do so. He knew Charlotte Dawes. As an old friend of his parents she had, over these lonely years, assumed a somewhat irritating proprietorial air over him. Her scoldings, her overbearing manner, concealed a genuine concern for his welfare. Though he had resisted, quietly, her efforts to jolly him into society, he had tolerated her for that reason.

Nevertheless he understood that she had the strongest hopes that her years of friendship would bring a reward. An alliance between the two families. A marriage between himself and one of her daughters. He had considered the possibility of marrying Joan. She was a cheerful, bouncy girl, who would certainly liven up his quiet existence, but he had regretfully put the idea aside. It would not do, much as he would have liked to please Charlotte Dawes. And since meeting Caroline he realised how sensible it had been not to rush into any attachment without careful thought.

He had not expected, at thirty-six, to experience the pangs

of love in the same clear way as at twenty. The intensity of his feelings surprised him. He was pleased and confused all at once, and, like any green youngster, very unsure of himself. Would she think him too old? Could she bring herself to care for him? All the caution in his nature told him to tread softly. She was young, unworldly. Go too fast and he would frighten her away. And it was best not to offend Charlotte Dawes with a too hasty abandonment of her daughter. Charlotte meant well. He would try to let her down gently.

He sought among the faces for the one he was most longing to see – and at last she was here. Charlotte, formidable in magenta, advanced with Joan and Maud. Behind, the pretty sister – and Caroline. He was gratified to see that the flowers he had sent matched her gown. And how the gown became her! It was modest in cut and material and trimmed only with narrow dark brown velvet at waist and sleeves, but the soft apricot colour warmed her pale skin, as the candlelight revealed the golden lights in her hair. She was very different from Nora, who had been tall and fair and willowy. He sensed in this girl an inner quality of strength that Nora had not had. Nora had been frail with a retiring delicacy of mind. He had worshipped her, protected her and in some ways she had been a child to him as much as a wife. Caroline was made of stronger stuff and that thought challenged and excited him.

"Such a splendid gathering – and how well the house looks." Charlotte's words poured unheeded over him as he looked past her to exchange a smile with Caroline. "You should have done this years ago, Edmund. But better late than never, as I am sure my girls would agree." Jane bridled as her mother rapped her archly with her fan. "They are such accomplished dancers that they will be in great demand. You must be sure to mark their cards early or you will be disappointed."

"How good of you to remind me," he murmured.

Charlotte swept Joan and Maud in the direction of the music, calling, "Come Caroline, Adele. Do not dawdle."

But Carrie lingered to thank him for his flowers.

"I trust you will have cause to remember tonight as a most special evening." He touched the card at her wrist. "May I? Thank you. I must obey Charlotte's instructions."

"She was referring to Joan and Maud. Let me disenchant you right away, Mr Brook. I am untried in the art of the dance. I might abuse your toes quite severely."

"Then we shall do well together, for I am sadly out of practice. We shall blunder along very happily and let our feet take care of themselves."

Her warm smile stayed with him long after she had moved away, and though he forced himself to greet, patiently, the remainder of his guests he longed to be free to see her again on the dance floor.

The evening moved on to the rhythm of the dancing.

Elliot Sanderson claimed Adele Linton for a waltz. They spun giddily to the insistent, heady beat of the music. They managed, breathlessly, a little conversation.

"Did the new orchid arrive?"

"The *Cypripedium*? Yes, it did. And in splendid condition," he said eagerly. "You will find it interesting to sketch."

"Then I must do so as soon as possible."

Their feet carried them across the floor as light as air. Adele saw nothing of the other dancers. She was giddy from his closeness, from the touch of his hand at her waist, of her own gloved fingers resting lightly in his.

"You waltz well," he breathed.

"We had a good dancing master at Malvern."

"All the dancing masters in the world will not compensate for lack of grace and rhythm. It is a pleasure to dance with you after my experience with so many clodhoppers."

173

She glowed with happiness. The music reached its climax, quickened and stopped. It was over all too soon. Just one precious dance. Out of courtesy he had claimed it, just as he would presently dance with Carrie. But he would not smile at her sister with his warm brown eyes, nor place her hand on his arm slowly, covering it with his own, as he escorted her to her seat, and leave go of it so very reluctantly.

"I shall have more free time after Tuesday," he murmured. They both understood, without explanation, that Margaret Gordon would depart for London on Tuesday. "It is in my mind to reorganise the hothouses in the coming weeks. I . . . I shall be happy to describe my plans to you."

"And I shall be happy to hear of your new arrangements. I trust that the weather does not prevent Miss Gordon from travelling."

"I hope so too," he said, adding hastily. "She and her mamma are very close. She is anxious to be with her family again."

"Of course," said Adele. "I trust she has a comfortable journey and is not inconvenienced by the snow." Her heart lifted. No restrictions now on their meetings. She could see him every day. He handed her to her seat and bowed. They smiled at each other and she saw the future spinning giddily golden ahead, for how could anything stand in the way of true love? She saw her own fairy tale unfolding in a romantic haze.

"Now to the clodhoppers once more," he murmured. "My deepest thanks for favouring me with this waltz. I shall hope to see you soon."

"Indeed," she whispered. Then turned to greet the next eager young man come to claim a dance.

Carrie danced a quadrille with Mr Sanderson. He looked tired this evening. His long sallow face had a greyish tinge and he seemed more stooped, more angular than ever. When the dance ended he was sadly out of breath. He passed it off lightly.

"I lack practice." He mopped his forehead. "It is warm in here. I think I shall take a turn in the hall where the air is cooler."

"May I stroll with you?" Carrie asked. "I am not engaged for the next dance."

"But some young sprig will soon seize the opportunity to snatch you onto the floor."

She smiled. "I am a little breathless myself. I have danced every dance so far."

"That is how it should be. I see young Brook has been attentive."

"I think he feared that I might be a wallflower. He has put himself out to ensure that Adele and I feel at ease. He is most kind."

Miles Sanderson glanced at her thoughtfully and said, "He lives in some style but he has played the recluse too long. He was deeply attached to his first wife. I am glad to see that he is taking a more sensible attitude, for one cannot grieve for ever. I know it. I thought myself inconsolable after my first wife died – yet once I met Dolly I found a contentment I thought I had lost for ever."

"Then I am glad my father had a part in your meeting."

He smiled. "I did not appreciate him at all, at first. I was impatient when this young man appeared, uninvited, in my office, insisting that it was my duty to assist an English gentlewoman in distress. He was afraid that when he left the island she would be friendless. And he was right. Her husband had been a rascal. Owed money everywhere and creditors were pressing."

The hall was airy after the press and noise in the drawing room. A few other couples strolled or admired the pictures set about the walls. Mr Sanderson led Carrie to a chair and seated himself beside her.

"Yes, your father was a persistent young man."

"But you did not regret his persistence."

"I was glad I submitted, if unwillingly, to his request to meet the lady." His eyes had an inward look. "She had such style, such character. On the brink of ruin she held up her head and kept her backbone straight as a ramrod. Had she met me with tears and tremblings, I suspect I should have got my clerks to sort out the mess and paid her passage home. But she would have none of it. She was a fighter. She wished to stay and make the best of what she had. I admired her for it and admiration quickly changed to something deeper." There was something almost boyish in his grin. "We set island society on its head. We married within six weeks of meeting." Twenty odd years ago Mr Sanderson would have been in the prime of middle age and not unhandsome. "We were both lonely people. She was in need of security. I had begun to long for the warmth of feminine companionship. There seemed little point in waiting half a year to see her out of mourning."

Carrie laughed. "Do I detect a certain smugness in having flouted convention?"

"Most certainly. A man has to take chances sometimes. In his private life as well as in business. Of course Dolly took a risk, too. I might have turned out to be a wife beater or a Bluebeard."

"Then Mrs Sanderson would not have been at all grateful to my papa for causing you to meet – and she would certainly never have given Adele and me a second thought!"

"Life is chancy. But we both have cause to thank Robert Linton. It was through his discretion and hard endeavour that she was able to come to a second marriage with her dignity intact and if she brought only a handful of useless papers as her dowry, at least they were enough to bolster her pride."

"And they did not remain worthless."

He was silent, his eyes looking into far-off distances she could not follow. Then he said, briskly, "Yes, of course. But it did not matter to me. Not in the slightest. It remained a matter of pride to her though, that the investments did well. Naturally, once she was my wife they became my responsibility. However, I always made a point of remarking how the business did and what the profits were. A small matter but it pleased her."

"And it was those same investments that rescued Adele and me when we were so desperately in need. We shall always be grateful to Mrs Sanderson for she had no obligation to assist us."

"A moral obligation may be just as binding as a legal one."

Carrie said, carefully, "I, too, feel something of a moral obligation."

"In what way?"

"Adele and I have been so fortunate that I feel strongly that, in turn, we should help others less well placed."

Mr Sanderson looked at her from under his heavy brows. "What had you in mind?"

She outlined her plans with enthusiasm. She had by heart the rough figures Jem had written down for her. In her mind she could see the house he had selected and tried to build a word picture for Mr Sanderson. "I have the papers at home. I will show them to you tomorrow. You see, I believe that after the initial work has been done that, with good management, such a venture would eventually show a profit of 5 per cent."

"You have been thorough."

"I could not afford to be anything else. I knew you would turn down my suggestion out of hand if I had come to you with some nebulous scheme."

He nodded. "True."

"I was greatly distressed to see children living in such dreadful conditions that day in town. I felt I must do something."

"I can understand that. You are a girl of sensibility. I have

177

often thought that had my wife and I been blessed with daughters, I should have been pleased had they turned out as you and Adele have done."

"That is a great compliment, sir."

"I should have liked a large family about me." Carrie stifled her impatience at the digression. "But it was not to be. Dolly had a bad fall which precipitated Elliot's birth. Both she and the child suffered severely at the time, though both recovered well. But the damage had been done. We were not to have another child."

"I am sorry."

"I reconciled myself to it long ago. Perhaps that is why I have taken such pleasure in looking to your affairs. You and Adele have been in some small measure the daughters I did not have." The music came to them with the thumping of feet and the muffled buzz of voices. "I care very much for your welfare. That is why I could not possibly agree to this scheme you propose."

"You need not make up your mind right away! Please, sir, give it some thought . . ."

"It is too chancy, Caroline," he said. "Besides, I have already made up my mind that your capital should be invested in railway stock."

She stared at him, shocked.

"But you promised I should have some say . . ."

"Not promised, my dear," he corrected gently. "I agreed to listen to your preferences. But this scheme — well, the initial capital outlay would be too large, the profits too slow in coming. I can do much better for you than that. I have been making my own enquiries and I become more convinced each day that railways are the coming thing."

"Notwithstanding the moral obligation," she said, unable to keep the disappointment from her voice.

"I applaud your idealism, Caroline, but your financial position is not so sound that you can afford to waste money."

"It would not be wasted. It would be used to help people."

"Charity, may I remind you, begins at home. Your aunt and sister should be your first considerations. What do they think of your idea?"

"I have not told them. I thought to wait until you had given your approval."

"And now you have my answer." His smile was benevolent and implacable. "You must trust my experience in these matters. I am not governed by emotional feminine impulses but by hard facts and logic. You must realise, Caroline, that the male mind is far more suited to the intricacies of business and finance. All the feminine traits which we males find so endearing – softness, gentleness, modesty and submissiveness – are intended by nature to suit a woman to duties within the home and family. A gentlewoman has her father to lean upon in her formative years – a role I have delighted in, and shall continue to delight in undertaking, until you marry. In marriage her husband provides the protective shelter in which she can find fulfilment as a wife and mother. The world outside the domestic circle is a hard, competitive one. It is best left to those equipped to deal with it."

There was no reaching him. His bland smile defeated her.

He said, "The music is ending. We must return to the dancing."

Miles Sanderson looked at the girl's crestfallen face. Pretty little thing when she smiled. Plain as paper when she was low. He did not like to see her down, especially tonight, but it could not be helped. Better a quick end to this unwomanly scheme of hers. It there'd been more time, perhaps, he might have indulged her. He saw time as in the big old-fashioned hourglass he had, with the sand trickling from one globe to the other. For him, the upper glass was almost empty. Running out fast, quicker than either he or the physician had anticipated. The least exertion now and the cramping, stifling pain caught him in his chest and arm and all the pills the doctor prescribed scarcely delayed by a fraction that remorseless flow of sand.

All his life he had been a practical man. He had built his business on efficiency and thoroughness and profited by it. Death he could face squarely. When the pain was on him he felt it to be a friend. But the thought of it catching him unawares, leaving untidiness and loose ends in its wake, troubled him mightily. Of course, Dolly's affairs, and Elliot's, were in order. Every facet of his business was as secure as he could make it, though how relieved and proud he would have been to have seen the reins in Elliot's hands. The old regret surged in him and was suppressed. No matter now. The boy was not suited to it. He had chosen his own path and despite his disappointment, Miles had the satisfaction of knowing that Elliot would be able to live comfortably, a gentleman following a gentleman's idle pursuits, confident that his father's agents and bankers were shrewd men who would advise him well.

In the fullness of time, perhaps, Elliot would father a son who might inherit his grandfather's interest and flair for commerce. The thought of that distant, hazy-featured youth comforted him through long nights. It was as well Elliot was to be married soon, even though he was not overly impressed with the bride-to-be. But she had breeding, excellent connections and gentility. Dolly had assured him that the match was in every way suitable. All the same he thought her tongue too acid, her manner too haughty and stiff. He would, from choice, have preferred for Elliot someone showing evidence of a warmer heart and kindlier spirit. But with the doctor's latest pronouncement ringing in his ears, he was glad he had not urged for a longer engagement as he had been prompted to do at first. With God's help he would live long enough to attend the wedding and see the boy nicely settled.

'A low farinaceous diet. No excitement, no stimulating liquors and above all guard against any emotion or agitation of the mind. Then you may live to see the year out.' It had been a shock to have his fate spelled out in such a dry, abrupt manner, but he had demanded the truth and the doctor respected him enough to present the facts squarely. Aye, and he was grateful.

Tomorrow he could begin upon the strict regimen of rest and quiet that had been imposed upon him. And he would be glad to. He felt very tired and old. It was a trouble, now, to rise stiffly to his feet and offer Caroline his arm. The disappointment in her expression awoke a sudden, uncharacteristic irritation. Why must she bother him like this? He was doing his very best for her. He forced the irritation away. No excitement. No agitation. It was not the girl's fault. Nor his. It was the sand slipping too speedily through the narrow neck of the hourglass. It was the knowledge of his own mortality.

Resentment was a useless emotion. Carrie fought it. Mr Sanderson had her best interests at heart. She tried not to let him see how he had dashed her hopes. She forced herself to smile and speak quietly and if her cheeks were flushed and her eyes overbright when she returned to the dancing it could only be due to the excitement of the occasion.

Both Charlotte Dawes and Dorothea Sanderson noticed her return. The former with a tightening of her lips, the latter with the flicker of a glance as she exchanged courtesies with a stout matron. Smoothly Dolly excused herself and moved across the drawing room.

"Ah, Caroline," she said, "a word with you."

"Mrs Sanderson?"

"I am having a few friends taking tea on Thursday next. Would you and Adele be free to join us? You would? Good. I shall expect you at half past three." This small manoeuvre accomplished, she said pleasantly, "You look well tonight. Your hair is most becoming."

Dorothea was indifferent to the matter but it was advisable that Miles should see her as friendly and interested. She had plans for young Adele. Already the hints had been dropped into the right ear, the groundwork laid, and though she could not envisage Miles having any objection, for he was anxious to see both tiresome girls settled, one never could be quite sure. Men were sometimes a little sentimental on these occasions. But he must not know that she had anything in mind but the best of motives. Indeed, if all went as smoothly as she hoped her role would merely be that of a helpful observer. No one need know of the casual remarks made to Charlotte Dawes and the equally light and friendly comment to the other interested parties. The seeds were sown and now she must await signs of growth. If all went as she hoped then Charlotte, never one to shun the limelight, would obligingly take the credit.

Charlotte Dawes watched the three of them with narrowed eyes. She was put out. Well might Caroline Linton have colour in her cheeks and a defiant look on her face, for she had quite ruined the evening that was to have been dear Joan's triumph. Two dances already with Edmund Brook, to poor Joan's one. *And* that so-important waltz that preceded supper. Caroline, instead of Joan, would be accompanied by Edmund into the room set aside for refreshment. And Edmund's manner when she had broached the subject in a tactful way, hinting that he had no need to be so kind towards Caroline for her dance card was full, had been evasive. He had excused himself by saying that he felt obliged, as host, to look after one so newly arrived in their social circle.

She fanned herself rapidly, nodding at a passing acquaintance More and more she regretted taking the Lintons under her wing. It was a pity, she thought sourly, that Miles had not handed the task to his own wife.

She had always had a great respect for Miles. His wife, on the other hand, was something less than a thorough lady she had always thought. She was handsome and had a proud manner. But there was something. It was hard to pin it down. She had an enviable stylishness, yet there was something a little too perfect, too contrived about it. Her manners were good yet one occasionally detected a schooled rigidity that was not totally natural. She looked, tonight, superb in jade-green lace, a tortoiseshell comb set high in her dark hair (suspiciously dark, for there was not a trace of grey in it and her age was the wrong side of forty-five). She had, Charlotte thought balefully, the look of an actress or courtesan who must set herself to be deliberately genteel in order to keep the public eye upon her, and an illusion of good breeding.

Charlotte eased her back away from the chair. These new stays might have cost all of five-and-twenty shillings but it had been a mistake to wear them tonight. There was a bone pressing unmercifully into her ribs. She would have to have a sharp word with the stay-maker who had sworn they would be as comfortable as a second skin. A burst of laughter drew her attention to the young men gathered in a group around her daughters and the other Linton girl. Previously she would have been delighted that her girls were part of such a happy throng of young people, but in her newly soured mood she saw with distressing clarity that Adele sat like a little princess at the centre of the group, with Joan and Maud mere handmaidens on either side, and the young men were practically tumbling over themselves for a word or a look from her. Mark Hughes she saw with a deep indignant drawing in of breath, was gazing at the minx with the eyes of a love-sick puppy.

She snapped her fan shut. It was too much. She had always thought that Adele needed a firm hand. She was far too flirtatious for her own good. Something Dolly Linton had mentioned sprang to her mind. She had previously dismissed it as being, perhaps, unsuitable, but now a further consideration of the matter did not seem at all an unreasonable idea.

Yes, the girl should be settled. And soon.

The thought comforted her. She was quite able, when Caroline returned to sit beside her, to put on a good face, and even when Edmund came to claim the supper waltz she hid her chagrin. In her mind Adele was already settled. It should not then, surely, be so difficult to find some way of settling Caroline also and so rid herself of two disagreeable burdens.

The refreshments set the perfect seal on the evening. Glazed hams, prime rounds of beef, raised chicken pies, a great galantine of veal and larded capons marched the length of the table that was decorated with epergnes of fruit and platters of rich pastries.

Edmund Brook waited on Caroline, fetching her plates of delicacies and refilling her glass with champagne until she laughingly refused to eat or drink another mouthful. "I shall not be able to dance a step after this," she protested. "It has been delicious and I am quite giddy from the champagne."

"Then I think we should take a stroll to recover from such excess," he said. "Should you care to see something of my house? I have a collection of landscape paintings I should like you to see."

"But your other guests . . ."

"Can manage without me for a few moments. Come, we may slip away out of the side door. I deserve a little time of quiet. Unused as I am to entertaining, this evening has been a strain upon my good nature."

They went across the hall and down a corridor, pausing here and there to regard a painting or a piece of statuary, then he led her into a small parlour where a fire glinted on brass fire irons and polished mahogany and on the gilded frames of pictures clustered together in groups on the walls.

"This was my wife's favourite room," he told Carrie. "She chose many of the pictures here though I have added to the collection." He ran his long fingers across the inlay of a rosewood escritoire. "The room remains much as she left it. At first – after her death – I came here often, for it seemed to me that her spirit still lingered where she had been so happy."

"Her loss must have been a great grief to you."

"It was and I took comfort from having her possessions about me." He lifted his hand in a sharp gesture. "But I did not bring you here to talk of the past. Tell me what you think of my landscapes."

He escorted her from painting to painting, pointing out a particular effect of light and shade, the way one artist had captured a spread of landscape, another an intimate vision of woodland or garden. Finally he stopped before a picture that, to Carrie, seemed nothing more than a blur of colour.

"This is my new acquisition," he said. "And of all my collection it is the jewel." Carrie stared at it blankly and he smiled. "I quite understand. It is not the kind of picture that has an instant appeal."

"I cannot quite see what it is meant to be," she said, apologetically.

"It represents a sunset over a stormy sea. There, you can make out the image of a ship almost lost in the spindrift and behind and around it, the fire and glare of the setting sun dipping behind storm clouds. Stand back a little more."

For a moment the picture was still a blur, then she took another step backwards and it sprang into life. Yes, there was the ship plunging into the trough of a gigantic wave, a small gallant vessel, almost obscured in a watery haze of light and colour.

"Why, yes," she breathed. "Yes, I can see it now. But it is so unusual. Nothing is quite clear, yet the wildness of the storm is almost overpoweringly real."

"The work of genius," he said calmly. "At least that is my opinion, though there is much controversy over the works of Mr Turner. In a hundred years the world will judge the better.

For myself, I feel only the privilege of owning a picture so beautiful." There was a pause, then, abruptly, "I thought you appeared a little upset earlier in the evening. Did something happen to trouble you?"

She was startled at the sudden change of subject. "It was nothing. It is quite forgotten."

"Then you *were* upset. I am distressed that it should happen when I particularly wished the evening to be enjoyable."

She shook her head. "I did not realise that my feelings were so transparent."

"They were not, Miss Linton, except to someone who has your well-being at heart. Should you care to tell me about it?"

His expression was friendly and encouraging. She said, frankly, "I had a disappointment this evening, Mr Brook, but it was my own fault for building up my expectations unwisely."

"And what were those expectations?"

"You will think them very unimportant." She told him briefly what had occurred, making light of it. "So you see," she finished, "Mr Sanderson thinks I am too much of a goose to make decisions for myself."

Mr Brook frowned and paced slowly across the room away from her. "He wished to protect you, of course," he said. "That is understandable."

"I did not think my idea so very foolish."

"Nor do I," he said unexpectedly and with genuine assurance. "I take a great interest in housing. I have just completed a small development for my workers." She looked at him in surprise. "If you had spoken to me of this before, I might have used my influence with Miles."

"I wish I had."

He kicked absently at a cinder fallen to the hearth. "Let me think about this for a while," he said thoughtfully. "Although that particular avenue is closed, perhaps there may be some other way . . ." He cleared his throat. "In the meantime, you might like to view the houses I have built for my labourers. I have incorporated all the most modern ideas. No dwelling has less than three rooms, its own scullery and water tap and I discourage the practice of taking in lodgers so that there is no overcrowding.

Despite his diffident manner she sensed his enthusiasm and said, warmly, "I should be most interested."

"Good. Then we must arrange a visit. Your aunt, of course, should be consulted."

"I shall ask her permission."

"It would be best if I called on her myself. I should like to assure her that her niece will be in trustworthy hands. I hope to see you at home when I call."

"The weather has kept us much indoors of late," Carrie said politely.

"Then I pray that it remains inclement."

She met his earnest gaze and glanced away, before saying, "Should we not be returning to the dancing? Your guests will be missing you."

"Let them," he said easily. "The company of one agreeable person is far more pleasurable than a roomful of chattering acquaintances."

A silence fell and lengthened. For the first time in the presence of Edmund Brook, Carrie felt a prickle of discomfort. To cover her sudden awkwardness, she said, looking at the picture, "The painting reminds me of the journey back from Malacca. We ran into bad storms. I was only small but I remember how I enjoyed the fury of the wind and water. I was never seasick, though the poor lady who was caring for us was laid below for days in dreadful distress and Adele was too frightened to stir from the cabin. I used to creep up on deck to wonder at the great green seas that seemed ready to swallow us up."

"You might have been swept away." Edmund found that thought intolerable.

"The captain once found me clinging to a stay, soaked with spray and teeth a-chatter. He swore the most terrible oaths, but later he laughed and had an empty apple barrel lashed to one of the masts and stood me inside it so that I might watch the rough seas in safety . . ." She was rattling on in a headlong rush of words to fill that unaccountably uncomfortable silence.

It was strange, the room that had looked so cosy a few moments ago, now seemed less so. The dark velvet drapes, the mahogany furniture, the precise patterns of the Turkey rug, the walls laden with heavy-framed paintings, closed her in. The atmosphere seemed ponderous, weighted with the memories of the woman who had loved this room – perhaps that was it. She felt an intruder here, in this overfurnished room. She longed, suddenly, for the things that had become familiar in recent weeks: Aunt Linnie nodding over her embroidery; Jane bustling in with a tray of tea; Adele quietly sketching; Jem standing in the doorway, ducking his head to avoid the lintel . . .

Starched skirts swished by the door. Mr Brook gave a nervous cough. "I dare say we had best return to the throng. I have so much enjoyed showing you my paintings."

The picture still held her. The turbulence of light and colour brought an answering agitation in her blood.

"The Turner quite takes you, does it not?" He sounded pleased. "I am glad, because of all my pictures it is my favourite. Whether or no Mr Turner becomes the rage, I shall never part with it."

"It is . . . it is strangely moving." The words were lame for the sensations that it aroused. Sensations that had only in part to do with the picture. In that haze of luminous rain and spray, a face seemed to focus and dissolve. He had come to her tonight out of the snow storm. Tired and work-stained, he had trudged

188

all the way to the lodge with the papers. He had given nothing for his own comfort. He had wished only to please her, and she had seen, for a few moments – before he had left to face again the cold and snow – the reason why. Only, then, she had not understood the fierce hunger in his eyes. Now she did. And the knowledge seemed both new and frightening and, illogically, to have been part of her for a long time.

Mr Brook was tucking her hand gently into the crook of his arm. From a distance she heard his voice. "I must play the host once more. Come, Miss Linton, we must brace ourselves for jollity . . ."

She saw again the dingy street and the howling urchins and felt the wild heartbeat of the dove, the warmth of its blood on her fingers. She saw him striding towards her, anger in his face. Felt the hardness of his arms as he swept her up and into the carriage. She closed her eyes, remembering the way he had held her against his heart, cradling her as she cradled the dove.

"I think it will be Thursday afternoon before I am free to call upon your aunt," Mr Brook was saying. "Will that be convenient?"

Thursday? There was something happening on Thursday. Ah, yes, Mrs Sanderson's tea. She was amazed that her voice was polite and ordinary, as she explained.

He looked disappointed but said, lightly, "I trust you enjoy it. Would you acquaint your aunt with the information that I shall call at about four o'clock?"

"Certainly."

She thought, I have been blind. *Blind*.

"Then I shall arrange for you to tour my housing development."

"Of course. I shall look forward to it."

The deep bubble of joy that suddenly surfaced would not be denied. It made her light-headed, dizzy from the tingle in her veins. She could not contain her smile. She looked at Edmund Brook but did not see him. She would be with Jem soon. Tomorrow — no, today, for it was gone midnight. This very afternoon!

Her face, so ordinary, took light from the inner radiance. It illuminated the whiteness of her skin, emphasised the delicacy of bone under smooth flesh, darkened her eyes to the colour of smoke.

Edmund Brook stared at her transfixed. If he had been a man timorously testing the waters, now he was helplessly drowning. And he welcomed the current that swept him away. Had not her smile spoken more than words? She could not smile at him like that and not care, for it was the smile a woman bestowed upon her lover.

He felt his spirits soar as he walked into the glitter and heat of the drawing room. How splendid an evening this had been. And there would be more of them. He would create for Caroline a world of splendour. She was a queen among women and once she was his he would dress her in satin and silk, pale, subtle colours to set off her white skin, and jewels in her ears and at her throat. Diamonds to match the sparkle in her eyes and amethyst and sapphire and glossy pearls to twine in the curling richness of her hair. He would take her to theatres and soirées. He would take her travelling. Together they would explore the quiet English shires, the ancient cities, old cathedrals. He would sweep her off to Europe. Show her the world, for the world was hers if she wanted it.

He bowed and shook hands and modestly accepted the congratulations of his departing guests, and the one face he sought, swept by in the crowd. Yet her few quiet words of thanks and the gentle touch of her hand on his remained with him after those with heartier grips and louder voices had said their farewells.

The door closed on the last guest. The icy draught stirred

and bent the candle flames. He shivered as the cold blast from outdoors touched him. He turned his back on it and walked to the small parlour. There, in the firelight, he sat, long after the servants had retired yawning to their beds. He thought of his wife and it seemed that the image of her pale beauty, so long cherished, had dimmed, become soft and featureless. Even this room, a shrine to her memory and unchanged except for the addition of a few paintings, was no longer hers.

Caroline had been here. Fresh and young, she had swept away the stale webs of old regrets and sorrows. Nora was dead and gone. Caroline was warm and living. His eyes strayed to the Turner, a faint glimmer of yellows in the firelight. Caroline had admired and understood it. From now on he would cherish it the more. One day he would set it aside in a special room. A room for Caroline, one that she should furnish as she wished, with the Turner as her inspiration . . .

The fire crumbled to ash. He sat on in the dying light and was still staring at the painting as the last candle shivered and went out.

Chapter Six

The low afternoon sun sent long blue shadows over the snow. Icicles hung along fence poles and twigs, glinting with the rainbow scintillation of diamonds. It was very still, the only sounds the crisp scrunch of the snow underfoot as he walked the empty back lanes from the town.

George O'Hara was feeling that mild euphoria of spirit that was always with him after a night in Sal's company. He wondered sometimes at the attraction she held for him. She was nothing but a whore, half tinker, not averse to picking a pocket when money was tight or having a clawing fight with one of the other sluts in Coney Alley if the mood took her. But from the beginning, from the night she'd hoisted him off to her lodgings after he'd been celebrating – mistakenly – the prospect of those brats bringing him in a nice plump income, something had kept them together. They could row and fight – and she gave as good as she got in that direction – they could slang each other, argue, but nothing ever quite snapped the thread of their friendship. He grinned. Friendship? Was that the word?

He thought of her firm-fleshed body, sallow-skinned and strong, of her sturdy calves, of her hair like jet silk spread across the pillow. Yet beyond the rolling, sweaty urgency of their lovemaking there was something else. Something that made an evening spent drinking porter beside the good fire she always kept in her room, or a stroll around the town arm in arm, or a shared mutton pie from the steamy-windowed shop in Deansgate, eaten with burning fingers as they ambled along back entries, just as pleasurable. He'd known a lot of women in his forty years. Known 'em, taken what he'd wanted from 'em and turned his back on them when they'd tired him. No woman had ever kept his interest for more than a few months, but he'd been calling on Sal, now, for what was it? More than two years. She had become in a way as much of a fixture as that bitch of a wife of his.

He swished viciously with his stick at a tuft of frost-bleached grass and wondered, as he so often did, why he'd been fool enough to marry the spiritless, whining creature. It had been a time of weakness he'd realised later – too late. He'd had a bastard run of ill luck that had ended with a spell in jail. Three months of prison brutalities and prison food, then the weeks on the run after he'd gone over the wall, had made the prospect of a nice easy berth with a doting widow rosily attractive.

A new name, a new beginning, a settled life. The widow had led him to understand that she was in comfortable circumstances. The cottage was neat and inviting. A rural retreat where no one knew him. The widow was not then unpleasing to the eye. Marriage? Well, why not. There came a time in a man's life, he had assured himself, when security meant more than freedom of the road. He'd had enough of living on his wits. It was time to settle, to breed handsome sons and pretty daughters who would be a comfort in his old age.

For a while the illusion had lingered. The first month or two had been to his liking. The widow, short of a man for so long, had come eagerly to the nuptial bed and he enjoyed the good food, the peace and the warm feeling of money in his pocket. Even the brats of nieces had behaved themselves, waiting on him at their aunt's bidding, fetching his slippers and his pipe. He felt he might grow quite attached to the little pretty one, though the elder was not very likeable. There was something too sharp and knowing about her. The way she looked at him was an irritation, as though she could see past the fictions he had invented. 'I know you George O'Hara,' her cold grey eyes said. 'You may fool my aunt with your fancy tales of a tradesman fallen upon hard times, but I see beyond the lie.' It had given him gratification later to show her who was master and he'd have ground down her high-nosed spirit had his influence not been challenged.

He might have known respectability would pall. The tameness of his new mode of life padded him about like an oversoft feather bed. His wife's spaniel-eyed glances, devoted and humble, flattering at first, began to grate on him. But it was her inability to carry a child to full term and the subsequent whinings he'd had to endure on account of it, that had turned irritation to anger and anger to indifference. Her looks decayed with appalling rapidity and the nest egg she had accumulated melted like ice in the sun, so that he was forced to take on carpentry work to keep him in ale money. He'd felt cheated, and found relief in bouts of drunkenness. It gave him some satisfaction as he staggered up Cheetham Hill Road, to see Linnie's acquaintances drawing their skirts aside, pretending not to see him. And he grinned the more when Linnie shrank back from the brandy fumes on his breath and melted to weak tears as his slurred, ribald songs rang round the cottage.

Yet this put only a thin veneer on the restlessness that was in him. He found himself turning to the pursuits that had enlivened his former existence, pursuits to be discovered in the town's rookeries. As he familiarised himself with the mean alleys of Angel Meadow and Deansgate, some of the tension in him began to ease. The brothels where the harlots smiled wolfishly, the low taverns where a man might make a deal and no questions asked, the roar and bloody sawdust of the cockpit – these were the sights and sounds that stimulated him. He could let his carefully cultivated tones slip to gutter language and nobody cared.

"You belong here, lad," Sal had said more than once. "You might pretend as how you'd like to be a cut above all this," she swept her hand round to indicate the rough drabness of her room, "but you're more comfortable here I'll be bound than up wi' the nobs at Crumpsall."

"My trouble is," he'd answered lazily, "that I've a foot in both camps and it's always been the case. What can you expect with the younger son of impoverished gentry for a pa and a slum-bred brat for a ma."

His father, so lordly even in his dissipation. He always boasted of his grand family who'd kicked him out when he diminished the family fortunes even further with his gambling debts. There remained something of the gent about him, even when his breeches were patched and his coat greening with age. With his height and broad shoulders and mane of tawny hair he would stride about the dingy streets greeting acquaintances like a squire condescending to his tenants. And his ma, daughter of ragtag Irish immigrants who had early lost the man of the family to the hangman's rope when he'd been caught with his hand in a market man's purse. His grandmother and the brood of children had lived rough in the stews of Bristol and his ma, the eldest and prettiest of the girls, had soon found an easy trade lifting her skirts for sixpence to any sailor who had the price. His parents had met when Pa, lately enriched by a wager on the number of rats a fancied terrier could despatch in ten minutes, had taken a liking to the fine blue eyes and Irish brogue of the pretty creature who'd accosted him outside the tavern. He'd taken her to his lodgings, persuaded her into a bath, togged her up in cheap finery and was well pleased with the results of his philanthropy. So much so, that the two of them set up house together in a couple of rooms and though Pa had too much of the wanderlust in him to stay in any place for long, it was to Ma he returned time and again to stay for a few months or a few weeks or a few days, and to note the progress of his lusty son.

How George had awaited with impatience his pa's visits, not the least because for a while, the frowsty rooms his ma always allowed to become a slovenly tip when they were alone, would, at Pa's admonishing, know again the touch of the scrubbing brush and the cleaning rag, and the men who came slinking in the night to his mother's bed were banished for the duration of Pa's stay.

Pa never came empty handed. However down on his luck, his pockets bulged with fat sugared almonds, oranges and nuts, packets of sticky sweet raisins; mysterious boxes might contain a troop of wooden soldiers, a painted tin horse with a real horsehair mane and tail, a spinning top . . . such bounty made George king of the alleys. Who else had such a fine pa? Who else could boast such splendid toys? He would strut among the urchins dispensing the largesse of fruit and toffee; noting how the craven, the sycophants, fawned upon him so that they might share in the bounty. He revelled in their greedy flattery, even while his mind filed away a name, a face, that might at sometime be of use: that one worked for a poulterer on market day and might be persuaded to part with a farthing out of his weekly fourpence; this one was the best pickpocket, should he be wanting a new kerchief or a trinket to bribe a favourite.

By night Pa, mellowed with brandy, would bring out a pack of cards and show George the way to conceal a card in a sleeve ruffle, or shuffle the pack so that you might deal yourself a better hand, roaring with laughter when his son proved deft with his fingers. He would cuff him lightly and cry, "Easy tricks, but not for you, George. An education, a trade, that's the way to get on in this world."

Pa paid his fees at a boys' day school. George bore the

condescension of the better-bred boys. He could see the sense of an education. The ability to read and number immediately set him above the level of the gutter children. Pa was an educated gentleman. There was nothing he wanted more than to be like Pa, to join him on his travels that took him all over the country and beyond it, sometimes, to France. To be a credit to Pa he must be smooth of tongue and clever. He practised with a pack of cards against the day when he would be grown enough to take his place at Pa's side in the gambling halls and cockpits, and he worked to ease the rough dialect from his tongue. One day it would be his turn to go back to the stews with his pockets full of bounty. He would be a man of the world. Travelled and sharp-witted.

But Pa meant it when he spoke of George taking a trade. When George was twelve he was apprenticed to a carpenter. Pa chaffed away his sulks. "You'll be glad someday, boy," he roared. "A trade at your fingertips. That's what I should have had. It would have kept me in order better than learning how to pay a lady a compliment, or the latest dance steps or the manner to order a servant. You'll not be making a sorry mess of your life like I have, if I've any say in the matter."

George's protests made no impression. He was angry that Pa could be so blind, so unheeding and he was puzzled to know why Pa thought himself a failure when he had such stature and ready wit and fine manner.

He stuck the carpenter's shop for four years. It was a prosperous business by the docks and he slept in a loft with four other apprentices who treated him with the good-natured contempt all newcomers received. It displeased George, who had been king of the alleys, to find himself given the most menial and heavy tasks, to be the butt of the oafish practical jokes played upon all new apprentices, to have to sleep on the pallet nearest the door where the draughts disturbed his slumbers. He found it politic to submit with apparent docility to this treatment, but his sharp eyes missed nothing. How the eldest apprentice, a grinning dolt, always had money in his pocket and a box full of plum cake and sweetmeats on his return from a half day spent with doting parents; the way another – the joker who sent George on senseless errands – mooned after the yellow-haired daughter of the house and the mutual blushing and bridling that occurred whenever the two chanced to meet; the beatings a third earned from their quick-tempered master because of inept work.

George bided his time. He had, he discovered, something in him that was to be of use all through his life. He had an acute sense of timing. An instinct that cautioned him to wait or to act quickly. In later life it was to see him out of many a tight spot. It kept him from the gaming table where there were other chancers more skilled than he; it told him the moment to cut his losses over some deal that had proved less profitable than expected; it kept him more than once ahead of magistrates and constables – ahead, too, of many a parent irate over the sullied charms of an erring daughter. It nudged him to strike when action would prove most rewarding or revenge the most cutting. He had ignored this instinct once or twice and the results were disastrous.

Now he chose his moment carefully. First he obtained a cosier pallet well away from the draughts. George was younger by half a year than the clumsy-fingered apprentice, Sam, but he was already a head taller and far quicker witted, with an unsuspected skill at carpentry. He was helpful to Sam. When his master's back was turned a ruined piece of wood was spirited away, an ungainly joint improved. George even took the blame for an overturned glue pot, knowing that the master would treat him with leniency for he was pleased with his new apprentice's progress. Sam, still sore from his last beating, was whimperingly grateful. It seemed the least he could do when George complained of another sleepless night by the loft door, was to offer to change places with him. It was a small suffering compared with the threat of the master's stick.

Nobody quite knew who introduced the subject of cards. It was opportune that the new apprentice had a greasy old pack when the big lad, Matthew, volunteered to acquaint them with faro. Matthew won quite often. Small matter for they could do nothing other than place their wagers in farthings or minor services or a renouncing of the noontide jug of ale. Yet George had his moments of luck. Flash in the pan, nothing more. But he would wager, loftily, to the others' amusement. His good boots against the seed cake Matthew had brought from home yesterday. A week's puddings – the fine apple dumplings and plum pies that the carpenter's wife made so well – against the new shilling Matthew had snug in his pocket. At such times, Matthew thought grudgingly, all the right cards seemed to fly unerringly into George's hand. Matthew never did puzzle out why, that last year of his apprenticeship, the favourite goodies his mother made so lovingly for him, more often than not found their way into George's stomach.

As for that other business, who could point a finger? Everyone knew that the master's yellow-haired daughter and Billy Becket met in secret behind the stables of a Wednesday evening when her parents went a-visiting. But who was it who whispered the news to the master who returned early and caught his daughter languishing in young Billy's arms with her bodice disarranged?

Miss Yellow-hair went around for weeks red-eyed and woeful after Billy had been thrashed and sent packing. The sorry business left a sense of unease for Billy had been an easy-going, likeable sort of lad, though given to practical jokes. Who had betrayed him? Still, it was forgotten in time and soon a new lad was taken on, a weedy little runt who was suitably in awe of the others and of George in particular because he was so grown and strong and well-spoken and given to awarding unpleasant punishments of his own devising if he was displeased.

Even now, with half a lifetime's scheming behind him, George could feel the satisfaction of being in command of a situation that had not, at first, seemed promising. He paused on the path as it rose, a slight indentation in the snow, through a spinney of ash and birch. Aye, he'd been a sharp lad. Pa was pleased with the master's reports of him as the best apprentice he'd had in years, with a natural bent to his chosen trade. George himself had been surprised at the pleasure he got from the handling of wood, from seeing a rough sawn plank planed, cut, jointed, shaped to a cabinet or a chest of drawers or a table, solid and sound and built to last. Underneath was always that restlessness, that suppressed resentment that he was destined for a different, more exciting life. Yet on Pa's rare visits he bathed in the warm glow of his approbation. "I'm proud that you've such application, m'boy. Always knew it was the best thing for you – here's a half sovereign for doing so splendidly and we shall take a chop together at the Griffin this very evening . . ."

And that night there would be the heat of unaccustomed brandy in his belly and the stimulation of the raucous company that drifted, as ever, to Pa's side. There would be bawdy talk of wenches, the more sober judgement on gamecocks and terriers and the latest prizefight, ribald joking, the easy boasting of the near drunk. He would feel elated at being considered a man in a man's world with his grand pa presiding, shabbily majestic, over the party.

"Take me with you, Pa," he would beg when the leave-taking came.

His father would slap him on the back, slip an extra sixpence into his pocket, declare him a fine fellow and bellow, "Not yet, boy. Not yet. You must work out your time first. Be a credit to me, that's what I want."

200

"And then, Pa?"

Pa roared with laughter. "You're a determined young devil. Aye, when your seven years is up, then I shall see about the rest of your education in the wide world."

And, had Pa lived, he might have gritted his teeth and plodded on at the carpenter's shop. But Pa did not survive an apoplexy that took him when, rumour had it, he was with an exotic import at a brothel by London docks. When, months later, George could think of his father's death calmly, he thought it appropriate that Pa had breathed his last in the arms of a black, beautiful Hottentot princess.

It was weeks before a seaman brought Ma the news. She screamed and wept then lapsed into her natural apathy. The Irish eyes that had once tempted James Robinson were bleary now, her complexion pitted. When she smiled it was the death's head grimace of the aging whore and that only for her steadily more decrepit customers. The rest of the time she sat mute and dull with the jug of gin at her side and even when George announced his intention of leaving the carpenter's she only shrugged and said, 'You must please yourself.'

She had always been a drab background figure in his childhood a grey shadow compared to his full-blooded, colourful father. Now he scorned her and wondered why Pa had never quite abandoned this draggled creature. Out of pity, he supposed. That was a mistake he wouldn't make. Pretty faces were ten a penny. He'd already noted how many of them turned in his direction. He'd never stay with any long enough to see them degenerate to this.

He grinned now at the irony, confined as he was in a loveless marriage to a self-pitying invalid. But there was a difference. It had suited him to stay put these last two years. Suited him to let that bastard, Sanderson, think he was reformed and submissive.

The day Sanderson had sent for him stood sharply engraved

on his brain, even after the passage of two slow years. He had gone to the house curious and pleased that he had been sent for, expecting to be consulted about the new financial arrangements. He had stared greedily at the splendid property and the beautiful gardens. Things were looking up, indeed, with acquaintances of this standard of wealth.

The interview quickly disillusioned him.

"I know about you, O'Hara," he said. "I know about that poor woman you lived with in Stafford and the savings you stole when you abandoned her. You were caught for that and put into prison, were you not?"

George froze, his sharp brain racing over the possibilities. He decided against brazening it out, as Sanderson went on in that same level dispassionate voice. It was obvious the man had been thorough.

George kept his head bent, his shoulders bowed at the right attitude of humbleness.

"I shall regret that deed all my days, sir," he mumbled. He was alarmed and shaken. Above all, he was angry. He had not reckoned with Sanderson's interference, nor with the strength of his influence. "It was a temptation of the moment. The woman — as you will understand as a man of the world — was of a certain class and had caused me much pain with her fickleness. Nobody knows how I suffered for love of her and she rewarded me by stealing money from my pocket at every opportunity . . ."

"The story that came to me," Sanderson said, "was of a respectable spinster whom you courted and cruelly abandoned, taking her life savings."

"She told a well-spun tale to the magistrates. She could turn on the tears at will. The magistrates were putty in her hands, sir."

Sanderson's long yellow face was stony. "Mr O'Hara — or Robinson or whatever you choose to call yourself — I am not concerned with the rights and wrongs of the case but with your treatment of your wife and her nieces."

"I have done all in my power to give them a happy life." He strove to give an impression of offended dignity. "I am not a rich man like you, sir, but I have done my best within my means. It is not my fault that my wife, an invalid as you will have seen for yourself, causes a terrible drain on my finances. This money the girls will have should ease the situation . . ."

"Indeed it will. Your wife and her nieces must reap every benefit from it."

"I shall ensure—"

"*I* shall ensure that they do. You protest your innocence in the matter of the Stafford woman. That is as maybe. I must be influenced only by the facts. You are a man who has been convicted and imprisoned for a crime. You escaped from prison before your term was up. By rights, I should return you there."

Silently George cursed the woman who'd kept him dallying in Stafford too long. His instinct had told him to cut and run. Greed had held him back until he discovered the whereabouts of her hoard of coins and jewellery. She had been too canny . . . and time had run out on him.

He said, "I beg of you, sir, think of my sick wife. I did wrong to deceive her, but it is not a confession a man makes lightly. I was – I am – determined to put the past behind me. You may think of me as you will, but respect my wife's feelings. It would grieve her beyond bearing – indeed it would be sadly to the detriment of her health – to learn of my . . . my fall from grace. To know that she has been married these past years to a man who has run foul of the law." He let his voice fall to a hoarse whisper, as though overcome with emotion. "I was punished, sir. For a civilised man, even the shortest spell in prison is a terrible price to pay for one small lapse."

"I am sure of it," Sanderson said, dryly.

George raised moist eyes. "I have learned my lesson, believe me. Returning me to gaol would serve no purpose other than to punish my wife as much as it would punish me." He let the small silence lengthen, then said, with dignity, "O'Hara is my real name. I chose to call myself Robinson for many years because that was my father's name and he was a real gentleman such as yourself. He and my poor mother never had the benefit of the marriage service read over them, but they were as devoted as any married couple. Had they both lived, I might have had a better start in life. As it was, I was orphaned and forced to leave my apprenticeship at the carpenter's. To be at the mercy of a hard world, penniless and homeless, is something a gently reared person cannot comprehend. That is when it becomes easy to fall in with bad company . . ." The glib half-truths slid from his lips. He was practised in the direct glance, the appeal of apparent frankness. Sanderson's expression remained stern. George presently allowed his voice to falter. He sighed. "I can see you are a hard, just man. You will have me do penance for a deed long forgotten, whatever the cost to my wife."

"Not so," Sanderson said equably. "I am fully prepared to accept that prison had a chastening effect upon you and that your admission of a reformed way of life is a true one. Nor would I submit Mrs O'Hara to any unnecessary distress. It might be best to keep your past decently buried, just so long as by your behaviour you show that you mean to live an honest life from now on. I intend to give you the opportunity to prove your words by offering you regular employment and such assistance as may be necessary to make your wife's invalid state as comfortable as possible.

George listened as Sanderson talked. He felt the net go over him and tighten and when Sanderson had finished he made but one effort to slide a foot out of the trap. "Your offer of accommodation in the lodge is overly generous, sir," he said, "but we are perfectly settled in the cottage at Smedley."

"When the girls leave for school, Mrs O'Hara will be much on her own. If you move to the lodge my own servants will be on hand if she is ill and it will be convenient for you not to have the walk to work each day." Convenient to have you under my eye, he might have added, George thought sourly. Sanderson's bushy grey brows drew down. "The arrangements are not to your taste?"

George curled his fingers into his soft, sweating palms. "You seem to have thought of everything," he said, unable to keep the grating of anger from his voice.

Sanderson smiled thinly, without humour. "You need not fear that anything will be made known of your past. You will start with a clean slate. Provided you conduct yourself in an honest manner, I shall not refer again to your unsavoury past. If, however, you behaviour merits it, I shall have no hesitation in turning you over to the authorities."

"That has the ring of blackmail about it," George said, softly.

"Indeed? It matters little to me personally whether you stay or whether you return to prison. It is the well-being of your wife and your nieces that concerns me. I would prefer to cushion them from the knowledge that you are a gaolbird. It might endanger your wife's health and perhaps reflect on the girls. However, with my patronage, it would not be an insurmountable problem. Once recovered from the shock, I dare say they would manage comfortably enough without you." Again the thin, knowing smile. "I merely thought that a man in your position, so impassioned an advocate of his innocence, would appreciate a helping hand. The law is not always as just as it would like to believe. I am prepared to give you the benefit of the doubt. The rest is up to you."

The cards were down, his bluff called. George swallowed.

Caution. The wordless voice poured its message into his brain, spreading its restraining influence into the fire of his anger. Wait, it said. Hold, now. He kept still and silent until he was able to say with calmness, "Your generosity is deeply appreciated. I shall do my utmost to justify your trust in me."

Sanderson's voice droned on, cautioning him not to exhibit himself in drunkenness on the highway, nor to put any impediment in the way of the girls' education. Then, to underscore his humiliation, the cool remote voice said, "I am told by the physician that your wife should not be got with child again. Take heed of it, O'Hara. There is room in the lodge for you to occupy separate bedrooms."

He ground his teeth together, but deep beyond the reach of Sanderson's words his anger curdled at the cold touch of reason. He must submit. But he would wait. He would bend to the gale like a reed and bide his time.

He walked from Sanderson's house a humbled figure, but his eyes and face were blood-engorged. He swivelled his head to look at the fine house amid its shaved lawns and mounded shrubberies. The house of a proud influential man who imagined himself invulnerable.

"I'll make you pay for this day, my fine friend," he had sworn. "If it takes me ten years, twenty, I'll have my revenge on you and yours. Nobody crosses George O'Hara and gets away with it."

He grinned now, showing his strong teeth. Not twenty years, not even five. He plunged his stick into a drift of snow piled between black tree roots, as though it were a sword sliding between bony ribs. The waiting was almost over. Only a little while longer and he would be free. He would leave Manchester and go where no one would care a farthing about his past. Where a man with a pocket of money and a grand air to him would be accepted without question. Aye, he had long thought the colonies the place for a man of his shrewdness and capabilities. In those vast new continents a man might shake off his past as he shed his old clothes. He could invent a completely new person, with a different history and, among others with perhaps more to hide than he had himself, would be accepted on his own recommendation. There were fortunes for the asking out there.

He had close-questioned every seaman squandering his pay in the taverns, every returned rogue lucky enough to have survived the transports and the hard labour of the penal colonies. He had combed the newspapers and periodicals for items about these far-flung virgin lands; storing the knowledge snippet by snippet in his mind.

Life out there could be cruel and unpleasant for the convicted felon or for the unfortunate soldier posted to some godforsaken desert or jungle, for the pioneer wresting a living among savages in a cruel climate. But in the growing townships and small centres of civilisation, a man such as himself might seek a more rewarding existence. There were parts of Australia, for example, where the climate was tolerable, where the eye might feast on scenery more spectacular than anything England had to offer, where the comfortably-off lived agreeably and the entrance to such society depended more on a person's depth of pocket than on his lineage. Where the bounds of class were blurred in the common aim to civilise and tame a wild new continent.

He thought with contentment of the leather pouch concealed in the secret compartment he had constructed at the back of the tallboy in his room. In two years the pouch had grown comfortably weighty. His wages from Sanderson were barely enough to keep a dog in bare bones, but he had benefited from his work about Sanderson's house. He had a small but acceptable commission from the timber merchant who supplied the mahogany and rosewood and walnut for the refurbishing of

Beech Place. And, should he have here and there overestimated – nothing greedy, mind, but the extra plank on a fair-sized order – even Sanderson's careful checking of accounts and his occasional descents upon the carpenter's shop could not detect this piece of walnut or that length of mahogany as being surplus to requirements. Many was the winter evening when, cloaked by darkness, the fretwork picture frame, a set of candle holders, a prettily carved figure of an animal or bird, were removed to the outhouse of the lodge until they could be transported to Deansgate and the dealer who grudgingly underpaid but asked no questions.

This outlet had been invaluable for the other items that he had acquired. A pocket watch or ring Sally had lifted from some drunken gentleman staggering along the alleys. And all the items he had come across amid the stored lumber in the attics of Beech Place, when he had been repairing the windows.

These attics were treasure trove indeed. He learned that when Mrs Sanderson had set so vigorously about the refurbishing of her home, everything not in the mode had been banished to the topmost floors of the house. The attics were aired and dusted but rarely. They were kept locked and Mrs Price, the housekeeper, had the key on the jangling bunch at the waist of her black dress. His good friend Mrs Prince who, when he found that the repairs were more extensive than had at first been obvious, had gladly admitted him to each quiet attic and stood, breathing a little fast, at his elbow while he examined all the window frames and spoke knowledgeably of spreading rot.

He had taken his time over the new window frames and despite Mrs Price's frequent visits to see how he fared, he had plenty of time to delve into the cumbrous chests and presses. Amid the detritus of years – frail silks and faded velvets, musty books, long-abandoned toys, age-darkened pictures – small treasures leaped to his eager fingers. A pair of gilt-framed miniatures lost under a jumble of cracked china, a threadbare silk case, that opened to reveal a set of finely chased silver embroidery scissors, a patch box, exquisitely enamelled in blue and rose, buried at the back of a drawer containing nothing else but old letters written in faded ink and tied with ribbon that crumbled at a touch.

Forgotten things, so easily slipped into the deep pockets of his canvas apron, to be haggled over later in the shuttered closeness of the dealer's back parlour.

So the purse became heavy. Heavy enough now to pay his passage to the antipodes and to ensure that he would not arrive penniless. Enough, too, to pay for Sal should she have a mind to throw her lot in with his. Aye, together they might do well. Dressed in fine clothes, tutored to take the coarseness from her tongue, she would make a flamboyant lady to equal the likes of Sanderson's arrogant wife. She would carry off her role with spirit. Why, she could ape the grand ladies of the town like any actress, swishing up and down her small room, dragging an imaginary cloak after her, upending her nose as she chastised some wayward servant, making him roar with laughter at her drollery.

The world would be theirs for the taking. Once the small matter of revenge was taken care of. He would not leave Crumpsall before he had left his mark, indelibly, on the Sanderson household.

And it seemed to him that affairs were taking a very fortuitous turn. Young Elliot, now, so idle and languid a fellow and yet so ardent in his cultivation of those weird flowers, and so indiscreetly meeting Adele. All those ardent glances and fond looks he bestowed upon her were scarcely the kind of behaviour to be expected of a man about to become the husband of another. If there was a way to grieve Sanderson and his high-nosed wife it was through that brat of a son. They might have plans for him, but what a fine thing it would be to disarrange them, and heap a scandal on their doorstep. His mind had already explored and rejected several interesting possibilities. The anonymous letter to the innocent fiancée and her mother held some appeal, but he felt that a greater drama, a more lasting effect was necessary. When the blow came it had to be deep and thrusting and painful. With a little luck, Adele and Elliot would weave their own dangerous web and he need only give a touch of encouragement, a delicate nudge in the right direction, before they found themselves impossibly trapped. Ah, he was lucky indeed that Adele was such a trusting, foolish creature.

He breasted a rise. The hill dipped to the lane that led to the lodge. The familiar landscape was strange and remote under the white mantle. The trees were sharp-edged in blacks and greys and dislodged snow fell in little flurries from upper branches as he passed beneath them. In the icy stillness the voices came to him soft and clear. Not the words, but the cadences of quiet conversation broken by gentle laughter. There was an intimacy about the sound that sparked his curiosity, for he recognised the voices.

He moved cautiously then; for so bulky a man he moved surprisingly lightly, his gaitered legs and broad shoulders scarcely moving the snow-weighted branches as he pressed into the thicket. From the concealment of a sturdy thorn bush he looked down upon the stile and the young man and woman who stood there, a little apart, she snug in her hooded green cloak, he leaning against the stile, tall and young and smiling. Shyly, she had turned her head from him. George could see the curve of her cheek, pink from the cold, and the soft brown hair curling in its wayward manner from under her hood. As he watched they fell silent and in the silence the boy moved his hand, a little tentatively, seeking her gloved one. Slowly she lifted her head to look at him and, less tentatively now, he took both her hands in his, pulling her towards him. George could sense the hot urgency tensing the young man's shoulders and wished, heartily, that Jem was a lustier lover, so that he would fling Carrie down in the snow and take her roughly and make her wince and cry, then stand over her and laugh at her despoilation.

How he would have enjoyed her subjugation. It would be a punishment well deserved for the way she slighted him and looked coldly upon him with her clear grey eyes.

Punishment.

George's ready smile deepened. The dark and tortuous workings of his mind had something else to ponder upon. Another delight in prospect.

Heartened, he moved from the thicket. He took a wide route down to the lane, so avoiding the stile, and returned to the lodge and his flutteringly attentive wife, in great good humour.

To Carrie the morning had dragged by. Adele, slow and yawning, wanted nothing more than to sit by the fire and stare dreamily into the flames. Aunt Linnie, who had kept herself awake until she heard them return from the ball, had nodded over the pages of the Bible which was the only reading matter she considered suitable for Sunday. Only Carrie was restless, her thoughts riding giddily high one moment and plunging the next as doubts nagged at her. Would he come? Was the snow too deep to prevent him walking up from Hendham Vale? Time and again she went to the window. Icicles hung from the iron gates. The snow on the drive was smooth and unmarked. No one from Beech Place had ventured forth today and no carriages had called. The sense of isolation was sharp. No one would be abroad without good reason.

Uncle George had not returned home last night and she was glad that they could dine at noon in peaceful ease. As they sat sipping coffee afterwards she quietly and casually mentioned that Jem might call to hear how she had fared with a plan she had to buy an old property and make it a fit habitation for poor people.

Aunt Linnie was relieved to learn that Mr Sanderson had turned down so ill-conceived a plan. "I am most upset that Jem encouraged you," she cried.

"It was not Jem's fault at all," Carrie said quickly. "He was quite against it, only I persuaded him to help me."

"Then it was wrong of you, Carrie, to take such an attitude," Aunt Linnie said. "I am distressed that you should have done such an underhand thing. It was deceitful."

"I did not mean it so. Believe me, Aunt, I only wished to help these poor people and it seemed the sensible way to be sure of my facts before I spoke to Mr Sanderson."

Two pink spots flared on Aunt Linnie's cheeks. She placed her cup on the table and gripped her fingers together, leaning towards Carrie. "You must not, *must not* offend Mr Sanderson, dear. I do not think you realise how very dependent I . . . that is we . . . are upon his good nature. It was he who rescued us when we were in such desperate straits and found employment for George . . . who saw to it that I was looked after in your long absence." Her voice sunk to a whisper. "I could not bear it if we were again reduced to the life we had before. I should not find, I think, the will to carry on if Mr Sanderson turned us out of the home we have made here."

Carrie was stricken. "I did not wish to cause you distress."

"You are young, dear, and it is the way of the young to be headstrong. But pray, Caroline, when you are taken with any other such foolish notion, banish it immediately from your mind."

"But Mr Sanderson would not make you leave this lodge," Adele said. "He is far too kind."

"And if he did," Carrie said, "we have our income . . ."

"Which is not under your control until you are twenty-one," Aunt Linnie said sharply. "There could well be difficulties."

By name, one George O'Hara, Carrie thought dryly. But she could see the genuine fear that underlay her aunt's fuss and worry. How wondrous a thing it must have seemed to Aunt Linnie to have had more than two years of security and peace. And how frail that security must appear when any disruption threatened.

She said, gently, "I shall try not to be so thoughtless again."

There was relief on Aunt Linnie's face. "I am glad – and not selfishly so. I want more than anything to see you both happy. I am quite without influence and my greatest delight is to know that in the capable hands of Mr Sanderson and Mrs Dawes you will be introduced to the right kind of society as I am sure your mamma and papa would have wished. I should not want you to jeopardise your chances in any way."

"Oh, you must take no heed of Carrie's odd notions," Adele said airily.

"Odd?" her sister said with a wry smile. "Odd to want to help people?"

"Not so *extremely*. After all, there is the sewing circle, which is a very suitable sort of charity for ladies to indulge in. Not to mention the entertainment value of such an occasion." Her eyes twinkled. "Miss Prince is a veritable divertissement on her own. And I dare say if you cast about, you might find other groups equally worthwhile."

"I am sure I would," she said quietly, and was glad when the conversation moved to easier subjects. She wished she had more of Adele's blithe acceptance and less of the questing, impatient spirit that always had so many questions to ask, that burned to know things, to do things.

She had often wondered from which of her parents she had inherited this quality. Had it been her father who, governed

213

by this inner drive, had sought his fortune in a foreign land? Or her mother who had seen in the sun-hardened, handsome stranger, a chance to escape from a humdrum existence? Time had smoothed over her images of them. They had been all of her child's world, yet they were remote and unknown. Only in Adele's fair perfection could she glimpse the physical attributes of her father, just as Aunt Linnie sighed nostalgically that she, Caroline, resembled her dear, dead sister as a girl. Of their characters she knew little, except that they had loved each other and that love had extended to warm and enclose their small family.

Carrie stared unseeingly into the fire. She knew so little of love. Oh, she loved Adele and Aunt Linnie and it was a quiet emotion, tinged sometimes with exasperation, sometimes with impatience, but it was a caring, settled, accepting thing. But of the other kind of love she knew nothing. The girls at school had blushed and giggled over young errand boys, or letters received from friends of their brothers, or cast languorous glances at the dancing master. But that, surely, had nothing at all to do with her feelings now. Had her mother felt like this as the fair, sun-browned man had bowed over her hand at that far-off subscription ball? Had Aunt Linnie, when the florid, smiling George O'Hara swaggered to her front door, been caught up in the same heady welter of emotions?

They were questions she could not ask. These overpowering feelings she had for Jem were something she must test for herself. It was new and undiscovered territory. Exciting and frightening all at once. Last night she had been so sure that Jem cared for her and the knowledge had carried her through the dying moments of the ball. But in the small hours, tossing in the big bed beside Adele, she had been riven with doubt. She felt as though she was slithering upon shifting sands, where nothing was certain; her emotions unsteady. Was this uncertainty, too, a part of love? Poets wrote of torment and despair. Perhaps this was what they meant. A necessary counterbalance to ecstacy.

She rose abruptly. "I need some air. I am quite in a stupor from the fire."

"But you cannot think of going out in this cold," Aunt Linnie protested.

"I shall wrap up well. I shall just go far enough to blow away the cobwebs." And far enough down the lane to see if Jem was in sight.

The air was as cold and fresh as sparkling wine. It nipped her cheeks and the tips of her mittened fingers and she drew deep, clean breaths of it into her lungs where it burned painfully and dispelled the clinging closeness of the lodge parlour. She raised her head to look at the blue cold arch of the sky and felt exultation at the fresh beauty of the changed landscape. She went into the lane, no longer a muddy and rutted runnel overhung with trees but a path of glittering white, roofed with a spreading tracery of frosted elm and beech and hawthorn, like an embroidery executed by a flurried, magnificent hand.

And there was a figure rounding the bend in the lane, head down, walking fast, not looking at her.

She stopped quite still. She could see that he wore his best blue coat, the brass buttons glinting in the sunlight and that he wore no hat and his unruly hair curled too long about his ears and needed the attention of scissors and that he had his hands stuffed in his pockets in a most ungentlemanly way, and that he looked exactly what he was, a working lad in his Sunday clothes, out courting. All these things she observed and she wanted to laugh with joy and to cry. Because he was coming courting her and because he did not know, yet, that she was waiting for him with her blood dissolved to water and the ache of her love coursing through her veins.

He glanced up, saw her and faltered, a frown driving down

his black brows. They faced each other down the glittering white tunnel.

Then, hesitantly, they began to move, step by step, over the crunching snow. As the distance fell away his frown lifted and he smiled, still a little doubtful, a little puzzled. She could see that his eyes took the colour of the sky, chips of clear blue, and she wanted to be drowning in their closeness.

This was the same Jem Walker she had patiently taught to write a clear hand, whom she had scolded for blotted copy books, who had been part of her childhood and adolescence like a patient, kind, understanding elder brother. The same Jem Walker, but so different now. Altered, as her inner vision had altered.

She spoke his name softly and her breath was white smoke on the frozen air. She saw an answering awareness kindle in his eyes. Half disbelieving he held out his arms and, with no effort at all, she flew the last few yards across the snow.

After that, there was no need for words. She had come home.

Chapter Seven

The snow and ice lasted for several days. Ponds froze, streams gurgled to a standstill, people crouched over their fires grumbling that with spring in sight it was extra hard to be cast back to winter. Young people dusted off old pairs of skates and prepared to cut a dash on the nearest stretch of frozen water. A few well-prepared gentlemen had their gardeners cut the ice from their private lakes to be stored in cold underground vaults for use in the summer. Roast potato and hot chestnut vendors did a brisk trade about the town and merchants and mill owners cursed the delays caused by snow-clogged roads and frozen canals and agreed over steaming rum punch at their clubs that it would be a damn fine thing when the railway system encompassed the whole country.

For those who had food and shelter the weather was an inconvenience. For the homeless and hungry it was a disaster. Each freezing dawn found its victims. A woman and baby shrouded by snow on the steps of a warehouse, an aged man rigid and lifeless where he had fallen. A crossing sweeper stiff and blue among the rotten detritus of the market gutter. And the twisted frame of the Malay might well have been one of those to be carted away for a pauper's burial, had not his stubborn thread of willpower kept him alive.

He was so close now. He had the house marked. He had seen the carriage bearing the *tuan* and memsahib and, once, in the distance, the young *tuan* and a strange woman he did

217

not know. His quest was almost over and he was weary to the bone, almost ready to let the cold take him, but for that nagging voice that whispered—as it had all these long, long months, never letting him rest – urging him not to let go . . .

For all his wanderings he had never known such cold as this. His thin blood yearned for the weight of the tropical sun, his flesh quivered at the biting touch of the bitter wind. His money was almost gone and no one would give him work. People turned from him when he spoke, some brusque, some pitying, some making the old sign against the evil eye. Yet he still must stay in this place until he had completed his task.

He did not seek vengeance for himself. Long ago he had lost all self-pity. The bruised and battered shell of his body housed a spirit numbed beyond repair. Blow by blow his dignity, his manhood had been driven from him. By the scum of the fo'c'sle on that first nightmare voyage. The ones who ignored his outraged screams as they pinned down his slight youth's body and used it in unthinkable ways – and those who stood by, leering, watching, and so appeasing their own foul lusts. By the master of the ship who had sold him in fetters to the slavery of a Queensland sugar plantation. By the overseer whose rule had been that of the whip and the curse. All this he had survived. He had made his escape on a clipper bound for Canton. Within a day of arriving there he had been taken aboard the ill-fated brigantine that was to take his youth and crush it into something scarcely recognisable.

They had abandoned him on Singapore Island, on a small half-moon of sand close by a mangrove swamp. There, the guardian of a small shrine hidden in a thicket of scrub, had found him. The crone had given him water and squatted by his side waiting to see if he would die. When he did not, she bathed his wounds and covered them with leaves, forced rice between his swollen lips and sat by his side fanning away the flies and mosquitoes. As he drifted between dreams and agonised waking it became difficult to find a reason not to let go and sink for ever into the hovering blackness. Then he would remember his round, brown, smiling mother and his crotchety grandmother and gentle little Fatimah from whom he had been so cruelly torn. He had to make his way back to the peaceful *kampong* in Penang. They would care for him, they would help to heal the wounds of mind and body. Then he would seek out the young *tuan* who had been his friend, his brother, for as long as he could remember. *Tuan* Elliot would know what to do. Through his father, a person of great influence, the wicked ones who had brought him to this state would be made to suffer as he had suffered.

So he mended. He shared the crone's rice and she brought him the meagre offerings of fruit left at the shrine, almost as though he were a god the great sea had washed up to her. Perhaps that was her belief, for on the day when at last he mastered the one hundred paces between two leaning palms and he told her that it was time to leave, she had set up a high keening and begged him to stay.

He shook his head. "You have been good to me, old woman, but I can rest here no longer. There is much I have to do."

"I am old and alone," she wailed. After me there will be no one to tend to the shrine as I have done all these years. The omen spoke to me of your coming. I saw a white buffalo come from the ocean to kneel at my feet. I drew the thorn buried in its neck and where the blood dripped upon the sand a great temple arose. Two moons after the omens had spoken so, I found you cast up by the sea. My time here is short now. You have been sent to guard the shrine when I have gone and to make it a place of pilgrimage."

"I am not the one," he said. "Look for another."

The wrinkles in her shrivelled face deepened in anguish. "Stay," she beseeched. "Here you will find peace, for the *semangat* of the shrine is powerful and protects those who stay close."

He laughed harshly. "What need have I of protection? Look at me! No suffering could be worse than I have already experienced I have been made into something so deformed that neither man nor woman shall look at me without loathing."

She blinked at him, her filmy eyes blind in the strident sunlight. "Oh, yes," she crooned, "there is worse. If you go you will wish you had not. There are things best left undiscovered. Knowledge will only bring torment. A man may move a rock that blocks his path, but in the moving may expose a nest of scorpions."

"I have had enough of riddles," he said curtly. "I have an unfinished matter to attend to. Time enough has been wasted."

She sighed heavily. "I am too old and feeble to stop you. Go and seek your vengeance. Perhaps it is that the pattern is not yet complete. The cloth has been a long time a-weaving. Life and death is woven into it, but the design, when it is finished, will not be as you expect."

She brought him food for his journey, a few coins and a faded cloth to bind about his head and shade the raw, twisted scars. Then when he thanked her she said, simply, "I will wait to see you again. The *semangat* will give me the strength to live until you return. For you will return. That I know."

He left her, impatience dogging his limping gait, dismissing her words as senile ramblings. A few days later, in Singapore town, seeking the mate of a vessel due to leave for Penang he entered a waterside brothel. Among the listless creatures in the rancid darkness, one drifted towards him with a face like a flower that no mask of paint could quite disguise. By her posturings and smiles he saw that she had been taught her trade well.

It was his first glimpse of the scorpions' nest.

In the gloom, his face shadowed by the enveloping cloth, she had not recognised him. He staggered from the shanty to vomit his horror into a rain gully. Then, when he had his belly and thoughts under control, he plunged back into the hovel. The ugly sow who took his money acclaimed his choice in loud coarse phrases. Her foul words beat in his head as he followed Fatimah into the curtained alcove. And when she turned to him with invitation in her face and body he, who had not wept through all his pain, began to howl softly like a tortured animal.

She did not understand. She stood back from him, frightened, her hand reaching for the curtain of split bamboo. He caught her wrist and called her name in a great sobbing breath, at the same time tearing the cloth from his head.

He saw his own horror mirrored in her face. Then, as recognition came, the rouge on her cheeks and lips seemed to stand out like bloodstains against the pallor of her skin. Her eyes grew enormous, wide dark pits, washed first by shock and then by a sick black shame that wrenched at his heart.

She pulled her wrist from his grasp and buried her face in her hands and, awkwardly, he patted her shoulder and tried to speak words of comfort. But there was no comfort, only the truth. So he spoke again, telling her without evasion of all that had happened to him.

When he was finished, he said, "That is my story, little sister. Now you must tell me yours."

She began to weep quietly, the tears gathering between her fingers and running down among the jangling bracelets on her wrists. Then, in a broken voice, she told him. Of the fire that had destroyed the house and the man who had arrived with a cart saying that Mahmood had sent him to take them to *tuan* Sanderson's house. They had been too exhausted and distressed to question him closely, but once away from the *kampong* they had realised they had been tricked. The cart had stopped and evil men had leaped out of the lallang. They had torn her, screaming, from the cart. She had not seen their mother and grandmother again.

"And then?" he prompted through a constricted throat.

"Then?" Her soft voice was suddenly edged. "I was taken to a house with locked rooms. An old woman waited on me and gave me food and strange drink that made me dizzy in the head, so that all that happened seemed part of a bad dream. And when she told me of what I must do and what was to happen, that also was part of the dream." Like a child, she knuckled her eyes with her fists. She had stopped crying but she would not look at him. "But it was real when they delivered me to the bed of the fat merchant. A man who, no doubt, paid well for the use of a virgin."

The groan burst from him. "Why?" he moaned. "Why did this happen? Why have we been chosen for such misery?"

"Ask Pereira that," she said flatly. "He who makes a fortune from the misfortune of others."

"Pereira?" He dredged up the name from a mind numb with bewilderment. "The one who destroyed the fishing sampan of our neighbour when he would not sell him that strip of *padi*?"

"That one. It was his men who kidnapped me. He owns this house and others like it. He sent me here when my usefulness to the merchant was past. I have seen him but once or twice. He has a smooth face and ready smile, but his eyes are those of a snake."

"I shall find him out," he hissed. "Make him pay. You shall come with me and hunt him down yourself."

She shrugged. "It would not alter things for me . . . for you." She swung round slowly, lifting her head. Tears had made rivulets through the rouge and smudged the kohl round her eyes. "See me, elder brother," she said softly. "See me for what I am."

There were jasmine flowers in her coiled black hair and her sarong was patterned in shades of crimson and gold. Her gauzy jacket was moulded tightly to her breasts and fastened with looped gilt ornaments. She was still slender, still a beautiful child. Only her eyes, full of knowledge, old, betrayed her. That and the small smile that touched her lips. The voluptuousness, the hint of corruption in the smile chilled him.

"I will not let you stay here," he cried.

"And I cannot go with you," she answered. "I would be a burden." She reached out and touched, a moth's touch, the raw flesh of his maimed face. "And you are burdened enough."

From beyond the curtain a harsh voice called that their time was up and others waited to make use of the cubicle.

"It is not so bad a life," she said. "Some of the men are kind. They give me gifts." She touched the bracelets, the ornaments on her jacket. "I am well-fed, well-clothed. Had I been married to poor Suleiman, I should have had to work hard in the fields. My hands would not be soft and smooth as they are now, but calloused and rough. Here I am idle and pampered. I do not cheat or steal as some of the other girls do, and I try to please the men who ask for me, so I am popular."

The words fell upon his heart like stones. He made to speak but she turned quickly from him and held the curtain aside.

"Go now. Do not remember me as I am, but as I was." Almost as though she read his thoughts she added, gently. "You cannot save me from my destiny. What is done is done. We cannot alter the past. No decent man would look at me now. Even if I went with you nothing could ever be the same."

He stumbled from the shanty and went to sit at the edge of the water. Dusk changed to torpid darkness. The lights from anchored boats dipped and bobbed. Lightning flickered in the massed thunderheads on the horizon and the sounds of the night – the whining of insects, the cries of food vendors, the carousing, the brawling in the liquor shops – roared like thunder in his ears.

He was still there at dawn, and in the pearly pinkness of the fresh day he picked his way down the rutted red earth of the lane. He could not leave without her. Whatever her protests he would take her away. It was his right. He was the head of the family. And how would he be able to face his mother if he left her to become one of those creatures rotten with disease or dull and stupid with opium? Nothing more should separate them.

Only death.

She lay on her pallet, the blood from her severed wrists making red wreaths on the floor around her, scarlet flowers on her sarong, wilting jasmine tumbling from her hair. Red flowers. White flowers. She had washed the paint from her face and removed the garish jewellery.

"She gave it all to me," a woman wailed. "Not an hour since. She said she had no more need of it."

Fatimah's eyes were wide open, her gaze fixed on a tear in the attap thatch. The slit of sky, smudgy-pale, translucent, was reflected in her eyes. Her mouth was a child's parted innocently on a breath.

She had made her escape – and given him a reason for remaining alive.

The cellar where he found shelter from the cold was scarcely more hospitable than the street outside. A sweep and his climbing boys had the use of it. The soot they brought in on their clothes and scrapers and empty sacks, billowed up in clouds from the filthy straw underfoot and ran in glistening streaks down the walls. The sweep was not an unkind man. In this, the slack season, he still fed his lads a hot meal every day. He was free with soothing syrups for the ones with grating coughs and rubbed strong brine daily into the raw knees and elbows of his newest 'prentice, despite his screeching, because that was the best way to harden tender flesh against the rigours of the spring-cleaning season ahead, when every prudent housewife would want her chimney swept.

His rough kindness extended to the Malay. In his life he had seen many a lad crippled or mutilated. Some burnt when bad masters lit fires in the grate to make the reluctant climb swifter, some ripped and scarred by falls in awkward flues, even one or two poor devils with their private parts eaten away by the sooty cancer. The sight of Mahmood looming out of the driving snow did not frighten or shock him. He looked at him with professional curiosity, heard his plea for work or food or shelter for the night and said, heartily, "Work I have none, but you're welcome to share our lodgings out of this storm." He had hoped for a few friendly yarns over a pipe with the foreigner, but he was disappointed. Beyond terse replies in his strangely accented English, the Malay remained aloof. Folded, coughing feverishly, in a thin rag of a blanket that he used to carry his possessions, he squatted for hours, one more grotesque shadow among the restless ones cast by the candle. By night he tossed, muttering, in the corner. The sweep dosed him with the syrup he kept for his lads and the Malay took it silently, without thanks.

He remained there for many days. The cold outside relaxed its hold. Ice melted. Snow turned to black slush and then ran thick and filthy down the gutters. One evening the sweep and his tired band returned to the cellar to the savoury smell of cooking. The lads warily tasted the bowls of rice and vegetables, spicy and strange to the tongue, that the Malay ladled from the pot. Then they fell upon the food until the pot was scraped clean.

"Soon I go away," Mahmood said.

"You're welcome to stay," the sweep said gruffly. "By God, you can have food and lodging for nowt if you'd cook us a meal

225

like that every night. Another mouth to feed's neither here nor there to me."

Mahmood shook his head and the sweep was genuinely sorry. He had grown used to Mahmood's taciturn presence and was appreciative of his attempts in recent days to clean the cellar and keep the fire going against their return of an evening. But later, when the boys were sleeping and the fire dying and he lay drowsy on his pallet, he saw glinting movement in the corner the Malay had claimed. A rough rhythmic sound caught his ear, the rasp of metal on sharpening stone. The fire flared suddenly and the Malay was haloed briefly in its last red incandescence. He sat cross-legged, the stone held awkwardly in his bad hand, the cruel blade swishing steadily, strongly against it. He paused, tested the edge against his thumb and smiled. The twisted smile was as cruel as the knife. In the lurid light it seemed to the sweep that some imp of hell occupied the chimney corner, crouching there in an aura of malignancy. He rose on his elbow, but the fire fell to ash and the light died and presently there were only the soft sounds of the Malay settling himself into his blanket.

The sweep had never in his hard and rough life had time to be fanciful, but now it seemed something chill and alien had crept into the cellar. For himself he was unafraid. The knife was not meant for him or his lads. But he knew with overpowering certainty that the evil smile boded no good for some poor sod.

He pulled the old sacks that were his bedding up round his ears, burrowing down into their familiar scratchy warmth, but he remained uneasy. Whenever he dozed the image of the curved knife and that ruined face twisted to its nightmare smile hung before him. Before dawn he heard Mahmood moving about and, as the first grey light filtered through the pavement grating, the click of the latch. Raising himself he saw that the hearth corner was empty and relief cleared the last clinging tendrils of his bad dreams. He stood and yawned, nudging the nearest sleeping bundle with his toe. With the single-mindedness of the simple man he decided to put all thoughts of the Malay from his head. Whatever Mahmood was planning was no business of his. He'd found out nothing of the Malay's past and he certainly wanted to know nothing at all of his future. So, whistling, he stirred the ashes of the fire, hurled a few loud good-tempered oaths at the still-torpid lads, and gave his thoughts entirely to the pleasant business of making the breakfast porridge.

When he returned to Penang he found the Sandersons gone away and a different family occupying the house on the cool hillside. It was a blow, but he set to work, patiently, to piece together the truth. Slowly the truth emerged. A hint of gossip, a word from a resentful servant dismissed from Pereira's employ, the chatterings of a garrulous coolie in the docks . . . He found that the men who had abducted his family were the same ones who had snatched him from a life of security and comfort to the hell his existence had become. But these men were merely mindless brutes who took orders. He had to dig deeper. He had to know why Pereira's hand had fallen so heavily upon his family. They owned no land that Pereira might covet, no business to compete with his. They had never crossed him nor were they possessed of any riches or influence that might have attracted his displeasure. There was something here that he did not fully understand.

The man who could tell him was Pereira's chief clerk, a lean, bespectacled Indian with a mouth like a taut wire. He was Pereira's right hand, the receiver of all confidences and a man, it was reputed, of equal unscrupulousness. He lived in a rambling house set in a compound stoutly fenced with iron palings and patrolled by several noisy and undernourished dogs. Driving about on Pereira's affairs he was accompanied by a burly Sikh who carried a sharpened dagger conspicuously at his waist. He was not, however, totally invulnerable.

The Indian's wife and his innumerable despised daughters, rarely set foot beyond the compound. The youngest child, his one son, the last despairing effort of his wife before she passed the years of childbearing, was four years old and grown enough to be taken on outings by his doting and devoted father. On one of these outings the boy had demanded and been given a large kite. The kite must be given room to fly freely, so father and son each evening strolled the short length of sandy track to the beach. And there from his place of concealment among a clump of banana trees, Mahmood stepped out to snatch the boy and hold a kris to his throat.

It took no time at all for the Indian to dig into his retentive and meticulously accurate mind and drag out the facts of Mahmood's abduction. He babbled them out, spittle gathering at the corner of his thin lips, his eyes riveted in terror on that fine edge of metal pressing against his son's neck. Names, dates, how much had been paid to whom and where – he was lost for no detail, however small. The mother, the grandmother? Why, they had been shipped to some island off Java to work in a nutmeg plantation, but the boat had been attacked by Bugis pirates. No one had survived. But that was not Mr Pereira's fault. Indeed, he was only removing the family as a favour to a . . . person. The knife moved; a thin line of red slid down the boy's neck. He gurgled under the claw Mahmood held clamped across his mouth. His father's reticence vanished in a strangled groan. A woman – a Mrs Sanderson – had come to Mr Pereira in distress. This Mahmood, a servant in her employ, had proved a bad influence on her son. She knew it was impossible to have him dismissed in the ordinary way, so she begged Mr Pereira to remove him from the island. He and his family also, for she feared some misalliance between her son and Mahmood's sister, the girl being nothing but a

common whore who had now settled suitably among others
of her kind . . .

Mahmood flung the child from him and stopped the Indian's
lying tongue for ever. He noted that the new kris bit true and
straight before he cleaned the blade on a banana frond and
turned his back on the fallen figure, the child whimpering
and tugging at the hand that still twitched convulsively in the
red dust.

*A man may move a rock that blocks his path, but in the
moving may expose a nest of scorpions.*

The perimeters of his mind were hazy with grief and loss.
But the core of his resolve hardened, became a purpose that
drove him in the months that followed. Whenever he flagged,
that remorseless voice rang in his head until it throbbed,
whispering that the soul of his mother and grandmother, his
sister, would not have peace until they were avenged. It drove
him over continents and seas in pursuit of the woman who had
so evilly betrayed him.

Now the kris lay snug in his bundle as he moved through the
streets in the grey dawn. The gutters ran with rain in the soft
drizzle from the west. While he had been in the cellar spring
had arrived. He felt it was an auspicious sign.

He knew a place where he could shelter close to the house
where the evil one lived. He raised his head and sniffed the
mildness of the wind and, as though satisfied, bent his head
to the drizzle and walked, ungainly but purposefully, through
the quiet back lanes heading north.

Carrie had discovered that falling in love was pain as well as
delight; that the few snatched moments with Jem, heady and
blissful, were counterbalanced by stretched hours of emptiness
when she must attend to household tasks and talk to Adele
and Aunt Linnie and work her embroidery in an agony of
impatience that must be repressed. She longed to talk of him,

yet even to hear his name casually mentioned brought hot colour to her face and she must turn away or bend over her sewing.

He had called twice on his way from work, inventing excuses. His mother was worried how Mrs O'Hara fared during the severe weather; he had mislaid the large red kerchief that he valued, being a present from his sister — had he dropped it in the kitchen?

There was no chance to be alone, no reason for him to linger beyond warming himself at the kitchen fire or drinking the mug of tea she pressed upon him. They spoke in politenesses that sounded stilted, but their eyes sought and held hungrily. His hand brushed hers and lit fires in her blood. They talked in hurried whispers at the door, the noise of the wind drowning their voices. And when he had gone the warm kitchen seemed desolate and empty.

She yearned for night when she could lie in the dark and give all her thoughts to Jem. Even that brought a kind of pleasurable torment. Over and over again she relived that time when they had clung together, uncaring of the snow sinking coldly into their boots or the diamond hardness of the icy air, and her body responded with such a flood of longing that she turned and tossed on the feather mattress like someone in a fever.

"Oh, Carrie, Carrie," he had whispered. "I have longed for this time."

"And I, too," she had said. "I have been blind not to realise it before."

His palms were warm against the cold skin of her face. He traced a finger gently against the silk of her eyelashes and over her cheek and across her lips.

"I thought . . . I thought it was too late for me," he said. "You were taken away from me a servant girl and you came back a fine lady. Far too grand for a poor carter's lad."

"Hush!" she said fiercely. "Hush this minute! I am still *me*.

Pretty clothes and pretty manners are things that society sets store by and they matter not a jot to me."

"You know what folks'll say if I come courting you, lass . . ."

"A fig for what people say!"

"They'll say you're throwing yourself away, lowering yourself," he went on stubbornly. "This Mr Sanderson of yours, for one. And as for Mrs O'Hara well, she's always been nice to me but she's talked to my mother about the fine match you'll make one day."

"Do you believe me such a poor spineless creature to listen to such things? Why do you speak to me so, Jem Walker?"

"Because they're things that must be said. Everything's got to be clear and straight between us from the start." His eyes did not waver from hers. They seemed to look clear into her heart. "Admit it, Carrie love," he said softly. "You must have thought of it – there, I see it in your face."

"But we should not think of the obstacles . . ."

"Better now than later. You're not of age and I've scarce a penny to my name. You're from a good family, though you've suffered hard times through no fault of your own. My family has ever been poor and struggling. It's not going to be an easy road for us."

"I know all this, Jem."

"There'll be opposition. People will do their damnedest to persuade you to turn your back on me." He spoke urgently. "If you have doubts it'd be best if you said straight out now. Best that we shake hands on it and part friends and never set eyes on each other again." He stopped, then went on in a harsh whisper. "God Almighty, Carrie, I'd move heaven and earth if you asked for it. Take on every blackguard who'd deny us. But you must be sure. It must be what you want too."

"Oh, Jem," she said softly. "Dear Jem."

"I have nothing to offer you but myself. No wealth. No fine

house. No grand name. Only myself and the promise that I'll work day and night to be worthy of you and to make you proud of me."

She could sense the tension in him. His face was taut with it, the skin drawn tight across the hard young bones of jaw and cheek.

She could not speak for the constriction in her throat. Slowly she lifted her arms, smoothing her hands over his shoulders then locking her fingers tightly about his neck. Gently she pulled his head down, raising her face. Against his mouth she whispered, faintly, "Is this answer enough for you?" And as her body and lips melted to his, she felt the shudder that ran through him and that, too, was part of the warm tide that spread wantonly in shivering waves through her own responsive flesh . . .

Later, much later, they drew apart and she breathlessly pinned up her tumbled hair, tucked it under her hood and fastened the strings of her cloak that had somehow come undone. Suddenly shy, she said in confusion, "The shadows have lengthened. I must hurry back. Aunt Linnie will be in a pother. Oh, dear, I . . . we . . . have lingered far too long."

"When shall I see you again? I could call on my way home from work tomorrow."

"Yes . . . no. Oh, Jem, we must be careful. We must make plans. Heavens, I seem sadly lacking in hairpins."

He took a stray brown curl that had sprung from under her hood and wrapped it around his finger. He sighed. "Aye, I suppose we should be prudent. I'll make sure my excuse for calling is a good one."

"For a while it will be politic to act as though we are merely the friends we have always been."

"My head tells me so. My heart urges me to sweep you up and carry you off and be damned to the consequences." He laughed ruefully. "I've been patient enough these last years

232

without the smallest sign that you cared for me beyond the ordinary. I thought that hard, but this . . . to have you so close in spirit and mind and yet to have to deny it . . ."

"You must keep your thoughts upon your work, Jem Walker," she said severely. "That is the way to serve us best." Then with a small sigh she dropped the lightest of kisses on his cheek and slipped away as his arms went to catch her. "It will be hard for me, too," she murmured. "So pray do not make it the harder for me to leave you . . ."

Then it was Thursday and they must present themselves at Beech Place. The drizzle had eased by the time Adele and Carrie made their way up the drive and a soft wind bent the sodden grasses patchily emerging from the snow. Carrie felt the moist fresh promise of spring surging up from the reviving soil. The winter was passing, the days would lengthen and the long evenings would bring the hope of walks with Jem.

She was cheered by the thought and by the plan they had contrived. Later she would say to Aunt Linnie, 'By the way, Jem is having some difficulty with his accounting at Carter Smith's. You know how much this new position means to him and he is quite unused to bookkeeping. I thought I might give him some assistance for I helped Mrs Clare often with her accounts and it is really quite simple when one gets the way of it. An hour or two a week would be such a help to him.' And if that hour could be arranged for a Sunday how easily it could be prolonged. 'Stay and have tea with us, Jem . . .' 'Come and see how the garden does . . .' 'But it is so late you must surely take a bite of supper . . .'

Yes, it would be a good beginning. Later they would make more such contrivances. Then, when Aunt Linnie had grown accustomed to Jem's presence, she might be persuaded to allow a trip to the mission in town where, Jem assured her, her presence as a helper would be welcomed and the ladies there most respectable. Yes, she would like that, being again with children, teaching them, caring for them as she had at school. But she would not rush nor build her hopes too high, as she had over her scheme for buying a house. She would tread softly, softly . . .

Later, ensconced on an elegant gilt chair of great discomfort in the drawing room of Beech Place, Carrie saw that watery sunshine was gilding the edges of broken cloud beyond the heavy silk curtains and she sighed, suppressing the longing to be out in the air, away from this overheated room noisy with the rattle of teacups and tongues.

"A little more fruit cake, Miss Linton?"

Mr Prince loomed over her, baring his long teeth that were so distressingly fang-like. His sparse greying locks were brushed smoothly over his scalp and had shed a mantle of white flecks across the shoulders of his rusty black coat. He leaned towards her in an obsequious half bow.

"Thank you, no," she said, bravely trying not to turn her face from the overpowering odour of camphorated oil that hung about him.

"Ah, you have not the healthy appetite of your charming sister," he said, waving a bony finger waggishly. "See how she enjoys the comestibles so generously provided by our hostess. It is a pleasure to see – though I trust Miss Prince will caution her over the consumption of too much rich fare at this time of day. It can be irritable to the nerves of the stomach, as I myself found in my heedless youth. Now, through disregarding the warnings of my elders, I must suffer the consequences and dare risk only the merest sip of weak tea. I should not like to see such a young and delightful creature as Miss Adele become a martyr to a poor digestion."

"Indeed not," Carrie agreed, catching Adele's eye across the length of the drawing room. As though she guessed the content of Mr Prince's conversation Adele smiled roguishly before returning to listen attentively to something Miss Prince was declaiming upon. Miss Prince had appropriated the seat nearest to the roaring fire and various of her cronies had hurried to place themselves around her. In their midst Adele, who had been imperiously summoned to Miss Prince's side, glowed like a new-blossoming rose amid a cluster of withered grasses. The whole assembly, indeed, was most drearily middle-aged, if not elderly. Even the Dawes girls would have enlivened such a dull company, but, Mrs Sanderson had explained, there had been some confusion over a prior engagement and Mrs Dawes had had to come alone.

"Even dear Elliot," she said, "is absent from home this afternoon. His papa, being indisposed, requested that he take an important document to his lawyers in the town." She did not add that she herself had devised the errand, discovering some letters of Miles's put out for the post, and chivvying Elliot out of the house with them. "The air will do you good, dearest, if you wrap up well," she had said cheerfully. "Besides, I know how you become bored with the tittle-tattle of elderly ladies gathered together. I weary of it myself, but one has one's obligations. If you remain here I shall call upon you to share my burden and hand round plates and carry cups."

He had been eager enough to escape. Would he have gone so contentedly, Dorothea Sanderson wondered, had he known that the younger Miss Linton was to be present? She watched Adele's face carefully as she imparted the information, noting the swift shadow of disappointment that drooped the soft mouth and lowered the smooth lids over the guileless blue eyes that a moment before had gone eagerly around the drawing room, doubtless searching for the one face she hoped to see. Hussy, she thought. Silly, infatuated child. Silly and dangerous and best disposed of before any harm resulted. "Come girls," she cried, sweeping them into the warmth and gossip, a strong hand under each girlish elbow. "You will liven up our little gathering. How charming you both look and I know you have the manners to match your appearance. It is so agreeable to us older folk when young girls set themselves to amuse and entertain, not least by being attentive and courteous listeners.

Carrie thought Mrs Sanderson did not look at all old. Despite the unusually sober colouring of her olive-green velvet gown, she managed to look quite striking as she moved from one to another of her guests. It was all to do with her straight back, the arrogant angle of her chin above the long neck, the commanding boldness of her handsome dark eyes that seemed to fling out a challenge, 'Look at me! See how rich and fine I am!' It seemed impossible that such a vital woman had bred a son as pallid as Elliot. He had inherited neither his mother's strong character nor his father's intelligence. Mr Sanderson was disappointed in his son and she had wondered why he had allowed his son to be ruined by spoiling, for that was clearly what had happened.

But looking at Mrs Sanderson now, effortlessly dominating the small gathering, she had a glimpse of understanding. It would be very difficult indeed to deny Mrs Sanderson anything she was set upon, particularly for someone who cared for her deeply as her husband obviously did. If Mrs Sanderson had put her mind to indulging and cosseting Elliot, there would have been no gainsaying her. The thought of such strength of purpose was vaguely chilling. In an odd way it reminded her of Uncle George and the cold and remorseless grip he had once had on those around him; the cunningness with which he sought out weakness in others and turned it to his own advantage. She smiled at her fancy. As if a lady of such breeding and elegance could be compared to Uncle George.

She watched Mrs Sanderson pause by Miss Prince's group, slip gracefully into the seat by Adele and, noting empty cups, summon Mr Prince to carry them for replenishment to the starched maid presiding over the silver teapot, at the same time injecting a lively note into the conversation that made even the dourest old lady break into a smile. Then she rose again and, urging Mr Prince to take the seat she had vacated, moved to join Mrs Dawes on the opposite side of the hearth where both ladies conversed in quiet tones, heads intimately together, as though their discussion was of the utmost seriousness instead of, Carrie supposed, chatter of the latest mode or a coming social event.

Yet, as she watched, both ladies glanced across the room. Brief glances, quickly veiled, as though they had spoken of someone and were drawn irresistibly to look at the object of their interest. On Mrs Dawes's heavy features was an expression of calculation that melted to one of smiling agreement at something her companion said, the laces and ribbons on her cap whisking vigorously as she nodded. Mrs Sanderson's expression was less readable. Her smooth features were a mask of attentive politeness. But her eyes were bright, filled with some secret amusement and more than a hint of triumph.

It was natural, Carrie told herself, following the direction of the ladies' glances, that Adele should be the focus of all attention. She was a pleasure to look upon, a shaft of light from the low sun tangling with her hair, turning it to a nimbus of silver-gilt and gilding the tender skin at the nape of her neck. Sitting between the gaunt black-garbed figures of Mr and Miss Prince she was quicksilver against drab lead, diamond glittering amid ashes. So very young and innocent . . . and helpless.

Helpless? A strange word to spring into her mind and with it a sharp picture, unbidden. A foreign port, somewhere on that long-ago journey from the Malay Peninsula. Tumbledown roofs fringed with hunched black shapes against a sky washed out with heat. Down below, amid the detritus on the quay, a small yellow-barred cat, a runt, a scrap of skin and fur dragging itself on dying legs towards the shelter of a cask. As it crumbled to a halt the shapes on the roof above bent their heads and tilted hard eyes downwards. The kitten lay still, its eyes open and glazing. Flies gathered in a fat, buzzing iridescent cloud. And, one by one, the big birds swung lazily down from their perch and dropped to the ground. . . .

She clutched her hands together, remembering horror and revulsion and, for a second, it seemed the drawing room receded. The heat was different and the elderly figures sitting stiffly on the spindly chairs ruffled their feathers and tucked cruel-beaked heads down onto their shoulders and fixed Adele with bright, knowing eyes.

The maid startled her, moving past with a swish of skirts. The room righted itself. A voice asked if she had seen the new play at the Theatre Royal and her own answered calmly. Everything was normal, ordinary.

Her imagination, she told herself, was playing tricks. The overheated room, the boredom, had caused her momentarily to slip into a daydream.

So she reasoned, yet there still remained a faint uneasiness that would not be dispelled through the rest of the dull afternoon.

The lodge parlour seemed welcoming after the spare elegance of Beech Place. Carrie thankfully removed her bonnet and cloak and sniffed at the smell of cigar smoke that hung on the air.

"Mr Brook made himself quite at home," Aunt Linnie said. "He took two glasses of wine and then begged leave to smoke if it did not incommode me." She paused, stared pensively into the fire and then up at the face of her niece. "Such a pleasant gentleman. Do you not find him so, Carrie?"

"Very pleasant. But are you sure his visit did not overtire you? You look a little flushed. Should I make you an infusion of camomile tea?"

"Later, my dear, later," Aunt Linnie said, for once not

regarding her health. "I am a trifle fatigued, but it is merely that I missed my afternoon nap. Yes, a nice person. So thoughtful. He pressed me to accompany you girls – though I had to tell him that I was too weak to venture outdoors . . ."

"Oh, Aunt Linnie," Adele cried, "Do you mean to say that I have to accompany Carrie?" She wrinkled her nose prettily. "To look at artisans' houses?"

"You are not schoolgirls now," Aunt Linnie chided her. "It would be unthinkable for Caroline to go unchaperoned on such a visit."

"But it will be boring in the extreme," Adele wailed.

"Think upon it as educational," Carrie said, mischievously. "It will be no more dull than this afternoon's tea party with scarce a person under fifty."

Adele tossed her curls. "At least the ladies can be nudged to speak of fashion or flirtations, or scandals that I am not supposed to understand but find quite diverting. I had rather listen to chatter of whether caps should be worn with or without ribbons this season than the price of bricks or . . . or drainage systems. Besides," she added pertly, "I am not sure that Mrs Dawes would approve."

"Mrs Dawes?" queried Aunt Linnie, "How do you mean, dear?"

"Why, Joan of course. She is quite set upon a match between Joan and Mr Brook."

"Oh, I had not realised . . . I did not . . . but Mr Brook said . . ." Aunt Linnie looked quite agitated. "I would not wish to set myself at cross purposes with Mrs Dawes."

Carrie sent a reproving look at her sister. "Adele is only repeating gossip, Aunt."

"It was Maud who told me so," Adele answered, unrepentant. "She said an announcement could be expected any day."

"Oh, dear," quavered Aunt Linnie. "Perhaps I have been too hasty in allowing . . . but Mr Brook was so insistent."

"Mr Brook," said Carrie calmly, "has merely invited me to view some houses he has had built because I told him of my interest in such matters. There is nothing in that that can possibly offend Mrs Dawes . . .."

Linnie O'Hara felt the headache begin to spread behind her eyes to add to the myriad other discomforts her body was prone to. The girls' bickering was really too much and she had not the strength to argue with them. While they had been away at school she had longed to see them, and their return had given her great pride and joy. Yet, now, her regard for them seemed so often tinged with resentment. They were so very wearing. They seemed to forget she was an invalid needing quiet and rest. Their very youth was an affront. More and more their chatter and exuberant good health proved to be a drain on her own strength. As for the responsibility of having two young women to care for, it was quite overpoweringly alarming. And today, this extra burden of Mr Brook's confidences was yet another worry to plague her nights.

She closed her eyes against the painful band that tightened round her scalp, suddenly filled with longing for the peaceful routine, the tranquillity, of the days before the girls had returned. Such good years after . . . after the previous troubles.

Her mind shied away from those dreadful times when they had been penniless and George seemed to have turned against her. He had changed so much since then. Had become the considerate hard-working husband she had hoped and expected him to be from the first time he had come knocking at the door seeking work and setting her heart a-flutter.

With the ready acceptance of the weak-spirited, it pleased her to believe that those bad days had been a mere lapse on George's part; perhaps a kicking against the traces of marriage, for had he not told her when he was so forcefully courting her, that he had never been the marrying kind and

240

it was her bonny looks and kind heart that had ensnared him?

Oh, he was a good man now. Even his *other* demands, those that she had welcomed at first but later come to dread, giving her trembling body meekly to his robust and painful assaults, even those had ceased. He had assured her solemnly, pressing a chaste kiss upon her forehead, that the doctor had advised separate bedrooms and though the sacrifice would mightily incommode him, he was prepared to subdue his own natural male needs for her good.

She had cried when he had removed his possessions to the room at the end of the landing. "Don't fret, my dear," he had said brokenly. "I shall be content. It is a small room, true, and draughty, but if I come in late I shall not disturb you." His martyrdom smote her. After that, she was careful not to remark on any absences he might make from the house, beyond a timid enquiry as to whether he had enjoyed himself. If he reeked of spirits sometimes, it was only to be expected that he might try to console himself in drink; if his good friend – a Samuel Quick of whom he spoke often as an honest open fellow, and a chapel-goer (who saw nothing wicked in a visit to a music hall or playhouse) – wished him to sample the entertainments the town had to offer of a weekend, then how could she possibly deny him? "You should bring the gentleman home for supper," she had said once. George had shaken his head. "Sam's an odd sort. I get on with him for I speak his language. But women? Well, he had a bad experience once. Jilted, I believe, though I don't like to enquire too closely. But it turned him against the sex. Prefers men's company. He'd turn red as a turkey-cock if I so much as hinted you wanted to meet him, and make a dozen excuses." George had paused, then said sadly, meaningfully, "I suppose that's why we get on so well. We both have . . . burdens to bear." And Linnie had lowered her head, easy tears flooding her eyes and guilt swelling her bosom. She never again mentioned Mr Quick unless George did first.

The sound of the girls' voices sawed painfully along her nerves. She realised now how used she had become to the quietness of the lodge while they were away at school. With George out all day and a maid to do her bidding there had been many long, restful hours in which to doze or embroider or merely to sit, hands in lap, staring into the fire. Mrs Walker had called two or three times a week when they could have comfortable talks devoted entirely to health matters, but she never stayed beyond a decently considerate half an hour. Occasionally one or other of the servants from Beech Place would bring baskets of fruit or vegetables in season, and Mr Sanderson would look in from time to time, but since the girls had returned there seemed to have been constant demands on her attention.

Of course she was grateful to Mrs Dawes and Mr Sanderson for their interest, but their visits meant fuss and formality and opinions to be given. And though the responsibility for the girls' social life was out of her hands, there were still many matters she must attend to, from deciding whether the bodice of Adele's ballgown was too revealing, to worrying about Carrie's self-willed ways. She was a good, kind girl for much of the time, but she was strong-willed, no doubt of it, as her mother, Celia had been. Dear gentle Papa and Mamma had been greviously troubled when Celia had wished to marry the handsome stranger who wanted to carry her off to foreign places. He had a smooth tongue and a bold eye and easy charming ways, but scarcely anything but his name to offer.

She remembered the raised voices from Papa's study, the silent meals full of reproachful glances, until the unpleasantness became too much for Papa and, on Celia's stubborn insistence that if she did not get her way she would elope with Robert, he had agreed to the marriage. So they had had their wedding in Papa's pretty little church and Celia had been a radiant bride and Robert the epitome of the proud, adoring groom.

Six weeks later they had sailed for the East Indies and after that the vicarage had never quite been the same. With Celia's going — Celia who had been quiet and reliable and studious and Papa's right hand, and who had rebelled in such a startling way — it seemed that something had gone from Papa leaving him pensive and tired. He had succumbed to a hectic fever the following winter and his grieving widow had followed him shortly afterwards. Linnie would have been quite alone had not the sudden deaths of her parents precipitated the local doctor's new assistant into a premature proposal of marriage. Linnie had accepted with alacrity and when a decent interval of mourning had passed had married him and moved to Manchester.

Linnie who had spent several uncomfortable months lodging with an elderly spinster in the village, had cried at her wedding. The onlookers thought it seemly and natural in one so recently orphaned. Only Linnie knew she cried because Celia's wedding had had sunshine and a church full of flowers and smiling guests and a dress of white with silver ribbons and her own was, of necessity, drab and quiet. There were no doting parents to provide a wedding breakfast and her gown was humble mouse grey and it was January and wet. And Bertrand, kind Bertrand, was not in the least handsome and had the beginnings of stoutness pushing out his waistcoat. Saddest of all he was not dashing Robert Linton. It was long after Bertrand's death, after Celia's children had come to her to be a comfort in her widowhood, that a bold-eyed stranger had come to the door and made her feel a girl again; a girl who, this time, might tempt and capture a handsome man and find unparalleled happiness.

She felt the distressing echoes of distant emotion aching in her brain. She must be sickening for a head cold . . . feverish.

She had not thought of these things for years. Why, she had almost caught herself thinking jealously of Celia. Jealous! They had been amiable companions as children, as young women. It was merely that Celia always managed, so quietly and enviably, to get her own way, whereas she, Linnie – ever more sensitive and indubitably the prettier – hated dissent and preferred people to think the best of her, bending to their wishes as best she could.

Yes, life was difficult for the tender-hearted – and hers looked likely to continue so, with Carrie proving headstrong. Look at that wild scheme of buying a house! It was a wonder Mr Sanderson, whose patronage was a bulwark against which she thankfully leant, had not been provoked to anger. At least Mr Brook had been merely amused. "She is young and the youthful ever rush into things without giving much thought to the consequences. For myself, I find it worthy that Miss Linton thinks beyond the social round and is prepared to extend a helping hand to those less fortunate than herself." Linnie had hastened to agree lest he think her overcritical of Carrie, but Mr Brook had scarcely seemed to notice her interruption. He was full of nervous energy, striding about the small parlour, brushing his long fingers through his thinning, light hair. "I speak in confidence, Mrs O'Hara, you understand . . . I feel that it is only proper that you should comprehend my feelings. Of course, nothing of this must be conveyed to Caroline – too hasty a declaration might startle one so newly launched into society – but your understanding your approval would greatly relieve me . . ."

She knew it would be a splendid match, Mr Sanderson had once hinted as much. He would be delighted to know Mr Brook had revealed his feelings so openly. But she felt only the burden of his confidences. She wished, fretfully, that it was all arranged, finalised, and Carrie dutifully bound in an engagement. Then she could rest happy knowing all parties were pleased. As it was, Carrie might well take against Mr Brook out of contrariness, where another girl would leap at such a chance. That would doubtless offend Mr Sanderson, let alone Mr Brook. If it had been Adele, now, she had always been so much more pliable more agreeable, as she herself . . ."

". . . and it will not inconvenience you, Aunt."

Aunt Linnie's thoughts, running like little harrassed rabbits round her brain, abruptly focused on what Carrie was saying.

"I am sorry, dear," she said. "I did not quite catch . . ."

"Oh, it is just another of Carrie's philanthropic schemes," Adele laughed, laying out her watercolours and preparing to improve a sketch of a golden yellow *Dendrobium fimbriatum* she had recently attempted. "Not content with schooling Jem Walker, she must now give him higher education. Bookkeeping, no less."

"Merely helping him to sort out a few problems. It is important that Carter Smith finds his work accurate."

"But you have so much on hand," Aunt Linnie protested, envisaging further interruptions. "You will overtax yourself, Caroline. You have helped Jem enough in the past and I think it quite selfish of him to expect more."

"We shall use the kitchen," Carrie said, uncannily gauging her thoughts. "We shall not be in your way, I promise."

She sat there straight, clear-eyed, determined. Linnie, embroiled in self-pity and physical discomfort, did not notice the faint tremor in the girl's clasped hands, nor the heightened colour across her cheekbones. Her irresolute mind sharpened to petulance. No, she would not be turned this way and that to suit a slip of a girl. She had more than enough to bear. She would have some say in the matter. Caroline was too self-willed for her own good. She must learn a little more humility. She had been away, indulgently schooled, for more than two years. She could not just return and rearrange household affairs to suit herself.

"I am afraid I must insist," she said. "There are other places Jem Walker can obtain instruction. His mother has told me of the lectures he attends at the Mechanics' Institute. There must be well-qualified tutors there – or even at the mission he goes to. It would be much more suitable if they helped him. I do not want Jem Walker hanging about the house at all hours. There have been too many visitors lately as it is. People seem to forget that I am not a well woman." She paused, hearing the querulousness in her voice and saw Carrie gathering herself to speak. "I want to hear no more about it," she said pettishly. "Not another word. You have quite enough to occupy your time, dear." Then, with a deep sigh she raised her pale, plump hand to her head. "All this argument is most upsetting. I trust you girls never have to suffer the anguish of body that I endure day by day, and it is not at all eased by your . . . your perverseness, Caroline. I think I must now go and lie down."

She saw with some satisfaction that Carrie had taken the rebuke to heart. She looked quite stricken, her grey eyes wide. "There, there, dear," Linnie said, elated by her small victory and prepared to be condescending. "I know you did not mean to be thoughtless, any more than you meant to be deceitful over that house business. Come, now, you shall help me to bed and bring me my valerian and pennyroyal mixture. Then I shall lie quietly until supper with a cloth soaked in vinegar and camphor water on my head and you may sit by me, Caroline. I have a fancy to be read to. Something light. A tale, perhaps, from the new book Uncle George fetched me from the circulating library."

Carrie did as she was bid and when her aunt was settled she sat quietly in the lamplight and began to read. The vapourings and swoonings of the prissy heroine soon palled and presently a soft snore announced that Aunt Linnie had nodded off. Carrie let her voice die and sat on, unmoving, the book open on her lap, her face turned to the window as though she could see through the stiff blind and out into the windy darkness. Jem had been spending the day in the yard, seeing that things ran smoothly while Carter Smith took his wife on a jaunt to order new furniture. Soon he would be locking the office door, fastening the gates, relieved that the first test was over, looking forward to a good supper after his walk home along the dark roads. She thought of him sitting in the cottage, his family listening eagerly as he recounted the day's activities.

Jem, she thought, dear Jem. You should be coming home to me. She felt far, far away from him as though the few miles were a thousand and mountain peaks and arid deserts separated them. And it might well be. She had bungled her chance. She had antagonised Aunt Linnie, causing her to bristle and prickle. She felt bewildered. It had all seemed so simple, but in a moment her little plan had crumbled to nothing.

Below, a door banged and she heard a man's deep tones. Uncle George home from work, and the shiver of distaste she could never quite master, ran through her. Aunt Linnie was snoring regularly, her face half covered by the damp flannel, her limp white hands crossed on her breast. Resentment, anger, fluttered away in a wash of pity. Poor Aunt Linnie. She would bring a tray later with all her favourite delicacies. A bowl of milk soup, rich with egg yolks and cinnamon, some bread and butter cut thin as paper and an apple baked with raisins and sugar. Heavy footsteps crossed the passage below. Uncle George making for the parlour fire and the first pipe of the evening. Soon he would be enquiring about the delay in supper and Jane, who always watched him with big scared eyes, would be flying into a pother and dropping saucepans and dishes. She would go and attend to things. It was always best to keep busy and while her hands set about the kitchen tasks her brain could busy itself too. It would not be tactful to bring Jem's name up before Aunt Linnie too soon. She must think along other lines.

Of one fact she was clear and certain. Nothing – nobody – was going to keep her apart from Jem for long. And if he could not come to her, then she must go to him. . . .

TO BE CONTINUED